Stephen J. Schrader

Published By
ActionTales.com
a division of CM Technologies, Inc.

ISBN 0-9723737-1-3

Stephen Schrader
3150 Valley meadows Dr. #171
Dallas, TX 75220
sschraok@aol.com

This is a work of fiction. Any similarity of characters or events to real persons or actual events, is coincidental.

***Vector**: An organism, possibly innocuous in itself;*
that carries, and disseminates, a dangerous pathogen.

Oh, what a beautiful allegory for man.

Prelude

The hatch door opened to admit the medtech. With a soft sigh, he settled into the swivel chair behind the console and began a voice recording of his personnel notations for this batch of Cryo-corpses.

"The twenty-fourth surface-exploration team consists of six personnel. Training at the World Space Administration stations in Antarctica, Death Valley, Oceana, and Brazil. Consisting of. . ." He stood and walked down the line of cylindrical cryogenic . . . Coffins.

"William Griffon, caucasian, of the North American Union, team leader. Thirty-eight years old, one-point-nine meters tall, seventy-two kilos, brown hair, hazel eyes." *What the hell kind of color is hazel?* "Veteran of the third Chinese intervention and the Detroit riots. After military service, received a Doctorate in Environmental Engineering."

He switched off the recorder and glanced at the readouts below the viewport. His gaze rested on the composed features of the rugged, cleft-chinned face behind the thick glassite. *An awful lot of former military types in the exploration teams it seems. I guess there's nothing like real-world experience in surviving hostile environments.*

"All readings nominal," he continued.

Stepping to the next cylinder, he said, "Saranah Kashem; african, South African Confederation, team biologist. Thirty-six years old, one-point-seven meters, fifty-six kilos, black hair, black eyes. Possesses Doctorates in Microbiology and Biology from Capetown University, specializing in general medical sciences. Ten years of service with the World Health Alliance, two years with the Center for Disease Control, Stockholm. All readings nominal." *Great, if more of them volunteered maybe I could get a shot at a CDC slot.*

"Fineous Telerim, caucasian, Central European Alliance, team driver/mechanic. Thirty-seven years old, one-point-six-nine meters tall, fifty-two kilos, brown hair, brown eyes." *Ah, a mousy, buck-toothed, little creep.* "Four years exotic vehicle operations, Mars Colony, six months, operator experience with the IO exploration team. All nominal."

"Number four: William White, caucasian, Israel; team environmentalist. Thirty-two years old, one-point-eight-seven meters tall, sixty-eight kilos, black hair, green eyes. Has doctorate's in Medicine and Biology Sciences, Lunar Colony. Helped design the Grannymede Botanical Research Center. Looking good."

"Gillian MacEntire, caucasian, Scot Republic, team electronics engineer and power systems tech. Twenty-eight years old, one-point-seven-four meters, eighty-six kilos." *Eighty-six kilos? Good Lord, the guy's built like a cinder block!* "Masters of Engineering from Glasgow University, six years in the development department of the Edinburgh Advanced Technologies Laboratory. Still nominal."

Suddenly, the room blurred as a stabbing pain shot up his neck and seemed to explode in the back of his head. Clutching the cryo-coffin for support, he shook his head trying to clear it. *Damn I've been pulling too many doubles. I'd better check with sick bay about something for the headaches.*

"Last but certainly not least: Dornieran Fritz, caucasian, from Germany. Team computer and sensor specialist. Twenty-seven years old, two meters tall, one hundred kilos, blond and blue." *Good Lord, there's a Viking ship short a crewman.*

"Doctorate of computer sciences, Berlin University. Nominal."

Continuing as he walked back to the hatch, "Team was put into pre-launch cryo two months ago and have another four months of Cryo/Bio-tests and monitoring scheduled before they're OK'd for transfer." The door slid shut behind him. *If those damned delays don't scrub the whole trip.*

Chapter 1

Dark
Dark
Pain
Dark
DARK
PAIN
GRAY
PAIN

He struggled and fought. Swimming up from. . . Every nerve throbbed and spasomed with unaccustomed stimulation.

Slowly consciousness returned, ripping outward in a wave of agony. Burning pins and poisoned needles stabbed and tore through his body.

He didn't dare open his eyes to the stabbing glare he knew was waiting in the resuscitation lab. Griffon groaned and slowly, gingerly tested each limb. Spears of agony ripped into his head and exploded in blue-violet bursts of nerve-light. *Man, a cryo hangover's bad enough, but this is murder!*

He carefully cracked an eye, to the glare of…*Dark*? Carefully, he opened both eyes wide, *nothing...Nothing*? *I've never been under for this long before. Maybe something went wrong? Is that why they're waking me? Did I go blind while I was under?*

In a sudden surge of panic, he quickly sat up and promptly smashed his head into the top of the Cryo-crypt. "Ow! Mother frackin!" Dropping back to the flat pad, dizziness rippled, and consciousness wavered.

Grabbing at his brutalized head, the nerve lights began exploding again. Half-stunned, he opened his eyes and slowly, carefully, began to pick out true light and dim shadows from the dying glare of nerve light.

I can see, he thought with a sudden wave of relief, which was quickly replaced by confusion. *What the hell's going on? Where are the medtechs? Why's it so dark? And why's this damned coffin still closed?*

Within seconds, he began to make out dim shapes, confusing forms in the darkness. Growing sentience automatically cataloged his surroundings. The familiar feel of the cryo sensor-web covering his body, the slick plastic of the pad he was laying on, even the cool feel of the inside curve of the closed top.

Closed? Why would they wake me? Why didn't they unseal my damned coffin? A sudden thought flashed into his mind, *This is another one of those damned psyche tests!* His anger grew at the endless inanity of *Bureaucratic "Frack"* masquerading as medicine. *OK, I'll play their damned game. But, I'm really getting tired of this crapola!*

He took a deep breath. Lungs long unaccustomed to working ripped into spasmodic coughing, *What the hell? Smells like smoke*. A brief surge of claustrophobia reared from his unconscious. Fire in a dark, enclosed space is one of the real primal fears of mankind.

Of course, these bastards want to make it a real test! Slowly, the necessary memories were dredged up. *The bailout bar's on the inside of the coffin, right about. . . here.* He pulled up the lever, and heard the seal crack. But, the cover didn't rise as it was supposed to. Through the crack around the cover, bitter, stale-smelling air seeped into the pod. The only light visible was a dim blinking red with a dull green overlay, from somewhere beyond his sight.

The viewport was covered by a thick layer of. . . What? Plastic? Noooo, it looks more like, dust. Dust? What the hell?

OK, this is a test, only a test. I wonder if I could get away with killing the asshole that thought this one up? Yes! I could claim I had just failed the test. Now THAT's an idea to perk you up!

Using both hands, he pushed the cover upwards. Slowly, with hinges squealing in protest, the lid lifted and, finally, locked in place.He listened, sniffed, and slowly raised his head.

Water was dripping somewhere near. A soft crackling from just outside the coffin. *Bitter smell. . .* Now he had it! *Burnt insulation!*

Carefully, he climbed out, the sensor net sliding away. Old, stale air brushed against his bare skin. He stood unsteadily, bracing himself weakly against the side of the coffin. The dizziness slowly cleared. He blearily peered around.

Five other coffins stretched before him, lit by dim green glows from their monitoring panels. Red letters glowed from his. He slowly bent to read the series of blinking lines:

Primary power circuitry failure. . .
Notification of monitors initiated. . .
No response. . .
Reinitiating. . .
System failure. . .
Backup power initiation. . .
Low backup power. . .
Emergency notification of monitors. . .
No response. . .
Emergency revival program initiated.

He straightened up, beginning to feel much better.

Looking around, besides the coffins, he could see what appeared to be some sort of console on the other side of his coffin. Dim red and green lights, gleaming on the console, outlined a metal door in the wall beyond.

He lightly ran his hand along the top of the coffin, picking up a thick coat of dust. *What the frack?* His fingers rasped along his chin.

A beard? Cryo's supposed to slow the aging process to a factor of one second for each hour of 'real time', and I've got a beard? How long have I been under? I feel like shit!

Carefully, he stumbled towards the console. His legs unsteady, but growing stronger with each step.

He scanned the waist-high console. As he came around it looking for a call button, he jerked back quickly.

Sprawled behind the console was a dim form lying in a blackish puddle, a pistol clutched in the right hand. It was a *very* dead body.

The only thought to come to mind. . . *What the hell?*

Quickly crouching, he checked the huddled form. It was a very, very dead man. The body was mummified, the blackish puddle, now the dusty remains of long-dried blood.

Something in his mind clicked. Thoughts began to run quickly, with machine-like precision.

Even the WSA wouldn't provide a body for just a test. OK, first things first.

With renewed vigor, he quickly checked the rest of the chamber. He found nothing but a flak-vest of unknown make and some sort of battle harness tossed under the console. He noted the corpse seemed to be missing its right leg below the knee, and there was no trace of bleeding from the wound.

Hitting what appeared to be switches by the side of the door proved useless. The lights and the door power were no longer working. Using the butt of the corpse's pistol, he smashed a dark plastic panel next to the door, revealing an emergency door release handle and light switch. He hit the switch and four bulbs began to glow wanly from the corners, doing little to penetrate the darkness. The door popped its seals, but refused to budge any further.

Unable to force the door, he went to each of the remaining cryo-coffins, smashed the panel marked "Emergency Resuscitation" and pulled the lever within. As his companions slowly began to awaken, he returned to his "coffin" and opened the bottom storage drawers. They contained a light-colored coverall; and most importantly of all, several one-liter bottles of Electrolyte Restorative, personal mixture by individual requirements.

The taste was as bad as he remembered. *Liquid crapola, but better than nothing.*

Gradually, the rest of the team awoke. With better light, and a familiar face, even if seen dimly through the dust-caked viewport, their awakening was without the panic he'd experienced. Though the confusion and language were equally graphic, and in four different dialects, remarkably, the most colorful commentary came from the usually urbane Saranah.

Quickly explaining what he had found, Griffon organized them into teams, with the four beefiest working to open the stubborn door.

After a seeming eternity of heaving and grunting, the reluctant portal finally began to surrender to their united efforts, sliding aside one metal-grinding inch at a time. A small shower of earth, stones, and assorted rubble explained the door's reluctance to open. The corridor beyond was almost completely blocked by a cave-in.

Once the portal was open enough for even the largest of them to squeeze through they took a break to discuss the situation.

As usual, the grinning, mousy, Fineous was the first to speak. "Well, if this is a test, it's one hell of a poser. If not, this is the beginning I always wanted to see in an adventure story."

Gillian reluctantly rose to the bait. "OK, what's that?"

"Stark naked, in the dark, and totally clueless," he answered.

Griffon interrupted their reverie. "OK, enough of the comedy interlude. First things first, does anyone know where the hell we are? Yes, White?"

"Sir, this could be any of a hundred places. It appears to be nothing more than a high-tech storeroom, with power outlets for the cryo-units."

"We went into cryo at the Brisbane WSA facility, but I never saw anything like this," Griffon responded.

"Yes sir, we were put under in the clinic. This is most likely one of the storage facilities they had there. But, I can't prove it," White offered.

"OK, well then, next, Saranah, what did you find out from our, ah, reluctant overseer over there?"

Standing, as if she were instructing one of her classes at the university, Saranah gave her diagnosis. "Initial examination of the corpse indicates that shortly before death, his right leg was severed and cauterized just below the knee. Why, or with what, I have no way of determining. Some time later, he appears to have killed himself, using his own pistol."

Griffon turned to Fineous. "Right. Finn, what's the inventory look like?" Fineous took a relaxed seat on Griffon's former coffin. "Well, we have one datacomp with disk and stylus, but no power, which was laying on the console. Several more disks from his haversack, but those and what appear to have been rations or some-such thing, are probably useless. They've spent the last few years being turned into a stalactite by stale body fluids and dripping water. One pistol of some sort, that seems to be functional. I checked it over with Gillian, and we agree that it's not like anything we've ever seen." He turned to the short, broad, redhead. "Gill, you'd better take it from here."

Rising from where he'd been squatting, Gillian continued. "Right, we stripped an' cleaned it. I also disassembled the clip. I've never seen anything like it. However, I did read about some similar prototypes being tested by the military. I'd swear that this was one of those. It's basically a miniature launch rail in the shape of a pistol." Demonstrating with the pistol, he explained. "The clip feeds into the handle like so and holds thirty, three-millimeter manganese-aluminum, ah, "needles". The magazine also appears to hold the power pack used in firing. If I remember the stats right, this thing will fire a hypersonic needle, with a lethal range of about one hundred meters, with little or no danger of either a ricochet or going through the target. It's got too much velocity, so the round just disintegrates on impact. It was supposed to be good against even armored targets, since the energy released on impact will knock the crap out of whatever it hits, armored or not."

The broad Scot shrugged. "Oh yes, because of the round's makeup, air friction ignites it. This gives a tracer-like effect as well as giving a good "burn" on the target. The bullet won't travel much beyond the lethal range. Too much gets burned up too fast and doesn't leave any mass to hold momentum."

Griffon nodded. "OK, what else do we have? Finn?"

"We have one clip holding six rounds with an expended power pack. Two others with thirty rounds each and good charges. They were still sealed in the packing. One automatic medkit, still sealed and hopefully still good. One flashlight, battery expended. One flak-vest, size small, with two canteens, emptied. One set of battle harness, old but serviceable. Also, a set of I.D. disks telling us our erstwhile companion was one William Jasper of the "Defense Group 23." From our coffins we still have six liters of "liquidlite," one coverall each, and a bit of wire salvaged from our Cryo sensor nets."

"OK, well in case any of you haven't noticed . . ." Griffon began. "Yes, Finn, something else?"

Now, looking remarkably nervous. “Yes, I ah, hesitated to mention it. But, if this is just some sort of elaborate ‘test’, I’ll look like an idiot, but if it isn’t, well. . .”

“Vell vat?” Demanded a usually taciturn, but thoroughly aggravated Fritz.

“Well, I checked the console, and the only thing that still seems to be working is the clock.”

Griffon shook his head, exasperated, “Annnnd?”

“Well, we went into Cryo in June of 2078, right?”

“Yes, and. . .?” Even Griffon was getting a bit irritated at the prevarication.

“Well, ah, the clock shows a current date of December third, ah, 2149.”

There was a stunned silence.

Even Gillian was subdued. “Seventy-one years?” he finally asked.

Fineous looked almost apologetic. “And five months, yes. According to the clock.”

White joined in. “What, like maybe it might be running a bit slow?”

“Well, maybe it was damaged or set wrong or something?” Said a weakly hopeful Griffon.

Saranah put her two cents in. “Well, judging by the accumulation of dust on everything, the state of the body, and your beards. . . I’d say that should be about right.”

A still unbelieving Fineous, quavered. “Wait, you’re saying that we’ve been asleep for over seven decades?” Panic started to tinge his words.

Griffon stepped in. “Now, wait up.” Earlier thoughts came back to him and calculations ran madly through his head. “That means we’ve been asleep for the equivalent of just about a week-and-a-half, our time. This might still be a test, though I’ll admit that’s looking weaker all the time. But whether it is or not, we’ve got to get out of here and find out.”

With a clearly defined goal, the team began the task of digging their way out. It took several hours and all of their remaining drink before they could worm their way through the blockage. Hunger was really starting to set in. Fineous finally worked his way past the last blockage and into the next chamber. The others, waiting in the cramped crawl-space that had been cleared, could only hear him mutter a subdued. “My God.” After what seemed an eternity, he finally slid into the relatively well lit room beyond.

Chapter 2

Griffon was bringing up the rear and therefore the last to slide down the rubble into the next room. His first impression was he had slid into some kind of weird hospital 'slumber party'. At least twenty individuals were comfortably laid out on various pallets around the room. Two bodies were sitting at large consoles, slumped-over in poses of slumber. A closer look revealed dried-out mummies that would never awaken.

Fineous seemed to be in a near state of shock. "What kind of place is this? Everybody's dead!" Growing panic could be heard in his voice.

Attempting to short-circuit a more general panic, Griffon barked. "All right people!"

Heads snapped at the command voice, overly loud in the relatively small room. "I want a complete check and room search. Now, people. By the numbers!"

"Finn, you and Gillian get me an inventory of everything that might be useful in this. Saranah, you and White check the bodies. I want to know who they are, and how they died. Fritz, start looking for a way out of here, check for elevators, stairs, air vents anything. There's nothing here but a bunch of old bodies we can't help anyway, and I don't intend to join them. Now, move it people."

They responded instinctively, as their training required. At first hesitantly, then with growing purpose, they set to the tasks at hand.

#

The first to report was Fritz, his agitation showing through a thickening of his already heavy accent. "Vell, the only vay out of here hist up dis old elevator shaft. Der iss no car and a losed iris hatch blocks da shaft. But I tink ve can crank it open manually."

Gillian followed. "Well, these people were pretty well-equipped with weapons. We found several of these assault-rifles. Also, four more pistols, and what looks like a grenade launcher. They all look like variations on the same magnetic rail-launcher theme. Lots of ammo I think will work fine, as soon as we get a chance to test 'em. Combat knives, mess gear, clothing, and battle harness for everyone and then some." He began to check off items with a stylus on a scavenged datacomp. "Several had knapsacks with datacomps, batteries, spare clothing, boots, and other assorted gear. I even found several flashlights and a compass that are still working." Looking up and grinning, he added. "I guess they made things right seventy years ago." He paused for a moment. "Also, we found two more sealed automatic medkits, with refills; and a full-fledged autodoc that reads green across the board. There's all the canteens we can carry, plus a pool of water at the back of the room. It runs in through a crack in the wall, and out a hole in the floor. We've got several packets marked Water purification tabs. We can clean up. We also found enough sealed packs of rations to last weeks. Just don't get too picky with the menu."

Fineous took over. "Rope, batteries, identi-disks, sleeping bags; that's the most important things. There's all sorts of other stuff, including these things I think are grenades." He held up a bag full of dull-green oblongs. "They each have a button on one end, covered by a safety cap. My guess is that you flip up the cap, push the button, throw, and, well. . . BOOM! That's only a guess of course, until we can test them." Pointing at a thin line encircling each oblong, "They all have these colored strips around them."

"What color are the strips?" Griffon asked.

"I found twelve with red strips, three yellow, six black, and one blue." Fineous answered.

Griffon nodded, "OK. We'll divvy up the loads as equally as possible among us. Do not test anything until we get a chance to do it right!""Yessir." He said with a grin. The old Fineous was coming back.

Gillian just sighed and shook his head.

Thinking back, Griffon looked at Finn. "What kind of ammo did you say that grenade launcher had?"

"Well sir, I found six drums, each with six shells. They all have red bands around what I guess is the warhead. I also found one drum with green-striped grenades."

The last to report were Saranah and White. After a cursory check of the bodies, they spent a great deal of time huddled over one of the datacomps. Even after everyone had broken out rations and began to eat; they still refused to be disturbed.

Eventually, everyone else cleaned up at the pool and settled into an exhausted sleep. The two doctors continued to huddle over the datacomp, stylus clicking away, reviewing disk after disk. Exhausted, they finally broke up, with red-rimmed eyes and slumped-shoulders. Saranah's normally dark-skinned complexion looked mottled and pale and White looked positively ashen as they approached the group.

"What's the matter?" Griffon asked. "You two look like you're being audited by the IRS."

Strained chuckles followed, merely in appreciation of the effort to relieve the tension.

"Armageddon would be more appropriate, wouldn't it?" Saranah asked.

"Excuse me?" Griffon asked in surprise.

"That's just what we've read." White said. "The history of the end of the world." He stopped to half-heartedly nibble on a piece of freeze-dried something from a ration pack.

Saranah nodded dejectedly, and started to absentmindedly eat. Her shocked gaze reaching beyond the confines of the room.

Uncharacteristically, everyone waited in silence, exchanging entire conversations with their glances. After a few minutes that passed with the leaden pace of hours, Saranah continued. "The most cohesive part comes from the disk left by William Jasper, a medtech assigned to this station. When the emergency developed he was drafted into the base defense force."

She took a long drink before continuing. "The rest of his disks are illegible, can't be read. But, the one he recorded just before he killed himself tells most of the story."

"So it was a suicide note," someone in the group offered.

"No, it was more of a letter to us. He hoped we would be found by humans, feared we would be found by the others, but left us a letter just in case what actually has happened came about."

#

"It was dated about five years after we went into cryo." Suddenly, she seemed to snap back to the present. "But, I had better start from the beginning, so it will make sense. Now, we have pretty well managed to verify what he recorded with the notes and files we found here." White nodded, still gazing towards an imaginary horizon.

Saranah continued. "Shortly after we went into cryo, there was a worldwide outbreak of a devastating plague. It was a modified DNA virus that was incredibly virulent, aerosol-transmittable, and almost 100 percent contagious." She paused for another sip.

"It seemed to spring up simultaneously on every continent. After the Hemoragic Fever outbreaks of 2024 and 2043, everyone knew a disease could be spread around the world overnight purely by volume of international travel. So, while significant, it was not considered particularly noteworthy at the time.

"Also, while almost all viruses are RNA-based, enough have been DNA to again delay suspicions. This virus was called 'Calle-12' after the microbiologist who first identified it.

"Anyhow, this bug was far from lethal. It seemed to specifically target the neural complexes, which make up the human forebrain. These also control most of the higher brain functions. Other creatures could be infected, but remained seemingly unaffected, acting as carriers or vectors. Symptoms started with severe headaches, and, what they called 'lapses', or alcoholic-like 'blackouts.' These 'lapses' quickly increased in frequency and duration, until all higher brain functions simply ceased."

#

For the first time, she looked directly at her stunned audience. "Imagine it, whole segments of the population, quickly and irrevocably, reduced to the mental level of low-grade chimpanzees. Worse, you have to remember that humanity was the aggressive carnivore and pack-hunter of the primate world. Their records indicate that within six months approximately 90% of the human race had been reduced to animals..." Then, very quietly, she added, "Or dead, over six billion people dead in less than six months."

Stunned silence greeted her statement, everyone thinking of their respective family and friends that were left behind in a world of horror.

White slowly continued the story. "Frantic efforts to develop a vaccine, to even attempt to slow or reverse the disease were finally, partially successful. They were able to create a vaccine that would prevent infection and could partially control the effect on those infected. However, nothing could reverse the damage. At a stroke, the teeming populations of Earth were reduced to wandering family-packs of aggressive, cannibalistic, savages. They even came up with a new name for them, 'Homo Regresses', or regressed humans.

"Because of the traffic between the Earth, the orbital stations, and even the Luna bases were infected. After having their passengers and crew reduced to animals within hours, they quickly died, as computers and systems were smashed and hatches were opened.

"The Mars colonies, Europa, Grannymede, and the other remote bases and stations were far enough away that they were effectively insulated. Any infected ships heading their way were dead long before they could be reached." Pausing for reflection, he added. "Being sealed systems, they couldn't be infected like the Earth was.

"Now, from the first, many had believed Calle-12 was not a natural disease. It was too specific, too virulent, and there was no record whatsoever about previous encounters. Most experts thought it was the result of an accident in bioresearch, or an accidentally released bio-war weapon, perhaps biological terrorism. The actual answer was even simpler and much more devastating."

Saranah resumed the narrative. "Approximately six months after the first cases were detected, when the ravages of the disease were at their peak, humanity had finally reached the point of trying to fight back. Then, the invaders came.

"The outlying stations were the first to be hit. They reported sightings, or some sort of incidents. Then, they just went off the air.

"Similarly, rescue and relief ships sent to investigate simply disappeared."

"It wasn't until the invaders attempted to attack the Mars colonies that the truth came out. It seems that there was too much on Mars for them to kill all at once.

"The Martians were able to mount at least some resistance. It didn't make any difference. They were eliminated within hours. Everything the remaining Earth forces were able to determine indicated total annihilation wherever the invaders passed."

"Then, they reached Earth. Their technology was recognizable, but far more advanced than ours. One of the remaining scientists referred to it as similar to. . ." referring to her Datacomp, "the Wright brothers seeing a Jumbo-jet."

"The first to come in were what they called 'Dagger-craft' or just 'Daggers'. Winged strike craft, small, incredibly fast and nimble. They functioned with equal efficiency in vacuum as well as in atmosphere. Examination of those that were brought down indicated they were fusion-powered, armed with pivot-mounted, rapid-fire, plasma cannons on top and bottom, and controlled by systems similar to cybernetics. Once their aircraft had wiped out any possibility of organized resistance, the invaders' ships landed and disgorged a full complement of similarly powered, and controlled, 'combots'. They came in every size and purpose-designed for every mission. Small, bat-like 'recon bots', surface and air transports; and three-meter tall, bipedal combots.

"Examination of these damaged bots, revealed each was piloted by a self-contained 'brainbox' made of some sort of ceramic-titanium alloy. Once they were finally able to crack these 'boxes,' they found they were capable of providing full life-support, and even protective cryogenic storage for the biological part of the system."

A frown of concentration ridged her brow, as she concentrated on phrasing the next part just right.

"Instead of the brain they expected, or even a possible miniature alien, they found the 'Brainbox' was full of, well, insects."

"Insects, like in bugs?" Fineous said incredulously.

"Well, sort of. They were about the size of a human thumb. They were six-legged, had a thin chitinous shell, and minimal organs to maintain biologic function."

Griffon asked. "What do you mean, 'minimal' organs?"

White, took up the biology portion of the tale. "Their respiratory, digestive, and, as a matter of fact, all systems were so crude as to be an effectively non-functional living being, in the normal sense of the word."

Nodding, Griffon said. "Go on."

White shrugged. "Well, these insects were physically incapable of surviving in anything resembling an ordinary, natural environment on their own. However, the scientific investigators believed that these were either... some form of naturally occurring, but specialized version of a natural insect. Much like the queen ants, bees, or termites. They are incapable of functioning without the support of their hives. However, they could just as well be some insects specifically mutated to perform a function. In this case, the insects in question were noteworthy in two areas. First, a third of their body mass was made up of, well, brain. They were each a tiny, separately living brain. Secondly, they were equipped with specially designed neuralogic antennae on both the head and posterior. These antennae allowed these bugs to, 'link' their neuralogic networks together. When they put two or more bugs together, they would 'link' to form a larger single brain. The intelligence and mental power of this 'brain' increased in direct, geometric relationship to the number linked together."

Gillian the engineer stepped in, his eyes flashing with inspiration, "So, these 'combots' were actually vehicles piloted by colonies of bugs, rather than being true robots?"

"Yes, I can't remember any similar technological or biological developments in the Earth's history," White responded.

Griffon returned to his main area of interest. "So, who was this 'enemy'?"

Saranah answered, looking very uncomfortable. "They didn't know. There are, ah... were all sorts of theories. However, as of the time of the attack on this installation, there was no proof. They never actually saw the true enemy. All attempts at communications were, well, fruitless. Whether the enemy refused to communicate or the humans and their technology were simply not able to communicate with the enemy was unknown." She took a sip before continuing. "They did note all the machines they examined had these 'brainbugs' running them. They also reported massive 'hivelike structures' were being constructed in the areas the enemy had conquered. However, whether these, ah, 'bugs' were the enemy, or some other agency, couldn't be determined. They simply referred to them as the 'Hive' or 'Hivers'."

After a moment's pause, she shook her head. "Now, where was I? Oh yes, anyhow, the remnants of human civilization were savaged and driven underground by the enemy attack. Several of the most heavily camouflaged installations were spared. Most were former, or current, military installations. The remaining ones were already on a near-combat footing because of the plague. What was left after the plague was still largely intact after the invasion. There was just not much that they could do about it."

White returned to the narrative. "First, the reason they had kept us in Cryo was to at least keep the old Challenger's crew from being infected. They had been putting additional, specially selected, and non-infected personnel into cryo. This was an effort to maximize the number of remaining uninfected humans while the experts worked to find a true cure for the disease."

"When they developed a serum for the virus, they introduced it into the cryogenic system to inoculate us." He looked up, smiling, at the others. "That should ease any trepidation over our exposure to the virus through contact with these bodies, or the items they had handled.

"Once the invasion hit home, the inability of humanities' remaining civilization to, 'cope' with the invaders became obvious. The decision was made to keep the 'cryo-corpses' on ice. At least until the chances of success were better. They didn't know what other biological 'surprises' the enemy might have.

"Thus a sort of global 'guerrilla war' started. With the invaders establishing themselves by exterminating the remnants of humanity and the surviving humans struggling to understand and provide for 'The Day' when the sleepers would awaken and, what they termed 'Operation Phoenix,' could commence."

He pointed to the surrounding room. "This establishment was a biological research center." He paused to drink a sip of water, making a face at the taste. "Once they had established themselves, the invaders started importing and releasing vast numbers of alien animals and plants from their home-world into our environment. This appears to be a planned drive to exterminate everything Terran in an effort to 'terraform' the Earth.

"They had identified over 1200 different species of plants, animals, fish, and, 'other species'. Captured examples of alien life were brought here, where they could be examined, in an effort to create a defense against the enemy."

He paused, thinking. "The enemy imported what appears to be a full eco-system. Everything from what we would call bugs and bunnies, to 'lions and tigers and bears'."

Griffon now stepped in to get them back on track. "So, what happened?"

Saranah answered. "About five years after this all started, the enemy discovered this base." She looked pointedly at the bodies. "They were attacked by the enemies' assault forces.

"Now, most of the cryo-corpses had been moved. Sort of a 'scattering the eggs to other baskets', as it were. We were the only ones left.

"Anyhow, they were in the process of being wiped out. The combat troops attempted to hold the line while the researchers retreated to this, the lowest level of the installation. Once the battle was lost, the combat troops blew the elevator shaft. They hoped the enemy would miss this hiding place in the general destruction.

"In addition, they blew the tunnel to our 'crypt' for the same reason. They were hoping after the enemy left, human forces would return and dig them, and us, out."

Again, she looked pointedly about. "But that didn't happen. They sat and waited, and prayed, and finally took lethal doses of painkillers from the medkits."

"So why was that other guy with us?" Fineous asked.

"According to his letter, he was the only wounded one who lived long enough to be evacuated down here. When the decision to seal the tunnel was made, he knew he was not going to survive with the injury he had, and no real medical aid beyond first aid available. This whole 'Massada' thing, was a suicide pact anyhow. The others agreed to let him seal himself in with us. I guess they viewed him like a guide for us into our 'Afterlife' or some such."

She ran down. Several moments ticked by before Fineous spoke with low and even certainty. "Bullshit, I don't believe in letting the enemy off by taking my own life. Not unless I can take a few with me." Several nodded in agreement, a couple looked more circumspect.

Griffon rose. "Well they gave us a chance, it's up to us to make it what we will. It's been over sixty years since these things happened. Let's get the hell out of here and see what's out there."

Looking around. "Everyone agree?" Nods all around, some more enthusiastic than others were.

White, hesitantly, asked. "And what will we do when we get out of here?"

Griffon's grin seemed far more confident than he felt. "Find out what's going on. Then... we start kicking some alien butt."

Chapter 3

It took several days to clear the rubble from the elevator shaft. While they worked in shifts at the hard, dangerous labor of "digging a well from the bottom up," as Fineous put it, they fell into a routine of rotating digging shifts; study of the available materials, and sleep. The relatively confined space precluded doing anything else without disturbing those trying to rest.

A test firing into the rubble-filled passage they had come out of proved the utility and lethality of their weapons. However, the confined space and precarious nature of the excavation prevented testing the grenades.

#

He was running, running, across a vast, dark plain. With a flash, reaching from the horizon a mighty light, seeking across the plain, like a searchlight's beam. People and other, less identifiable figures were trapped in the light. Horrible, lingering, dismembering death followed the beam.

Suddenly, it speared directly into his eyes. He ran, twisting and dodging, seeking in vain for shelter. It caught him, blinded, pinned in the beam. A vast shadowy form loomed through the light, as a massively clawed hand stretched forth and....

"Hey, Skipper, wake up!" Fineous shook Griffon's thrashing form.

His eyes shot open. Gasping for breath, he knocked Finn's hand aside and leapt up, trying to flee, but frozen into sudden immobility. He shuddered; consciousness returning as his eyes slowly focused on the present.

#

Fineous, the ever-present sardonic smile on his lips, held out a steaming mug. "Care for a hot cup of seventy-year-old, simulated coffee-flavored drink?"

Griffon just blinked at him for a moment, sighed, closed his eyes, and nodded.

Fineous held up a fist-full of packets. "With or without seven-decade-old simulated cream-flavored additive or not? We're out of the simulated sugar flavor."

Sitting next to the diminutive figure, Griffon could only smile. "With, if you please, it'll help cover the taste of our chemically purified water."

"That's the spirit, Sir." Looking at the others still curled in various poses of slumber; he pointed over to where Gillian and Fritz lay next to each other. They seemed to be holding a "power-saw symphony". Smiling, he said. "Sir, it's your prerogative to snore in your sleep. However, I do believe this moaning and thrashing about exceeds the parameters for 'acceptable behavior'. I'll point it out to you as soon as we find a rule book."

"Sorry, nightmare." Griffon mumbled blearily.

Fineous actually looked thoughtful, as he nodded. "Yessir, apparently the same one twice tonight, and for the last three nights running."

Griffon shrugged, looking a bit sheepish. "Is it that obvious?"

Nodding, "Yessir, it is. Now, everyone is showing signs of the strain. Yesterday you had to practically pull Gillian and Fritz apart, fighting over whose turn it was to dig, and whose to haul the debris away. Or, when Saranah practically ripped White's liver out when he didn't have any more of the lemon-flavored fruit drink. . .

#

The little man poured a fresh cup, and took a sip before continuing. "The problem is that you seem to have this idea you have to be some sort of lock-jawed hero from the 'Tri-D' or something. You may be able to cover it for a while, but your dreams are giving you away."

Griffon looked at the perpetually cheerful face over the curve of his cup. "You think so? And why does Mister Pop-Psychologist think that?"

Fineous answered, chuckling. "Now don't go getting defensive on me, this is just between you, me, and the imitation coffee sludge. Let me see if I got this right, you were one of those strong, athletic hero-types in school. Captain of the team, president of the Chess Club, dated the head cheerleader and all that." He glanced at Griffon's embarrassed grin. "Yeah, go ahead tell me I'm full of it, go ahead!"

Smiling, Griffon could only shake his head. "You're wrong. She was the number two cheerleader. The first slot was held by a big sweaty guy named 'Bubba'."

"Yeah, just what I thought." Pouring another cup, Finn added the contents from a second packet. "Skipper, it's my unofficial opinion, as 'pop-psychologist', that you've never had to worry about anything but winning, or losing." Raising his hand to cut off Griffon's objection. "Now, I know you've seen quite a bit of combat and all that. However, there you were part of a team, and there was always someone who was more experienced than you to help until you learned the ropes. To abuse an old quote, 'The only thing you had to fear was fear itself.'"

"I never thought of it like that, but I guess you're right." Griffon answered thoughtfully.

"Yeah, well I read the 'Red Badge of Courage' too." Fineous mumbled around a sip of coffee.

Griffon emptied his cup before asking. "So, Doc, what's my problem? Why the nightmares?"

Fineous nodded. "For the first time, you actually have to worry about survival. Not for just yourself, but for all of us. That, and the fact that right here, right now, there's nobody that knows more than you, and you're perfectly aware of how little you know about what's up that hole. Right or wrong, your subconscious is punishing you for not being better prepared."

Pouring his second cup, Griffon thought for a few moments. "You may be right." Looking at the mousy little man squatting across from the camp stove, "So Doc, what do I do about it?"

Smiling, Fineous answered. "Damned if I know. The psychiatrists have always said stress affects everybody differently. What very few of them seem to realize is that everyone stresses over different things."

Grateful for the opportunity to move the conversation away from himself, Griffon said. "Oh, like what?"

Fineous paused before answering. "Well, take Fritz over there, he's one of those German 'Supermen'. Oh I know he'd rip his own lungs out before he'd admit it. But, all the same, he's always trying to prove it." He gestured with his cup towards where the Scot was rolled in his sleeping bag. "Then there's Gillian, he seems to be suffering from the 'little-man's syndrome'. He's always got to be stronger, tougher, and smarter than everyone else."

Fineous now nodded towards where the two doctors were sleeping. "White, well he just seems to be out of his depth, and grasping at anything that might offer stability in a 'world gone mad'."

With a chuckle, the little man continued. "Saranah, is in the same boat. It's amusing that all these 'winners' seem to be a bit lost, and desperate, when the rules of the game changes."

Griffon smiled as he asked. "And what about Fineous? Why are you immune to all this?"

The grin got larger. "Hell no! I'm just approaching the problem from a different perspective."

"Oh?" Griffon glanced over to where the others were starting to stir. They still had a few minutes of privacy left, and the conversation did seem to be relaxing him a bit.

Fineous' expression looked positively feral as he continued. "Sure, you see I was always the smallest one in my reform-school class. When you're a deer instead of a wolf, you look at the woods differently. Fear becomes a survival trait. You also learn to always be prepared for the worst."

After taking a sip, he continued. "Don't tell Saranah, but I have four packets of lemon-flavored drink mix in my pack. It'll be used as a bribe if needed." He chuckled and tossed the dregs from his cup.

A sudden thought hit Griffon. "Oh, and do you have any packets of imitation sugar-flavoring in your pack?"

The mousy little man chuckled as he rinsed out his cup. "No, sir! As a matter of fact, I just drank the last of it."

The others could only wonder why the team leader was suddenly doubled over with gales of laughter. However, good humor is contagious, and soon they were all having a good laugh. They needed it and knew it.

They broke camp for the first time and prepared to leave the morgue that had been their introduction to this strange New World.

The group gathered around the elevator shaft as Fineous carefully worked his way up, using a scavenged piece of rebar to pry the last few stones from the passage.

Once cleared, he quickly wormed his way to the next level, moving out of their view, assault-rifle at the ready.

Griffon followed him up. He stopped in the sudden gloom as he tried to orient himself.

"Pssst!" He could barely make out Fineous motioning from behind what appeared to be a doorway. Moving quickly, but cautiously, he crouched next to the dimly lit figure.

Continuing to scan into the darkness ahead, Fineous whispered. "Get the others up here quick and tell them we're not alone."

Peering vainly into the gloom beyond the doorway, Griffon whispered back. "What do you mean? Who's out there? How many? Where are they?"

Fineous' voice was tense. "Gimme a moment, sir! I just heard something scuttling about and some crunching, like gravel or something. I wanted to make sure I had some backup before I used a flashlight."

The others were working themselves up through the opening in what was now the floor. Saranah was next. She went to the opposite side of the opening in the wall. The others followed, scattering as best they could about the cramped room, responding to whispered instructions and aiming their weapons at the doorway.

Griffon's eyes were slowly becoming accustomed to the dim light filtering up from below. It was becoming apparent that they were in the remains of what appeared to be a large freight-elevator. It had crashed onto the rubble that blocked the shaft. Smashed and broken, the walls bucked, the outer doors had been ripped completely out of their tracks. Outside the door, he could dimly see they were on the inside of the angle formed by two corridors that were almost completely choked with rubble. What appeared to be piping, cables, and tubing trailed down through the remnants of a false ceiling to mix with the rocks and debris layered on the floor.

He could now make out the sounds of scuttling as well. Small, shadowy forms seemed to be moving about in both corridors.

Crawling to the doorway, Griffon whispered. "Well, we can't just hole up here. Let's use our lights and see if we can surprise our visitors. Any questions? Good.

"White, you and Saranah get on the other side of the opening, Fineous and I'll work from here. On the count of three, we'll shine our lights down the opposite corridor. Now, be ready to fire, but mark your targets, I don't want to fire unless we have to."

Quickly, and quietly, they slid into covered positions, awaiting his signal.

In a tense whisper, Griffon said, "On three. One... Two... THREE!"

In the relative darkness, the flashlight beams flashed brilliantly. Spearing into the corridor they pinned, a... nightmare. About half a meter long, something glistened black in the white light. The creature's scales rippled as six crooked legs sent the serpentine body across the rubble-choked floor. Large insect-like eyes flanked a bony, fang-filled beak which opened to a hissing scream.

Everyone froze in shock. Even the creature seemed stunned by the sudden brilliance. Then... bedlam!

The monster seemed to blur in movement and four rifles ripped stuttering barks. Everything was strobe lit in brilliant bolts of light. Dozens of the creatures scrambled backwards, for the safety of the darkness beyond.

Then, darkness, and silence fell like a blanket. Their flash-blinded vision slowly returned to normal. The flashlight beams were now appearing relatively dim and weak. Their ears quit ringing, and they could hear the crack and rattle of rubble still settling outside the doorway.

Fineous was the first to find his voice. "What the hell was that?" His knuckles were white where they clutched the assault rifle. White spoke up. "Well, judging from the description, I'd say it was what the researchers called a 'hexrat'." Griffon carefully moved forward and gingerly poked at a horribly mangled corpse, "A hexi-what?"

White followed him closely and knelt to peer and poke at another blasted corpse. "According to the researchers, most of the creatures the invaders have introduced are three or six-legged. They also combine several features we normally associate with one genus or another, like these scaled hides and insect-like, multi-faceted eyes."

Fineous had moved past them to peer down the right corridor. "How the hell does a three-legged animal walk?"

Absorbed in studying the creature before him, White answered. "Quite well, apparently. They report creatures that they called 'tripes' or 'Tripoidal Carnivores' that are described as chitinous, three-legged, terrestrial octopuses, with skeleton, and three-fingered, clawed hands. They believed they were cunning pack hunters and semi-arboreal, much like our baboons."

Griffon turned in disgust from the stinking, gutted remains. "And what is this thing?"

White looked up from his studying the creature. "A hexrat. They believed it filled the same niche as our rats."

Griffon nodded. "OK, and what's it doing here?"

White paused for a moment, thinking.

Gillian and Fritz had now joined them, but Griffon noted Saranah hadn't come out of the elevator yet.

White continued. "I can only surmise that this was a research facility where they studied captured specimens. Some of them must have survived the fighting and have now overrun the facility." He paused, his brow furrowed, "Either that or specimens of invading species may have made it down here over the decades."

In a quiet voice, Fineous said. "Maybe you should tell us what else we may run into. After all, these may not be the only such critters down here." Meanwhile, he continued to verify that all the creatures in sight were in fact dead.

Listening to the conversation behind him, Griffon returned to the elevator. Saranah was still crouched in the position she had fired from, just holding her rifle and rocking back and forth.

He knelt and touched her elbow. "Are you OK? Were you hurt?"

She turned to him, shuddering. "Oh, I'm OK. It's just that I have this thing about rats. I have no problem working with lizards, but seeing all those... little monsters... Ugh!" She stood unsteadily. "I'm all right now." She looked at him with deadly earnest. "Let's just get the hell out'ta here, OK?" She glanced out through the doorway to where the others were still discussing the hexrats. "If you mention a word about this I'll personally guarantee that you'll get a chance to get up close and personal with a tree-limb." Her brilliant smile gleamed in the dim light, "OK?"

Grinning, Griffon feigned a shudder of his own. "Yeah sure, whatever you say." He leaned in close and whispered. "Just remember this. Especially if we have a run-in with any giant spiders, OK?"

Relieved, they carefully stepped over the rubble to join the others. White was cataloging some of the more noteworthy specimens the research center had once held. "Well, the most impressive were the 'jabberwocks', which were shaped like a horizontal capital letter-'T', with three heavily clawed, three-toed feet. They walked on the front two, using the hind claw as a counterbalance, curled up over the back like a scorpion's stinger. The head was bullet-like and projected forward from the top of the 'T'. It had two large segmented eyes and a full set of fangs. They said it was a stalk-and-pounce pack hunter, reminiscent of the ancient terrestrial Raptors. They would pounce and grip with the forward claws, while gutting with the rearmost."

"I hate to break up the zoology class, but we'd better be moving out." Griffon announced. He checked the antique compass, and nodded towards the right corridor. "For want of a better way, we'll head north. Fineous, you take point, I'll follow, then the others. Fritz, you bring up the rear with the grenade launcher. If anything comes up behind us, you put it down."

The big German grinned. Unslinging the grenade-launcher, he hefted it, like a toy in his big paw. "Ja, I vill yust shove it down da gullet."

With a decidedly distasteful expression, Fineous readied his assault-rifle, heaved his pack onto his back, and prepared to move out. "Any idea why the lights were on down below and not here?"

Gillian spoke up, shrugging into his own pack. "Well, if this facility was powered by either geothermal or fusion power, and barring major breakdown, there's no reason why there shouldn't be power for another century. I'd guess from looking around that the circuits were cut on this level." He kicked at a stone which turned out to be a well-gnawed front half of a human skull. "This area looks like it was pretty heavily fought over, probably the rear-guard for those below."

With nothing more to go on, the others could only nod. They began to make their slow, tortuous way down the clogged corridor, pausing to check blasted rooms and cross-corridors.

The party tested their grenades at the first cross-corridor. The red-striped grenades were high explosive. While the yellow were illumination rounds. The white ones were some sort of smoke round, but they only had one of the hand-held blue-striped one, and didn't want to waste it. Occasionally, they came across small packs of the hideous hexrats, which proved very happy to scuttle away. After the first couple of encounters, Griffon decided firing at them was just a waste of ammunition.

After a couple of hours, light appeared in the distance. Approaching carefully, they saw what proved to be a less devastated area. Brighter areas loomed in the distance. The amount of rubble significantly declined in the brighter areas. The small pockets of heavy damage surrounded the largest piles of human bones.

Several hours of thorough exploration had revealed many stairways and elevator shafts to the higher levels, all blocked. They noted the locations on their rough map, hoping to find an easier way to the surface.

Eventually, they decided to break for the "night." Selecting a relatively undamaged room with a doorway that was easy to block; and set a rotating shift for watch FOUR

It was at the end of the second day that disaster struck.

The team was continuing with their exploration, when they spotted a different sort of light in the distance.

It was a broad shaft of almost cheerful yellow light, streaming down through a large hole in the ceiling. It was located deep in one of the larger areas of blacked-out devastation; otherwise, they might have missed it.

They had been exploring for several hours already, and were looking for a place to hole up when they found the breach.

As the team noted, the very heavy battle-damage surrounding the light. It came from a three-meter wide shaft that had been melted through the intervening rock, ferrocrete, and steel. Rusted pools and heaps of slag mounted up beneath the vitrified walls of the gap. Looking upwards they saw what seemed to be greenery choking the sun-drenched upper end.

Gillian, Griffon, and Fritz went into an immediate debate over exactly what kind of energy or tool could have burnt a hole through six meters of solid rock.

White and Saranah kept watch while Fineous set about exploring the area.

Off to one side he found what appeared to be a heavily barricaded doorway, with signs of extremely heavy combat. Human remains were heaped around the barricade among rusted, broken, and useless implements.

However, Fineous' interest was in what lay beyond the door. He called the others over, pointing out that the people had obviously fought ferociously to protect what lay beyond the still intact barricade.

Setting up camp to one side of the gap in the ceiling, they began to dig with scavenged tools at the barricade.

Working in shifts. Two at a time, to clear away the mound of material. Fritz and White were the ones to finally uncover the top of the warped and blasted door beyond.

Later, no one could quite remember what had happened, though all had it burnt into their memory.

Fritz was kneeling, looking into the wide gap at the top of the door. White turned to call to the others. Suddenly, a sun-bright shaft of red light burst upwards from behind the barricade.

Fritz was instantly decapitated; everything from the middle of his chest up was simply... gone.

His smoking remains were slammed backwards by the force of the blast.

White caught only the very edge of the beam. He was tossed aside like a doll. His limp form smashed into the far wall and tumbled into a heap. His right arm ended in a smoking stump.

The others were momentarily stunned. Griffon was just beginning to guess that they had tripped some kind of trap, when a horrible grinding and screech of metal ripped from the fire-blasted gap.

A huge clawed, metal hand appeared at the gap atop the barricade and started to tear it away. The weakened barrier quickly collapsed.

Within seconds, a massively armored form crawled out of the enlarged gap. It rose unsteadily on rusted, warped legs.

The apparition was humanoid, maybe three meters tall, heavily armored. The left arm ended in a rusted, tangled wreck just below the shoulder. The right had what appeared to be a large bore weapon in the forearm, just behind the clawed hand. Where the head should be was a conical turret, mounting what seemed to be a multitude of sensors and lenses. The upper body pivoted at the waist and first the cameras, then the blast cannon, were aimed at the stunned humans.

They were already moving. Gillian had been on watch and immediately began to fire short, controlled bursts into the armored form. Griffon and Saranah both dove to recover their own weapons and rolled behind bits of rubble for cover. Fineous hesitated a-moment, then dove away from the others and scuttled beneath the combot's view. Ducking behind it as it faced the others.

A brilliant hail of fire flashed and smashed against the armored form. Glowing divots exploded from the thick ceramic.

The blast cannon spoke in return. The pile of rubble Griffon had ducked behind exploded into a sun-bright burst of ash and cinders. He scuttled backwards, vainly seeking further cover.

Gillian shifted fire, walking tracers into the sensor turret, trying to blind it. The combot's fire burned high, blasting into the wall behind Griffon. The shock knocking him flat.

Seeing his chance, Gillian leapt forward, pulling the stylus of the datacomp at his belt and charged up the pile of rubble as the combot blindly fired in wild swaths. When it paused, he shoved the stylus into the gapping maw of the blast cannon and leapt clear.

The blinded combot pivoted, seeking movement through the scarring of its visor. Suddenly the face-shield seemed to blur, quiver, and shift. Leaving behind unmarred transparency. With blinding speed the Combot reacquired a target and fired.

There was a massive explosion. Red-yellow fire gouted outward. Shards from the ruined arm struck Gillian, tossing him into a limp, unconscious heap, his flak-vest molten and smoking.

The enemy staggered back, swinging it's ruined arms in futile threat. It stumbled over the rubble and crashed down into a broken heap.

They continued to fire as it steadied, then began to raise itself up on the ruined stumps of its arms. The sensor-turret exploded in a ball of flaming wreckage.

Blinded, the creature began to rip at the rubble around it with the jagged remnants of its arms, tearing huge divots from the floor and walls. The humans scrambled away from the maddened giant.

A second blast of white-hot fire and the combot dropped, smashed and sparking.

Behind it stood Fineous, Fritz's grenade launcher held lightly in both hands. He worked the action, aimed and put a third round through the back of the prone and helpless Combot.

It jerked, quivered, and died.

Fineous stood, snarling at the smoking form before him. He spat and muttered something the others could not hear.

Quickly tossing her weapon aside, Saranah rushed to where White lay. The stub of his arm was still smoking. She felt the side of his neck for a pulse and called to the others to bring her the autodoc. Fineous was kneeling by the moaning Gillian, helping the broad Scot as he feebly tried to peel off the smoking remains of his flak jacket. Griffon leapt to the pile of packs and started frantically searching for the rolled autodoc.

They unrolled the plastic, sleeping bag-shaped unit. White was quickly stripped. After cutting the remnants of his clothing away, they rolled him into the Autodoc. An oxygen mask snapped over his face as the tapered, mummy-like tube inflated. Probes and sensors automatically began to perform their checks. The computer quickly processed the information, and almost seemed to "tisk" as it began administering anesthetic and antibiotics. Hook-like feelers began to clean and debride the charred flesh around the wounds.

Gillian received the more prosaic attentions of a medkit.

He gave a doped up smile through his reddish whiskers, mumbling. "I'd do a whole lot better with a wee bit o' malt." Griffon smiled. "You can buy the first round." Gillian chuckled weakly, as the painkillers took hold. "Cheap bastid."

Once the wounded were treated, and in an anesthetized daze, the others tended to what was left of Fritz. They carefully gathered up his remains, zipped them into a sleeping bag, and laid them in the empty room behind the barricade. Then, they carefully rebuilt the wall. It wasn't much, but it would keep the Hexrats out.

Standing before the rubble-blocked doorway, Saranah and Fineous turned toward Griffon. They all bowed their heads as he began. "Oh, Lord I'm afraid that we don't have a Lutheran chaplain available to give the proper rights for our comrade. I can simply say that you've got a good man with you, a good friend, and someone that could be trusted to do the right thing, and that's the best I can say about anyone."

He picked up a handful of gravel and tossed it on the rubble blocking the doorway. "Ashes to ashes, dust to dust."

Later, they settled down around the camp stove, eating and speculating about the combot.

Griffon, who'd carefully examined the blasted and twisted room behind the barricade, thought for a moment before responding. "The best I can figure, that thing's been trapped here ever since this place was overrun. I think the humans were able to wound it, trap it in there, and just seal it off. The other alien forces either didn't know it was in there or didn't care."

"So it was able to remain activated for almost seventy years?" Fineous asked as he dished up a plate of the reconstituted meal.

Saranah shrugged. "Judging from the notes we found, those things are fusion-powered. The thing simply went on 'stand-by' until it heard someone trying to dig it out. It knew it couldn't be its forces, so it just attacked."

Griffon looked across the steaming pot at Fineous. "By the way, where'd you get the idea to use the grenade launcher on that thing?"

Fineous looking embarrassed. "Well, when I saw it climbing out from behind the barricade, I saw that it had been pretty-well chewed up, and I realized that it hadn't really stopped it at all. So, I thought we'd need something a bit heavier. We had used hand grenades to drive off the hexrats, and that the red-striped ones had been high explosive, while the yellow had been incendiary. I suddenly remembered Fritz had been carrying one launcher clip with nothing but green-striped grenades. So I went for it and hoped they'd be armor-piercing." He shrugged and looked toward the huddled forms of their wounded. "I guess I got lucky."

Saranah, in a rare display of femininity, walked over to him and lightly kissed his forehead. "We got lucky."

Griffon grinned at the fiercely flushing Fineous. "Good going truck-driver."

Desperately trying to regain his composure, Fineous waggled the thumb of his free hand at his crotch and muttered. "Ahhhh, drive this."

For the first time in hours, they all laughed. The sound echoed down the darkened corridors.

It was several hours before Gillian recovered enough for the medkit to release him from the painkiller daze. He slowly began to respond to his surroundings. After a mug of freeze-dried stew and a large shot of reconstituted coffee, he was back to his old self.

He quickly became enamored with the alien Combot. The others could only smile as he poked and prodded at the complex machinery. He absentmindedly thanked Fineous for bringing him his next meal. Then, immediately sat it down, and forgot it. The others arranged watches and slept. One of them kept constant watch over White, encased in the soft folds of the autodoc. Gillian worked on.

Occasionally he'd exclaim to himself, other times he'd curse and wrench at a bit of damaged metal that resisted his best efforts.

After hours of this, he finally staggered over to the camp stove. Sitting, he seemed to inhale a full pot of stew, tasting none of it as he stared off into the distance. Then, muttering to himself, he rolled into his sleeping bag and seemed to doze off. The others couldn't be sure. He'd shift from snoring and muttering in his sleep to mumbling over what he'd found, and back to snoring without missing a beat.

Finally, after two days of this, he was roused from his fixation by the excitement of the others. White was finally released by the autodoc. The doctor was pale and weak. His questions died when he discovered his right arm ended just below the elbow in a pink skim of scar tissue.

The others had been well briefed by Saranah on the psychological help they would have to provide a mutilated companion.

However, they never had a chance to try it out. Gillian pounced on White with questions about the effects of Cryogenics, time, and various radiations on the alien life forms. He didn't allow the wounded doctor to dwell on his injuries.

His efforts, while self-centered and almost monomaniacal in nature, did more than all the pop-psychology the others had been planning to use. White never had a chance to feel like a cripple before the redheaded little giant convinced him of how much he was needed, with or without his arm.

After a short while, the others managed to get White away from Gillian. The Scot stalked over to the partially disassembled and wholly smashed remains of the combot. He seemed to be sulking as he started tracing wiring and mechanisms, waiting for his next chance at the doctor.

Once White had eaten, drunk, and managed to speak a few words with the others, Gillian pounced again. He wanted to know all that the doctor remembered from his review of the records found below.

After a while, Saranah insisted Gillian allow White a chance to rest.

As the doctor began to breathe softly, the others gathered around the stove. Griffon finally dared to ask Gillian to explain what he'd been able to find out.

Nodding, Gillian stalked over to the remains of the combot and waved the others over. Using a meter-long piece of rebar as a pointer, he began to dictate his findings.

"This is just fantastic!" He said, as he pointed at the battered, barrel-like torso. "Inside, here is the most efficient powerplant I've ever seen. We'd need a fusion reactor the size of a house to match its output."

He spun toward the wrecked arm, almost decapitating Fineous with his pointer. "The magnetic fields they could form and their ability to manipulate them is simply amazing. For example, the weapon it used. . ." pointing at the blackened remains of the blast cannon in the forearm; "isn't even a weapon as we know it. They used a form of 'Liquid Metal' heat sump to cool their reactor."

"For example, we know both mercury and lead have relatively low-melting temperatures. However, they also have extremely stable atomic structures. Therefore, they can both absorb massive amounts of thermal energy before the atomic structure breaks down."

"In counterpoint, to say, uranium or plutonium, have relatively high melting temperatures. But, when excessive heat and pressure are applied, their unstable atomic structures cause them to break up, creating the, 'chain reaction' used in early fission systems."

"What we have here are 'base metals' with their lower melting points, being used as a cooling system for the fusion reactor. As the metal melts, it absorbs the excess heat from the reactor. It is then run through a rather efficient radiator system which allows the excess heat to be bled off, lowering the temperature of the metal to just above the melting point. It is then recycled through the system to receive more excess thermal energy."

"Now, what we have here is a, 'tapping' of some of this 'liquid metal' coolant into a special magnetic bottle. A 'high compression', thermal chamber as it was. Instead of being allowed to circulate through the system to radiate its excess heat, it is exposed to greater and greater amounts of heat. Like in a steam boiler, the metal is brought through vaporization, to the point where even these stable metals are on the point of atomic breakdown. Thus, they create what is known as a, 'high energy plasma'. They then simply, 'vent' this plasma down through this directional tube, ah, barrel where it's expelled as a 'Plasma Bolt'."

He shook his head. "This is a brilliant concept. Not only does it provide a remarkably simple weapon of tremendous destructive power; it also provides an emergency cooling sump for situations where the normal cooling system cannot handle the load. Simply put, they can use the excess heat to charge the weapon. Then they can choose to either discharge the weapon, or simply hold it, and recirculate the vaporized metal through the system when the emergency is past."

Griffon could only smile as he looked at the blackened scars gouged from the walls. "They used a high-tech steam cannon?"

"Well, yes! They're able to channel and direct the plasma like we would a bit of steam. This thing can launch a blast like a cannon, or a fine stream of welding energy, without effort." Gillian stepped back and looked down at the sprawled form of the Combot. "This is amazing, simply amazing." Hesitant as any schoolboy, Fineous raised his hand. "So how could it remain functional for sixty years?"

The broad Scot's face split in a huge grin. "Ah, that's the beauty of this system. Our own fusion reactors are capable of running for a couple of centuries, but they are the size of a building." Pointing. "Here we have a reactor with the same capabilities and output the size of a good computer monitor."

Griffon's turn, "What about that shield, or whatever it was, it had over its sensors?"

Gillian only missed a beat. "Oh, that. For over a century we've had the ability to treat glass and transparent metals with polarizing chemicals."

The others looked at each other blankly.

Exasperated at having to explain what he considered to be obvious, Gillian answered. “The windows that can be made clear or opaque at the flip of a switch.” Seeing that they finally got it. “What happens is that the electrical current runs a magnetic field over the chemical coating and realigns the molecules. In one direction it’s transparent, in another it isn’t.”

Walking over to the shattered remains of the head-like sensor turret, he added, “Here we have a thick layer of extremely advanced transparent metal.” Looking up at the others. “Like our ‘Transparent Aluminum’, only much denser and harder. Whenever it’s suffered damage, or otherwise become opaque to the sensors, they would use some form of current or interaction of magnetic fields, to realign the molecules. They could ‘fix it’ almost at will.”

Saranah asked. “So why didn’t they do that with all the armor?”

Gillian shrugged. “That’s easy, while much denser than anything we use, the faceplate is still rather. . . ‘soft’, as it were. The armor actually consists of relatively easy to replace, pre-formed, ablative, ‘sandwiches’ of various ceramics and metals. At least that’s what I’ve been able to make out here and from what the records we found said.”

Perplexed, Fineous asked. “‘Ablative’?”

Nodding, the broad Scott answered. “Yes, that means while it is perfectly capable of protecting and absorbing kinetic impact. Its primary design consideration is to ‘boil away’ under energy attack. While it obviously erodes the armor, it is really a most effective means of protecting from high-energy weapons.” Pointing to the arm-mounted energy cannon, “like that.”

Saranah asked. “If it’s so well protected why was it so easy for Fineous to blow it apart?”

This caused Gillian to pause for a bit, thinking. “Ah yes, well that’s because of two separate, but related things.” He picked up a piece of discarded armor, and pointed at the obvious pitting from battle damage. “These plates are meant to protect the Combot for one or two actions. They’re really very good at it. But, even while surviving repeated impacts and energy bolts, they will develop microscopic fractures, and inevitable separation of the various sections of the metal-ceramic, ah ‘sandwich’.”

Rotating the piece of armor to show the broken fasteners. “These were designed to be replaced after being damaged. This. . .” Pointing back at the combot; “never had a chance to get replacements from the last action. Basically, it was blasted to near ruin in its last fight, and Fineous just took up where it left off.”

Griffon asked. “You said there were two things?”

“Oh yes.” He picked up one of the green-striped Grenade rounds ‘borrowed’ from the launcher. “This is great. I really love this. Basically, it’s a titanium-alloy ‘sabot’, or needle positioned in front of a ‘shaped-charge’. The explosive jet ‘injects’ the solid ‘sabot’ straight through the armor. This prevents the jet from being redirected or scattered by the various channeling aspects of the ceramic sandwich."

Griffon looked up. "So, what you're saying is that Fineous was able to kill this thing because of a superior armor-penetration round and old, worn-out armor?"

Gillian looked a bit confused. "Well, yes."

"So, why didn't you just say so?" Fineous said. "Why the lesson in beginners physics?"

A bright red flush started at Gillian's collar and rolled all the way to his receding hairline. "My apologies for being an engineer. Maybe next time we'll just communicate in grunts and barks!"

The others traded smiles as the angered engineer stalked back to their camp, muttering. They were able to make out a few phrases, "Philistines", "Cretins" and "Liberal-arts majors", were among the more generous.

Later, as conversation turned to the more immediate concerns, they decided to wait two more days before trying to climb to the next level. To allow White's wounds a bit more time to heal and to prepare ropes and harnesses they would need for the climb out.

On the eve of their assent, Griffon awoke with a sudden start. He couldn't place the sounds which had awaked him. They were low, rhythmic, and almost animal in nature. He looked up and saw Fineous sitting by the camp stove, the ever-present cup of coffee steaming in his hand.

Trying not to wake the others he whispered. "Hey Finn, what the hell's that noise?"

Fineous ginned and gestured over his shoulder, toward the screens where White had been laid so as not to be disturbed. "Now, now sir. They think they're being discreet."

Perplexed, Griffon asked. "What? Who?"

Fineous gave him a wink. "Saranah and White."

Griffon shook his head, still confused. "What are you talking about?"

Sighing, Fineous muttered sarcastically. "You know, I helped colonize three worlds. I survived half a century in cold storage. I even survived Armageddon..." sipping his coffee, "and the only human female in the known universe wants a doctor."

Still a bit slow on the uptake, Griffon began. "What the hell are you talking abou... Oh!"

He shared a look and a nod, with Fineous. "Ah yes, I see. I guess we'll just have to let them keep their privacy."

"Good job sir." Fineous added, with a grin. "Now why don't you go back to sleep, it's still a couple of hours until your watch."

Tossing aside his covers and fishing for his boots, Griffon grumbled sotto-voice. "You have got to be kidding!"

Gillian rolled out of the sack also, grumbling. "Well if everyone else is going to get up..." Looking apologetically at the other two, "Sorry about the pun."

They shared a laugh, not disturbing the two lovers at all.

Chapter 4

They began the ascent. White was recovering well, but still too weak to risk climbing on his own. Therefore, Fineous, being the lightest of the team, climbed through the opening above, a strong, light cord coiled over his shoulder. Once he had reached the next level he secured one end and dropped the other back down. Gillian and Griffon went next. Saranah secured White in a harness and they hoisted him to the next level. Saranah followed and helped steer him past the few obstructions in the gap.

The top of the shaft was almost choked by a thick blanket of strange vines and creepers trailing down the shaft. The predominant type was a peculiar, green-black color, with massive purplish veins which were warm to the touch and seemed to pulse and flex with any movement of the leaves.

Another plant had odd reddish-orange leaves, with a green-shot yellow border around their saw-toothed edges. Fineous learned, by accidentally brushing his arm against one, the red-orange leaves burned the flesh. The contact left behind massive blisters which quickly formed into pus-filled knots. His cry of pain alarmed the others. Though clenched teeth, he managed to give quite a colorful warning to the others.

On the next level, they found themselves in a cave-like room. The walls, ceiling and floor were covered with thick layers of alien plantlife. Gillian brushed off a twelve-legged spider which had dropped onto Griffon's back. Six-winged beetle-like insects took flight.

The yellowish light was streaming through an opening several meters to the left, while the dim glow of another opening appeared down the corridor to their right.

In single file they slowly, carefully, worked their way through the riot of alien growth to the nearest opening.

As usual, Fineous was in the lead and reached the opening first. The others heard him gasp, and quickly following, each was frozen in turn by the sight that met their eyes.

At first impression, it seemed they were standing at the bottom of a mighty canyon. However, as their eyes became adjusted to the brilliant yellow light, they saw this was only an illusion.

Great banks of lights formed rank upon rank across a vaulted, catwalk-lined ceiling. The wall behind them curved on both sides to form a near perfect oval. They could make out several stories of evenly spaced windows, the glass missing from most. The far end of the room was at least a kilometer away.

The floor sloped gradually to a large lake or pond in the center of the chamber. What appeared, at first glance, to be a mighty tree rose from the center of the water to the ceiling two- to three hundred meters above. Closer examination revealed it was actually a girded pillar, supporting large bundles of pipes and tubing.

To both their left and right, walkways were supported by arched pillars running radially from the central column to the walls. They had obviously been covered at some time; the remnants of the transparency left splintered bits around the twisted frames.

Thick foliage covered everything. A riot of groundcover remained only partially identifiable as plants. Huge, tree-like objects lifted multi-spired trunks above the lesser plants. Thorny, vine growths twisted among the multiple stalks.

Everywhere, animals could be seen forcing their way through the growth, climbing among the branches and vines, leaping in the waters, and flying through the air.

In the distance was a small family of massive, gray-black, six-legged animals which most resembled a rhino with overlapping, spike-fringed, armored slabs protecting their flanks and great tusked heads, which they lifted to tear at the foliage.

They spotted a group of large, three-legged, yellow-detailed russet-colored creatures that could only be the "Jabberwocks" White had described.

Griffon ducked as a six-winged dragonfly, with a two-foot wingspan flew past his head, lashing at his face with a barbed tail.

Suddenly, a large bird-creature swooped down and snatched the dragonfly. It fluttered about before landing on a nearby branch, turning its insect-eyed, fanged face towards the party to emit a buzz-hiss of a scream. It was clutching its prey in its fore-claws. The wings were actually two central legs, elongated like a bat's wing.

Other, lesser creatures could be seen moving through the alien jungle. They lived, bred, and died beneath an unchanging, simulated sun.

Fineous, was the first to recover. He turned toward the others and, in a hushed voice. "I don't think we're in Kansas anymore."

The spell was broken and Griffon reached out and punched him in the arm.

Grinning, the little man rubbed his injury. "Hey! Ow! Somebody had to say it."

Gillian, automatically cataloging the engineering details involved, turned to White, "What is this place?"

The doctor shrugged. "Well, the notes we found said this had been a biologic research facility to study captured specimens of the invaders' flora and fauna. I can only guess that, while the environmental support systems still work, the detention facilities must have broken down. The creatures have been left to fend for themselves for the last sixty or so years."

Saranah, in a small, awed voice. "So this, in a very real sense, is what the aliens plan for Earth?"

White shook his head. "Maybe not, that'd be like judging what a city looks like by touring the zoo."

Griffon, in a much more practical vein, motioned the others back. "I think we'd better get back in the tunnel, or corridor, or whatever it is, until we can figure out what to do. Some of these things are carnivores."

As they turned back towards the cave-like entrance, Griffon spotted movement in the darkness. "Hold it, something's in there." Unslinging his assault-rifle, he moved past the others. "We don't have enough grenades to be tossing them at every shadow. Saranah, you and Gillian check six. White, overwatch, Fineous with me."

Before anyone else could react or speak, he sprinted towards the shadowed opening.

Ducking into the low entrance, he caught an indeterminate-sized group of bizarre, three-legged creatures in the beam of his flashlight.

They looked like half-meter-tall, three-legged, cross between an octopus and an insect. As he froze in place, the creatures began to scuttle back deeper into the darkness, emitting a high-pitched, hissing scream as they went.

He roared and charged after the creatures, firing burst after burst into the heaving mass of panicky monsters.

Outside the tunnel, the others only saw him charge into the darkness. As flashes lit the entrance of the cavern, Fineous muttered. "Mother, frackin..." and followed, unslinging his own weapon. Gillian and Saranah traded looks and flanked White who looked nervously on as all hell seemed to break loose in the tunnel.

Griffon had charged deep into the blackened corridor. He was well past the hole in the floor before he stopped, breathing hard.

Sounds of scuffling feet and the rattle of claws on rubble faded before him. He tried to shine the pathetic beam of his flashlight into the tunnel. Even so, it was several seconds before his flash-dazzled eyes were able to recover enough to allow him to just make out the dim, hulking mounds of vine covering rubble and debris. The after-image of blue-white streaks from his own tracers still danced before his eyes.

A heavy mass crashed against the back of his legs. Spinning he drew down on. . . Fineous, sprawling at his feet.

Spitting dust and grit, the mousy little man reached up. Grabbing Griffon by the battle harness, he pulled himself up and he shone his flashlight into Griffon's eyes.

Fineous seemed to be quite irate. He sputtered and hissed as he loudly whispered. "Will you hold up!" He bent down to gingerly probe a ragged tear in his leg. A spreading red stain told how deep the rusty piece of metal had cut. "What the hell do you think you're doing?"

Griffon ginned as he turned back to face the creatures still retreating down the corridor. "I chased them back, didn't I?"

Hearing a soft sound, Fineous looked up from his first aid. His flashlight reflected back from the mass of greenery growing among the bundles of pipes, cables, and tubing which lined the ceiling. "I'm not so sure."

"What do you mean? They took off like rabbits." Griffon turned as a pebble from the overhead bounced off his head.

They both started to sprint for the opening.

Shrieking, foul-smelling, brownish-white bodies dropped from above as others leapt from hiding places and boltholes in the piles of rubble. They could hear the shrieks and crashing charge of the creatures which had previously fled up the corridor returning, with a vengeance.

Their retreat cut off; the two stood back-to-back ripping loose with burst after burst. Firing blindly into the strobelit mass surging towards them.

Griffon's vision blanked out as a heavy mass dropped over his head and shoulders. His mouth and nose were assaulted by the stupefying stench of the creature. He dropped his rifle, grabbing at the chitinous-armored limbs clutching at him. He felt a stabbing pain as the beak of the monster tore into his right shoulder.

Grappling with the creature, he managed to rip his combat knife free and began stabbing and slashing at the beasts. His legs were knocked from under him, sending him crashing to the debris-cluttered floor.

The red haze of battle-lust settled over his vision. He seemed to step out of his body. Looking down he could see himself moving in slow motion. An endless mass of ripping claws, snapping beaks, and writhing bodies the color of rotting puss heaved and surged over him.

Suddenly he snapped back into his body and heaved himself to his feet.

Tossing the slashed and dismembered remnants of his attackers aside, he glanced about. His eyes, now adjusted to the dim light, managed to make out the sickening remnants piled in heaps around him. Fineous was off to one side, back to the wall, eyes wild, as he seemed to be trying to look in all directions at once, his rifle smoking in his hands.

Looking at the pile of ripped bodies scattered around Fineous and the carpet of sickening flesh and stinking ichor that trailed into the darkness, Griffon could only wonder at the feeling of white-hot fire rushing through his veins. Everything was in the sharpest focus. Startled, he realized he felt alive. He could feel his heart pounding, the stench-laden air drawing into his lungs, the grit that had seeped into his boots, the blood trickling down from his shoulder.

Fineous started as Griffon raised his blood-covered blade, threw his head back, and unleashed an inhuman scream.

Griffon gave a wild, blood-streaked grin to his still-shaking companion. “Now, the corridor’s clear.” He chuckled and offered Fineous his hand as he started towards the opening to the main cavern.

Bodies of the alien creatures were strewn all the way from the exit to where the other members of the party stood. A small barricade of several still-quivering carcasses marked the spot where the last had reached in their charge towards the others.

White, Gillian, and Saranah stared in amazement at the tattered and stained apparitions that walked towards them. After a moment’s hesitation, they rushed to help. Griffon’s savage grin was made hideous by the spattered gore.

Probing and patching with a vengeance, Saranah could only scold. “What the hell did you think you were doing?” Grunting under the ungentle ministrations, Griffon caught a muttering Fineous’ eye. “Wow, man, like ‘deja-vu’. She must have the same script you do.”

Fineous looked back as White awkwardly worked on him one-handed. “No, we all have the same reaction to a madman. What did you think you were doing?”

That brought them all to a pause, as Griffon looked up into the hooded eyes of his team. “Didn’t you guys smell them when we came up?”

The others looked at each other. He pointed at the opening. “Look at all the bits and pieces around here.”

They only now noticed the piles of discarded bits, hair, and other remnants heaped about the entrance to the tunnel.

“That shit’s piled all the way back past where we came up. I thought you’d noticed it. The tunnel’s the lair for those things.”

He pointed with his unbandaged arm at the pile of creatures. “I’d thought they had run off when we came up. Then I saw all the remains. I realized there were no signs of any Hexrats or other predators around, so I kind of figured these were really bad guys. Then, when we started to head back toward the tunnel, I saw them moving inside the entrance. With all that. I concluded we were about to be rushed.” He grinned at up at them. “I just figured we’d get the rush in first, and maybe run them off without a fight.”

Now Fineous muttered around a finger probing a loose tooth. “That didn’t work too good. Did it?” Griffon shrugged, still grinning. “Well, no, I guess it didn’t. But, hey, it wasn’t for want of trying.”

Spitting blood from the lip split when his tooth was loosened, the little man gave a sarcastic snort. “Judging from that scream and what I saw in there, I think you just wanted a fight.”

Flexing his fingers and checking the feel of his now-bandaged arm. “Yeah that’s right. I just wanted to run into the lair of a bunch of filthy alien monsters for the fun of it. You're just mad because you didn't spot the ambush."

Fineous waggled both thumbs at his crotch. "Ah, mad this. . ."

The others could only chuckle as the two fast friends bickered and ranted. Gillian gathered up the scattered gear while White and Saranah examined the hideous creatures.

They had to almost pry White and Saranah from the piles of creature parts. White was waving a severed arm in front of Saranah's nose, pointing and going on in some heat about indications the creature had a chameleon-like color-changing ability.

Saranah, with her own sizable chunk of creature, seemed to be stressing that; yes the creature had definite color-changing capabilities, but it was far more limited. Much like the way a fish will maintain its basic color pattern, but will vary the overall tint in relation to the ambient light available, etc., etc., etc.

For a while the others were content to just let them argue.

Chapter 5

After a while Griffon noted the pile of carcasses was starting to attract a remarkable number of pseudo-insects and smaller vermin. The proximity of the humans seemed to make no impression on the scavengers. He became alarmed when, a spider-like animal, with a body the size of a bowling ball and way-too-many-legs leapt from cover and pounced on a small Hexrat that had snatched at a bit of meat.

He walked up to the two scientists, who were oblivious to anything beyond their argument, took them each by an arm, and led them away from the heap.

Without missing a beat, the two continued their argument.

Griffon could only shake his head in wonder. *It's time to leave, before something tries to make a meal out of us*. He grabbed his assault-rifle. "OK, we'd better move out. Fineous, take point, Gillian you have the rear." He pointed to the nearby raised walkway. "We'll climb that, and use it as a road to the center column."

Fineous shouldered his pack and asked. "Ok, I'll bite. Why are we going to the center of this overgrown salad-bar, anyway?"

Griffon pointed to the outer ring of the walls. "We've been almost a week just reaching this level, how long will it take us to make it up those next four?" He then pointed at the tall central spire. "We should be able to climb those girders and make it up to there." He now pointed to the maze of walkways dimly visible behind the banks of lights. "Where, with any luck, we'll be able to get to the next level and be that much closer to getting out of here."

Fineous looked up, then back at the team leader, and started to chuckle.

This, for some reason, irritated Griffon. He had to ask. "OK, wise-guy, what's the problem?"

The little man started towards the raised walkway to their right. "I was just thinking about a quote from one of my favorite books."

"Which is?" Griffon asked, as he checked the area again.

"Short cuts make for long delays." Fineous answered over his shoulder.

Shaking his head, Griffon could only smile and direct the two scientists, who were still arguing in low tones, after the mousy little man.

It took only a few minutes to reach the walkway. They could hear a rising cacophony coming from the direction of their recent battle with the tripes. Gillian put it most succinctly. "Tah beasties seem to be disagreeing over the dining arrangements."

The walkway was made up of heavily worn and pitted ferrocrete. It rose three meters above the floor of the cavern and ran over a series of pillars straight from the second level of windows to the central spire.

It was also covered by large, leprous-looking patches of blackish-red mold or moss.

The two scientists were still fully engrossed in their argument. They were now debating why the alien "insects" were able to grow so large, and be so energetic, as compared to their earthly cousins. White held that it was obviously, due to their having a fully developed respiratory system. Of course, Saranah disagreed. She believed it must be due to their being in an environment with lower gravity and higher oxygen content than where they had originally evolved. The others just noted that the critters were disgusting.

White suddenly snapped at Fineous when he saw him reaching towards one of the patches of mold. "Freeze! Do not touch that!"

Fineous froze, turning as White and Saranah hurried up behind him.

White quickly began to explain. "The records we found said that one of the alien plants they'd encountered was a type of mold that seemed to have a real affinity for the particular combination of silicates and calcinates used in human construction."

Perplexed, Fineous could only ask. "Huh?"

Gillian stepped up, looking closely at the plant in question. "He said this stuff liked the sand and limestone we use in our concrete."

Saranah put in her two-cents worth. "Yes, that's it exactly. They said the moss literally eats the concrete by dissolving it with a complex organic enzyme."

Fineous looked back at the stuff on the pillar, and said. "And anything that'll eat concrete. . ."

White finished, nodding. "Is liable to eat right through your skin."

Griffon bent over to get a closer look at the vile stuff. As he got closer, he noted a particularly strong smell which made his eyes water. “Sort of like the vine that burnt Fineous before?”

Saranah pulled out her datacomp to bring up a particular page of notes. “Actually, yes and no. This is a plant, where that vine you brushed in the tunnel was an animal.”

Fineous, looked at the others, White was nodding. “Animal? It looked like a plant, it hung there like a plant...” Looking at White, now shaking his head, he ended weakly. “It must therefore be an animal?”

Saranah nodded. “Yes, it’s a lot like the coral fans in the Earth’s oceans. They look like plants, but are really animals.” She stepped over to a large tree with black-green leaves. Its trunk was covered with the colorful leaves and twisted tendrils of the vine that had burned Fineous before.

She used the stylus from her datacomp to point out various parts of the tree. “Just like its terrestrial counterpart, this is an actual tree. It’s made up of a complex cellulose structure covered by a tough bark. It feeds on a combination of water and various compounds absorbed in the roots with sugars produced by sunlight-activated chlorophyll in the leaves.”

She now used the stylus to carefully lift a couple of the ‘leaves’ of the enveloping ‘vine’. “Now, see here? This thing is, ‘drilling’ into the stem of this tree. It injects a digestive enzyme that dissolves the cellulose that makes up the main part of the wood. This enzyme is also the, ah, ‘vines’ primary defense, it exudes a thin layer over the stems and leaves as well. That’s what burned Fineous when he touched it before.”

Gillian stepped up for a closer look at the ‘vine’ in question. “So why is it plant-shaped, and why did they call it an animal?”

Saranah looked at her stylus for a moment, perplexed, before bending to wipe it clean on a bit of “grass”.

She continued. “All this enzyme activity generates a lot of heat. The leaf-like extensions along the stem act as a cooling system as well as providing excellent advertisement of the danger for anything that tries to eat the creature.”

Gillian repeated. “And, why is this an ‘animal’?”

Pulling out her datacomp, Saranah consulted her notes again. “Because, it literally ‘creeps’ around and up the tree, feeding as it goes.” She looked around before pointing at a nearby stump. “Since its feeding style tends to kill the host, it’ll move on to the next, victim. This is a very slow-moving and very nasty parasite.”

Gillian looked back at the moss on the walkway. “Are all these alien plants and creature so hostile?”

White jumped in. “Oh no! Not at all. Though it does seem an inordinate number of the known creatures were destructive in nature. That may just be that the invaders wanted to do as much damage to the terrestrial eco-systems as quickly as possible."

Gillian pointed to the moss. "So they just happened to have a plant that likes our concrete?"

Saranah rechecked her notes. "The researchers weren't able to determine if this was simply a natural plant that served their purposes, or a genetically engineered species developed by the enemy. They just didn't have enough to go on."

Griffon lifted his assault rifle and looked at Fineous over the huddled forms of the others. "Is it just me, or do they actually want to stay in this godawful place?"

Fineous grinned back. "Maybe you'll remember not to bring any research scientists for the next Armageddon?"

Griffon could only smile. The others continued to look at, and discuss the minutia of alien plantlife. A pair of flying creatures with six, half-meter long wings and huge faceted eyes, hovered just behind Gillian's shoulder. They seemed be studying the scientists.

They all jumped as a scream tore from somewhere in the jungle they had just came from.

Fineous spun around, snapping his assault-rifle up to firing position.

Loud crashing sounds came from their back-trail, followed by another, louder scream. After a moment of silence, they heard what sounded disconcertingly like crunching, snapping, and slurping.

White, his pale complexion doing a remarkable effort to prove his name, asked in a low quivering voice. "W-What in the world?"

Griffon in a firmer, but equally low, voice said. "Something just reinforced its position in the food chain. I'd say we'd better move on before we find out where we fit in."

Quickly organizing themselves, they moved off towards the center of the chamber, following along the walkway.

Their journey was slowed by having to constantly work around the larger plants, and very carefully push past the lesser ones.

They were constantly on guard and often startled as they flushed several small creatures, winged, arboreal, and ground bound. Constant clouds of tiny insects, many biting, hovered around their heads.

After about an hour, Fineous found where water from a broken pipe high up in the ceiling had cascaded off the walkway and washed away the stone-eating moss.

They decided to climb onto the wet-slick walkway, despite the problems caused by avoiding the patches of moss and other plants, all preferred to take the "high road."

Fineous, the point man, scrambled onto the walkway and secured a rope to the rusted remnants of the banister for the others to climb up. One-armed, White gamely wormed himself up.

They saw that they had almost reached the halfway point. The lake in the center of the chamber was much nearer, and they could make out many of the details of the girded central pillar.

The party made much better time along the top of the walkway, carefully stepping around the patches of moss and easily avoiding the few branches overhanging their path.

As they approached the central lake, Fineous suddenly squatted in the center of the walkway and motioned for the others to halt. He seemed to be carefully studying something the others couldn't see.

Griffon worked his way past Saranah and White and duck-walked up to the mousy little man. He stopped while still well behind him. Peering over Fineous' shoulder and whispered. "What have you got?"

Fineous gestured with the muzzle of his rifle. "I'm not sure. I saw what looked like spiderwebs down in the bushes back there, none crossed the walkway until now. But the main thing is, I have no idea what to make of... That!"

Griffon raised himself, and looked over the little man's shoulder at a huge brownish mass; at least two stories high, which totally encased the circular platform where the four walkways joined the central pillar. He could make out a few irregular holes in the sides of the mass. Some were as large as his head and scattered about in no discernible pattern. Other, much smaller, holes pitted the entire surface. Looking closer, he could see the entire surface seemed to be crawling with some sort of beetle-like insects.

Between them and the structure, there appeared to be several golden spiderwebs made up of extremely fine threads which were stretched across the causeway. They swayed slowly in the soft breeze from the distant ventilators. Glancing about, he noted that in places, the webs were so dense they seemed to drape the jungle on either side.

Stepping back, he looked about again, confirming a sudden suspicion. The webs seemed to be of a uniform design and size. They were placed to provide overlapping coverage and appeared to completely encircle the small lake. Glancing up, he saw they stretched to the very tops of the trees. The webs made up a complete tent-like structure surrounding the central mass.

He also noted the beetle-like insects crawling along the threads making up the webs were the same as the ones which covered the hive-like structure on the walkway.

There were several different types of beetles. The predominant ones were between one and three inches in length, a good third of which was made up of jaw.

He saw one of the winged, four-legged bats try to swoop down on the beetles. It slammed into the almost invisible web, which ripped free of its moorings and quickly, entangled the wildly struggling creature, scattering beetles in all directions.

He turned and motioned for the others to come up, a loud whisper warning them to be careful.

Fineous picked up a dead branch lying across the walkway. As the others worked their way forward avoiding patches of rockmoss, he carefully reached over with the branch and snagged the nearest web. He pulled back, easily popping it from its anchor points. Once it was free, he spun the stick sharply, neatly wrapping the web around the end. Several beetles were sent spinning into the brush. Griffon pointed out the webs and the mass on the walkway, as well as the bat-creature, now weakly twitching. It was completely wrapped in webbing. The whole mass was swarming with beetles.

Saranah pulled out her datacomp. "I have no idea what that thing is. The records did speak of. . ." She found the entry she wanted. "'Large hivelike structures,' in the areas the invaders had seized." She looked up and pointed with her stylus. "I guess this is what they were talking about."

Gillian stared at the trees around them. "I've never heard of webs being used by swarming creatures."

Fineous gestured with the stick he still held. "Yet, still. . . This isn't a web, it's a net."

He handed the stick to Gillian. "Look, it's not sticky, it seems to be made from some sort of very fine nylon or something, and the threads are actually knotted together to make the net."

The others gathered around Gillian, fingering the net in question.

Fineous turned to the doctors. "Could these bugs be those 'brainbugs' you told us about?"

Saranah looked up. "No, they're not." Swiftly the stylus flew across her datacomp, bringing up the applicable files. "They reported that they were, 'large round-bodied, pulpy, and hardly able to walk.' The description sounded more like some kind of blood-full tick, only being all brain instead of all stomach."

White, interrupted "Yes, but they were also a type of swarming insect. Now, in our own world all swarms come with several variations of the basic insect." Thinking quickly. "For example, termites have warriors, drones, and queens; and the adult queen is incapable of doing anything but laying eggs. She's even incapable of walking."

Griffon examined a three-inch beetle, a full inch of which was made up of savage-looking jaws. "So, these could be different versions of the one species?"

Saranah, still checking her notes. "Or, they could be some other species entirely." She looked up. "Just because they appear to make and use nets and hives doesn't mean they are the same species as the one from which the 'Brainbugs' came from."

Fineous pointed to the place where the captured bat-creature lay. "Yes, but they do act like ants."

The others looked and saw a long column of beetles, weaving it's way from the mass of webbing, up one of the support columns and along the walkway to the hive. Each was heavily burdened with what appeared to be a chunk of flesh.

Fineous looked over his shoulder at Griffon. "Sir, I really don't like this."

Griffon gave the hive the once-over, then scanned the webs. "I don't either." He gestured with a thumb over his shoulder. "But, we're here, and I don't think it'll be any safer going back the way we came. We'll just see if we can make it up the tower or not."

He caught the others attention by slapping his rifle. "We'll just all be careful doing it. Right?"

The rest of the team nodded, distracted by their own thoughts.

"All right, let's move out!" He announced as he gestured toward the hive, "Fineous, you got point. Saranah, you and White are the most familiar with what info we have on these things, you two come next. Gillian, you're 'Tail-end Charlie.' OK? Any questions? Yes, Fin?"

Fineous held his hand up like a kid in class. "What do we do about the nets and bugs?"

Griffon, glancing along the walkway. "We'll use a stick to take down the nets over the walkway, and brush the bugs we can't avoid out of the way."

Saranah nodded vigorously. "Yes, whatever you do, disturb as little as possible. Earthly ants signal their deaths to others by emitting a cloud of danger-scent when they're crushed."

Fineous, gesturing towards the huge mass on the circular platform. "And what do we do when we get up to that?"

"Well, if it's solid enough, we'll use a grapnel and simply walk up it to the tower." Looking at the hive. "And, if it's not, we'll use incendiary grenades to burn it clear and then climb the tower."

Fineous muttered. "I always like a man that appreciates the finer points of 'Scorched Earth'." He started toward the central tower.

They had just reached the edge of the water when Saranah suddenly yelled and clutched at her leg. A beetle had crawled up her pant leg and bitten her. Burning like a wasp sting, the bite caused her leg to spasm and collapse. She stumbled and fell into a large patch of rockmoss that covered much of the top of the walkway.

For a brief instant, she stared in horror at her hands sinking into the green-black mass. Then she screamed in agony, and wrenched herself back onto her knees.

The skin of her hands crisped and blistered, Griffon stared in horror as the flesh cracked, oozing and peeling, the muscle underneath bubbled and popped.

Saranah, screaming in agony, lurched to her feet as the acidic moss burned through her coveralls and into her knees.

Fineous had spun at the first scream, rifle ready for any attack. Then started towards Saranah, reaching for her, dropping his weapon.

White rushed forward as Saranah staggered to her feet. He was fumbling left-handed for his medkit as he tried to steady Saranah with the stump of his right arm.

Her mind ripped by the agony of her flesh, she could only grasp at the water lying just ahead. She started to stagger ahead when White wrapped his stump around her waist, attempting to wrestle her down so he could treat her wounds.

Maddened by the pain, she kicked out, knocking White back into Griffon, causing both to fall to the walkway.

Screaming in agony, she turned, off-balance and staggering, toward the water. In her rush toward relief, she knocked Fineous, spinning off the walkway, ripping through the nets to crash into the mud at the edge of the lake.

Still screaming in unimaginable agony as her flesh bubbled, cracked, and began to slough off the bones. She staggered forward to tumble into the cool beckoning water.

White, screaming her name, frantically struggled to free himself from Griffon. In blind fury he struck and kicked at the man pinned under him.

Gillian, blocked by the flailing, realized the doctor was totally berserk and struck him behind the left ear with the butt of his rifle, dropping him where he lay.

Griffon, stars bursting behind his eyes from White's blows, rolled the unconscious form off of him and staggered up to race down the causeway.

He ran forward, carefully leaping over the lethal patch of rockmoss. As he reached the point where the causeway passed over the water, he heard the tone of Saranah's screams change.

Looking down, he saw her tattered form rise above the surface. The water bubbled and boiled. Dim forms surged from the depths, scales flashed, fanged jaws slashed.

Saranah, blindly, spasmodically, screamed toward the heavens, the bony remnants of a hand thrust upwards.

The surging mass of creatures under the water heaved and ripped in a boiling frenzy. The black-green water and white spume turned a sickening pink.

Griffon dropped to his stomach and tried to reach Saranah's hand, only to see her yanked beneath the surface. He saw the creatures close in on her. Her last breath was torn in a bubbling shriek as it was ripped from her lungs. Then, the bloody water and scaled bodies blocked his view.

He froze in shock, hand still stretched forwards for what seemed an eternity. The sight of Saranah being pulled beneath the surface by ripping fangs replayed in his horrified mind.

Slowly, he came back to his senses as he remembered the others needed him. He turned his back to the fading pink stain in the water.

Gillian was just starting toward him. White still lay sprawled on the walkway. Griffon rushed toward the place where Fineous had been knocked from the walkway. He shouted to Gillian, pointing at White. "She's gone. I'll get Finn, you watch out for White!"

Gillian nodded sharply and squatted over the unconscious doctor, his rifle ready, scanning the jungle to either side for any threat.

Griffon looked over the side of the walkway to see Fineous lying on the muddy shore of the lake. He was draped in three or four of the nets and moving only slightly.

Griffon quickly secured the rope he was carrying to a piece of rebar jutting from the walkway and dropped beside his fallen comrade.

As he landed, he saw Fineous was slowly cutting away at the strands of the net with his knife. "For God's sake, don't move around, it'll just wrap you up tighter."

Fineous looked up, carefully using the thumb and middle finger of his left hand to flick away a three-inch beetle crawling up his leg. "Well, Duh! Why don't you teach me how to suck eggs while you're at it?" Slashing through several strands, he said. "Just get me out of this shit, OK?"

With the two working together, he was quickly freed from the nets. Before they were finished, they had more trouble beating off the growing horde of beetles than cutting the nets. Both suffered several stings for their trouble.

Climbing back onto the walkway, they found Gillian still squatted beside a sobbing White.

In the changeless artificial sunlight of the chamber, they had no idea how long it had been, or how long it was before they were able to pull themselves together.

After being treated by one of the medkits, Griffon stood, rubbing the still swollen and tender bites on his arms and legs he peered at the tower and the massive hive encasing its base. Then, he turned and studied their path and the serried rows of broken windows in the far wall.

Making a decision, he shouldered his rifle. "OK, mount up people!" He jabbed a thumb over his shoulder at the huge hive. "Since we don't know what will happen if we disturb that. . ." He nodded at the lake surrounding the base of the tower. "And we definitely do know what will happen if we get dumped into that. . ." He pointed down the way they had come. "We're going to change tacks. We'll go back to the wall and use the grapnel and rope to climb from one level to another. We should be able to climb with no problem and avoid wandering through the rubble on at least four floors."

White glared at him through red-rimmed eyes. "That's what you said about the tower!"

Looking back at the tower, Griffon nodded. He felt his eyes burning, his vision blurred with unshed tears. "At the time, and with what we knew, it was the right decision."

He turned back to his three companions. "And now, trying the wall looks like the right decision. At least we have some idea what's behind us." Turning back toward the hive, he said "But, with these nets. . ." He pointed towards the water. "And that. I'd guess they're using that as some sort of moat..." Pointing at the surrounding jungle with the muzzle of his rifle. "And the fact there are none of the major animals anywhere near this place. I'd say whatever those bugs are, we don't want any more of it."

White leapt up and stood nose-to-nose with him. Griffon braced himself for a possible attack. Instead, White thrust the stump of his right arm towards the nest, "What're we going to do about that?" He was barely under control. His face was red, as he sputtered vehemently. "Those shits killed Saranah! What are we going to do? Just walk away?"

Not budging an inch, Griffon ignored the shower of spittle. His voice was low, and firm, "Yes, that's exactly what we are going to do." He kicked the pack at his feet; "We don't have enough ammunition to blast everything in sight!" He continued his tone now even. "We have to get out of here, we have to live. We will have our payback, but not today, not like this. If we waste our chance to get out just to kill a bunch of bugs and lizards, we will not be doing anything for Saranah's memory."

He put a hand on White's shoulder. "Her memory will die here, with us."

White stared at him, eyes bulging, his face growing redder and redder. Clenching and unclenching his fist, he raised the stump of his right arm as if he was going to strike the taller man with his missing hand.

Then, with frightening suddenness, some sort of internal switch flipped. He seemed to deflate. His face went deathly pale. He lowered his arms and turned towards the tower and the nest encircling it. Tears ran down both cheeks, as he said in a deadly cold voice. "You're right, of course. We have to get out of here."

He turned back to the puzzled Griffon, his eyes blazing from the almost serene face. "But, I will hold you to your promise that we will avenge ourselves on the aliens."

Griffon nodded and held up his right hand, his eyes locked on White's. "I promise, we will avenge ourselves on the aliens, come what may."

White turned to Gillian. "And you?"

Gillian, his eyes never wavering, raised his right hand. "I, too, promise for Saranah and Fritz."

White then turned towards Fineous. "You?"

Fineous, his features solemn, and his eyes strangely burning answered. "I promise we will avenge ourselves on the enemy. Whoever it may be."

Satisfied, White struggled into his pack.

As they all prepared to move out, Griffon spoke up. "Right, Fineous you've got point. I'm next, then White; Gillian, you have our six. Any questions? Good, lets go."

They carefully retraced their footsteps along the remnants of the raised causeway.

It took only a short time to reach the wall of the vast chamber. They looked at the cave-like entrance where the walkway entered the second floor of the chamber. Griffon halted Fineous wordlessly with a light touch on his elbow. "We still want to avoid working our way up through that maze." He pointed up at the shattered windows and pitted wall of the third and fourth level. "We'll use our grapnel and climb up here. " Turning back to the others. "That should save us quite a bit of wandering."

Gillian took out the grapnel hook he'd cobbled out of the lightweight, but very rigid angle, of some metal framework that had been shattered in the ancient battle. He eyed the next two levels. "Aye, this ought to do just fine."

The grapnel soared through a shattered fourth-level window on the third try. It caught and held when Gillian heaved downwards with all his strength.

Fineous, as usual, climbed first, followed by Griffon. White, to the amazement of all, took a quick wrap of the rope around one leg, pinning it with the opposite foot. Then shimmied up the rope with some skill, even one-handed. Gillian then secured their packs to the end of the rope and had them pull it up before taking his turn.

On the new floor, they found almost total darkness, the only light coming from the brightly-lit room behind them. Winged creatures, of several alien designs, startled by their appearance, flew, buzzed, and hissed around their heads and out into the larger chamber behind.

Hexrats, pseudo-insects, and other... Things scuttled off into the darkness.

As their eyes slowly adapted to the dimness, they saw a scene of almost total destruction. The partitioning walls were shattered stumps, burnt and twisted. The litter of battle lay in heaps everywhere. White bones and twisted wreckage of the combatants were piled everywhere. A grinning skull leered at them from the top of a chest-high heap. Further back, they could just make out several holes blasted from the floor above.

Griffon, checking his watch. "We've had quite a day, let's take a break here. . ." He pointed towards the shattered ceiling. "Before we check out what's waiting up there."

They synchronized their watches and settled in for the 'night'. It took some time before the disturbed occupants finally settled down.

Chapter 6

Climbing through one of the holes blasted from the level above, they found themselves in of a vast garage-like structure. A vehicle scrap-yard of rusted metal strewn across the floor. Weak beams of sunlight were streaming through the twisted remnants of massive doors. Eagerly, they made their way towards the weak, yellow, beckoning light.

Wading through the heap of wind-blown debris that lay before the battle-scarred valves, they exited from the dungeon into the weak sunlight of a winter's dawn. Fineous was the first one through; he spread his arms and drew in the sweet breath of the chilly breeze. The others celebrated in their own way as they left the nightmare behind.

The camouflaged entrance was carved into the head of a gully. Only traces of concrete paving could be seen peeking through the thick layers of sand and doss washed down from the red sandstone sides of the cut. Thin strands of rank, yellowed grass and brown leaves were drifted and piled everywhere. Yellow-fringed leaves of green-black alien plants were mixed with the honest red-brown and yellowed remnants of their terran counterparts. Stark skeletons of twisted, smallish, oak-like trees crowned each side of the gully. Their view downhill was blocked by the natural-seeming twists and turns of the cutting.

Wearing a crown of brown, like some elfin beggar, Fineous bent and heaved twin handfuls of dead leaves at Griffon's' head. With a whoop, the larger man tackled him, tossing the little man into the nearest pile of debris. Gillian broke out in some incomprehensible Scottish ditty and danced a brief jig. Even the morose White smiled as he fingered several leaves. They carried on like this for a couple of minutes, when the sight of a small brownish form streaking from under a fallen log returned them to the present.

Startled, Fineous rolled to his feet; his pistol at the ready, dead leaves trailing behind. Griffon reached out and slowly pushed the barrel down. "Hold it! That's a monkey!"

The others looked at the familiar, tailed figure as it streaked up the side of the gully, then paused on the crest and looked back at them. It gave a hooting laugh and disappeared over the crest.

Quizzically, Fineous asked. "So what does that mean? Are we in Africa, or South America?"

Griffon, looking at the trees. "I'm not sure. . . Those really look like the blackjack trees I saw in North America. I think it was Oklahoma, or Texas."

“So? I remember such trees in Europe too.” Commented Gillian. They turned to their life sciences expert, White. He was staring thoughtfully at the point where the monkey had disappeared. “I don’t think we have enough to go on right now. This is December and it’s chilly, so we’re in the Northern hemisphere.” He looked up at the others. “Or we could be at high altitude in the Southern Hemisphere.” He pointed to the spot where the monkey had disappeared, “We can’t judge too much from a monkey being around here. After all, every zoo and animal-park on the planet had monkeys, and some probably escaped when everything collapsed.”

Stooping to pick up a brown leaf at his feet. He said. “And these trees could be any of half a dozen scrub types, from almost anywhere. I just don’t know enough about them to tell.” He turned to the others. “I do think we should climb out of here and see what we can see though, don’t you?”

Nodding in agreement, they shrugged into the packs they’d discarded in their roughhousing. As they prepared to move out, Fineous looked back at the black opening behind them. “You know, I was just wondering. . .”

Griffon looked up from adjusting his pack straps to ride easier. “What?”

Fineous said, thoughtfully. “Well, that place was really something.”

Gillian glanced up. “Yes, and...”

Catching the others’ eye, Fineous continued. “Oh, I just wonder what that place was originally intended for.” He pointed at the gaping doorway. “A huge underground installation, camouflaged entrance and all that. Sure was an awful lot to do when everything’s going to crap.” He shrugged, settling his backpack in place, and starting. “Yeah that’s it. . . It just happened to be here.”

They decided to work their way down the gully. As Griffon put it, “We’re just as likely to find some clue to where we’re at going that way, and we’re more likely to find fresh water.”

They had walked for only a short distance when Griffon spotted a red-breasted robin. That seemed to be rather convincing evidence that were somewhere on the North American continent. Exactly where remained a mystery. After about an hour’s trudging, the gully opened out into a wide, shallow canyon stretching down to a lake, the water gray-blue under the scuttering clouds.

Large cottonwood trees lined the shore. A troop of monkeys had claimed them for their temporary home. The screaming creatures took exception to their invasion, protesting in the raucous tones familiar to many a zoo patron.

The team worked their way through the grove of trees, toward the shore. Fineous suddenly stiffened, dropped to one knee, and aimed his rifle at something in the brush to the far right. The others immediately froze the surrounding trees and brush blocking any view of his target.

He carefully squeezed off a single round. The blast silenced the screaming monkeys, who went crashing off through the trees. A bellow of pain, another shot, and a great thrashing from the direction he was shooting.

Then, pounding hooves, crashing brush, and noise fading off in the distance.

Whooping, Fineous sprang to his feet and raced in the direction he'd shot. Not knowing what to expect, the others moved up, just in time to see him stop and fire a third shot at something in the brush at his feet. He waved them over. They moved closer, curious to see what he'd killed. He proudly stood over the rangy, red and white form of a long-horned cow. Pulling his knife. "Now, we have fresh water and fresh meat." Griffon stopped him before he made a big mistake, telling him how they should 'bleed' the carcass before butchering it.

While White stood watch; and Gillian set up a camp, drew water, and started a small fire; they skinned and butchered the animal. After some time, the monkeys started to filter back, more subdued this time.

After their experience with attracting scavengers in the installation, they set up camp, well away from the site of the kill. When they'd cut away most of the tough, stringy beef, they wrapped it in the hide and walked to where the others were waiting.

Pulling out various pans and packets from their packs a satisfied Fineous prepared to "treat them to their first 'Real' meal." A tired Griffon could only smile as he shrugged out of his pack and set it at the base of the cottonwood they were camping under. He turned, sat, and leaned back.

He was surprised when, he kept falling back until his head smacked into the trunk. He saw his pack scurrying up the tree, on top of a large, red, monkey's butt.

With a startled yell, he jumped up, and started a remarkable stream of curses at the mischievous primate. The others could only laugh as he shook his fist at the monkey rifling through his pack.

He grabbed a rock and threw it at the monkey, but missed. The monkey was not amused, and started screaming back. The monkey howled. Griffon cursed. The others were rolling on the ground laughing. This did little to settle the ire of either of those involved in the confrontation. Griffon grabbed up another rock and hurled it at the monkey.

The ape answered by defecating in its hand and hurling it at the irate human. His aim was much better.

Quickly the rest of the troop joined in; pelting all the humans with feces, twigs, and screams. The humans were quickly driven from their intended camp. One in red-faced fury, the others almost incapacitated by laughter.

Eventually, Griffon was able to recover his pack and most of the inedible contents, much the worse for wear. Even after he'd spent several hours cleaning and soaking his gear, he still complained he could smell the stench of monkey excrement and urine.

After a while, things began to quiet down. They picked up their gear, cleaned off the monkey dung, and set up a new camp under the overhanging bank of the gully they'd come down. As he grilled steaks over their fire, Fineous was driven to observe. "Well, so much for proving our superior intellect. I suppose there's still hope for the opposable thumb." The others pelted him with whatever was handy. An occupation made difficult by the fact all were doubled up in renewed gales of laughter.

With the dawn they climbed out of the gully and got the first real view of the world around them. Long, low, rolling hills cut by brush-filled and tree-lined gullies. They could just make out a series of low mountains crimping the northern horizon. With nothing else to pick from they headed for them.

They weren't able to make very good time. The plains proved to be virtually teeming with wildlife. Twice they had to make major detours, downwind. Avoiding large herds of American buffalo or Bison. On the second day, Griffon shot a pronghorn antelope. Herds of longhorn cattle, sheep, and horses ran wild. On occasion, the plains seemed to be creeping with life.

Alien creatures were also in abundance. On the third day, they watched as a pack of Jabberwocks expertly cut a young bull from a herd of Bison. The ferocity of the attack was awesome; the young bull was gutted before it hit the earth. It collapsed bellowing in pain. A cloud of bloody spume and whipping intestines followed. The first massive chunks of flesh were ripped out by razor-like claws and shoved down fang-lined mouths as their victim was still thrashing in agony.

On several occasions, they saw the solitary forms of six-legged Behemoths striding along, ripping through one clump of trees after another.

Among the winter-browned stretches of terrestrial flora, the black-green and purple-veined alien plantlife clustered in close-packed and spreading clumps. They finally reached the foot of the highest mountain in the small range at the end of their fifth day, making camp in a brush-choked draw.

Griffon had the last watch of the night. He sat bundled up against the chill, their small cook-fire dying down to dim embers. The eastern sky was only just beginning to lighten from black to deepest purple when he was startled by a brilliant, blue-white streak that strobe-lit the countryside, ripping vertically into the earth far to the west. The others leapt up, bootless, automatically reaching for weapons laid at hand.

A massive fireball rose beyond the horizon, seeming to hover before it slowly spread into a dimming mushroom cloud. Griffon silenced the questions of the others with an upraised hand as he continued counting. "One-one-thousand-forty-six, one-one-thousand-forty-seven. . ." A heavy rumble and a blast of the shock wave washed over their hidden camp. Small stones, dust, and bits of debris tumbled into the gully.

Griffon turned to the others, the glowing cloud rising behind him, the top lit by the sun of the newborn day, the bottom by the fires beneath. "Ok, it's about fifty miles away, and the wind's out of the northwest." Looking back at the cloud. "We should be safe fr..."

He was slammed to the ground, the others were knocked back. The fire exploded into a shower of sparks that was sucked, whirling, into the hostile sky. Three metallic-black forms blurred by, clearing the out-thrust ridge by scant meters. The shock wave from their hypersonic passage was a rolling explosion of violence. Small plants were ripped out of the ground, and larger trees cracked. The team was buried by a small avalanche of rock and earth torn from the upper edges of the gully.

Their ears shocked numb, they felt dazed, stunned. Then, thrashing and tearing, they fought from their shallow wrack-covered graves, weapons out, eyes staring wildly about for the next assault. . . Nothing.

Slowly they became aware of sounds sinking into the remains of their camp from beyond the gully. Thundering hooves, roars, and bellows of fright and panic. The animals of the plains were tearing the earth and themselves apart in blind panic. A Jaguar, flushed from the slopes of the mountain behind them, knocked Fineous sprawling as it tore through their camp, blind to all but the need to flee.

Luckily, the nearest herds of Bison and cattle were panicked into stampeding away from their camp. Trapped against the foot of the mountain as they were, they would have died under the thundering hooves. Gillian helped Fineous up, while Griffon and White scrambled up the side of the gully for a better view. A dozen or more panicked deer bounded between them, knocking Griffon and White sprawling back to the bottom of the gully. Fineous dove behind a nearby rock. Gillian went down, blood spurting from a hoof-slash on the arm. For an interminable time they were pounded and riddled by stone and earth cascading over them. Choking clouds of dust roiled and boiled, blotting out the still-dim dawn.

Gradually, things began to settle and quiet. They dug out, brushed off, and took stock. White slapped a medkit on Gillian's still-leaking arm.

Finally, they recovered, clearing their weapons, and climbed to the rim of the gully to look around.

Fineous was the first to speak. "Well, what the frack was that all about?"

Griffon responded. "How the frack do I know?"

Gillian, holding the hastily cleaned binoculars to his eyes said. "Well, I'd say there was some sort of combat going on. Somebody launched some sort of nuclear attack, followed up by some sort of armed aerial response by somebody against somebody."

The others just looked at him. Fineous was the first to speak. "Well, no shit, Sherlock! Maybe the great engineer could tell us something we don't already know? Like what type or size of nuclear attack? Or what kind of aircraft?"

Gillian was perplexed at the vehemence of the retort. "Oh, I do apologize."

They looked back at the mushroom cloud, now fully lit by the newborn day. It was just starting to lose its definition in the soft breeze.

After thinking things over, Gillian continued. "Well, there's no indication it was an actual nuclear attack. In fact, with the immediate movement of the aircraft towards the area of the strike, and the vertical streak, I'd say what we witnessed was probably a simple 'Orbital Kinetic Strike'. Also, since those aircraft were following immediately on the tail of the strike, I do believe they were probably on the same side as the attackers."

The others exchanged glances. White just grunted and turned to study the plains lying below them, looking for any approaching threat.

Fineous spoke. "Ok, what's a 'Orbital Kinetic Strike', and why do you think it wasn't a nuclear hit?"

"An 'O. K. S.' was a fairly common tactic. It was simply dropping a large mass from orbit on a surface target. You could use a small asteroid, or a purpose-designed missile. The combined orbital and gravity-accelerated velocity would be so great, it would be instantly converted into energy on contact, with, well," gesturing at the distant cloud, "catastrophic results." Was Gillian's thoughtful response.

Griffon now spoke up. "Why do you think this was one of those?"

Standing for a better look, Gillian answered. "Well, first, the vertical streak was nearly instantaneous, which indicates it was either an energy or hypervelocity weapon. Second, unless you're trying for maximum surface disruption and fallout, a nuclear surface burst is actually counterproductive. Third, it's doubtful the follow-up forces would have been racing into a dangerously 'Hot' environment. A kinetic strike, while still 'Hot', is much less radioactive than either a fission or a fusion weapon."

"And why do you think those aircraft were from the same people as the ones that made the strike?" Fineous asked.

"I can field that one." Griffon said. "Even if they were traveling at hypersonic speeds," He gestured to the surrounding countryside; "there's no place nearby where they could have come from. So they were either fortuitously patrolling nearby, or..."

Gillian finished. "They were part of a comprehensive plan to follow up the strike with an immediate aerial assault."

Fineous, looking back and forth between the two, said. "Sooooo, what do we do about it?"

After a few moments of thought, Griffon spoke up. “We avoid the area. We still don’t know where we are, who’s fighting, or what the fight’s about. I really don’t feel comfortable with walking blindly into what is apparently a major battle.”

Gillian and Fineous nodded. White finally spoke up. “Well, we’d better be moving out. I don’t know if those jets, or whatever they were spotted us or not, but they may return this way. Or, there may be follow-up troops.” He scrambled back toward their camp, asking over his shoulder at the others. “Does anyone want to be here when they come?”

Quickly, they tried to get themselves together, but it took a long while to dig their gear out from the shattered and buried camp. Finally, they could set out.

Fineous, settling his pack in place, asked. “Which way?”

Griffon, shrugging into his own pack, said “That way,” pointing north. “The strike is there and they came from the east.” He now gestured towards the south as he picked up his weapon. “We came from there. That leaves north.”

Fineous grinned. “Roge-O. Yeah, I know, ‘Finn, take point’.”

Gillian chimed in. “And Gillian take, ‘Tail-end Charlie’, right?”

White snorted, and Griffon grinned. “Ok, So we’re in a rut! Let’s just move out and sort it out later.”

Fineous turned to skirt the mountain’s shoulder on the east side and said over his shoulder. “Speaking of being in a rut. . . I think we’d be smart to keep making camp in gullies or depressions.”

Next in line, Griffon asked. “Why, to hide our fire?”

Fineous nodded. “Well that, and to keep from being killed by low-flying craft.”

Bringing up the rear, Gillian spoke. “That’s right. The shock wave from those craft, at that speed and altitude, would have killed us if we hadn’t been protected by the sides of the gully.”

Griffon could only smile. “Sort of ‘aerial roadkill’ huh?”

Gillian grinned at the back of his head. “In a word, yes.”

Chapter 7

Once clear of the right shoulder of the small, rocky mountain, they made good time across the prairie stretching to the horizon. Even when they detoured from a true northerly course to take advantage of cover, they didn’t have to worry about the herds of animals that had caused so much concern before. The creatures seemed to have fled the carnage and panic of the night before.

As evening fell, they sought out a shallow wash, a thin stream threading its way along the bottom. Once they'd made camp and cooked the evening meal, Fineous sat beside Griffon. White and Gillian were cleaning their weapons and discussing the possible advances in Artificial Intelligence they might find when... if, they reached civilization. "Sir, I was wondering, what with all that happened last night, shouldn't we be moving at night?"

Griffon looked up from cleaning his assault rifle, a steaming cup of coffee sitting on the log beside him. "I thought about that too. However, I didn't want to hang around there and wait for night. If they have aircraft and space-based weapons, we have to figure they have night vision equipment, or some form of sensors. Whoever they are. Since we don't, we'd be giving up too much by walking out blind. At least we can see the animals and where we're going in daylight."

Fineous nodded. "Guess so. By the way, do you think it was just coincidence those jets, or whatever they were, passed over us last night?"

Before answering, Griffon snapped the pieces of his weapon back together. Then, leaning the fully reassembled rifle against the log he was sitting on. He took a sip from his cup. "No, I don't. However, I think we both went to the same point for different reasons. That mountain was the highest point in the area. We wanted it to get a look around. I think they were using it to stay below the sensor horizon of the target area, or maybe as a checkpoint for some sort of terrain-following course they were using. After all," he added grinning. "We aren't dead."

Fineous nodded, grinning. "Yet."

Griffon curled his upper lip in a mock snarl. "RRRRRrrrrrrr."

Over the next three days, things were seemingly normal. The herds, packs, and prides of the various animals they encountered returned to their regular routine, living and dying, feeding, sleeping, hunter and prey. The team was able to catalogue a large array of creatures, most of which were classic North American: Bison, wild horses, and cattle. Many others were of African, Asian, European, and even Australian origin, more monkeys, baboons, lions, tigers, kangaroo, even rhino, and some elephants. Some, far too many, were of clearly alien origin.

The hunting was good. To stretch their rations, they started eating what they could kill. In addition, they were able to augment their evening stew with a few wild plants- onions, potatoes, and such, that they could find along the way.

On their third night from the mountain, the weather turned nasty. The clouds grew ominous. A slow, soaking drizzle started. As the temperature dropped, the rain turned to sleet. Everything that was soaked now grew a thin layer of ice. Just before dawn, a light snow began to drift down.

Without tents, they huddled under their thin, mylar, emergency blankets. Life was miserable and none could sleep. Clustered around the pathetically small fire for whatever warmth they could find. Bundled into every stitch of clothing they had.

The next day dawned bleak and frosty. A bitterly cold wind blew from the north in irregular gusts. As they choked down their lukewarm breakfast, the conversation turned to their course. It was decided they needed to find some sort of shelter. As there was none in the immediate area, they decided to move on.

Within the first hour, they came across their first evidence of civilization: the remains of what had once been a major highway. The cracked and warped remains of two ancient strips of macadam peeking pathetically from the browned prairie grass and sifting snow. The road cutting ran arrow-straight across their path.

The cracked and broken pillars of a more modern elevated magrail system followed the same route. The endless line of shattered ruins faded into the distance to the east and west. Surprisingly the ceramic rails, though pitted and twisted, still stretched between most of them.

After another debate, they decided to follow the highway eastwards. They still needed shelter, and their best hope lay along the ancient route. The direction was decided by the fact they were still extremely leery of what lay to the west.

Just as the pathetically dismal sun started to fade, they came across the shattered, moldering remains of a town. While most of the buildings were little more than heaps of overgrown rubble, some of the buildings in the center of the town had been of construction that was more substantial. They were able to wait out the rest of the storm in the cavelike cornice of two walls that still had a vestige of a roof, canted crazily overhead. It wasn't much, but it was out of wind and rain.

After three more days, the dreary winter storm finally passed. A weak sun rose wanly into a gray-blue sky. Few sights can be more glorious to the weary traveler.

Setting out again, still headed east. The warming temperatures quickly turned the red clay and sandy soil into a slippery, gluey, mess. Their path became harder as the ghastly stuff clung and sucked at every step. Before long, Fineous was complaining that he didn't mind walking across the prairie, he just resented having to carry it with him.

However, difficult, the way was far from impassable. The ancient highway made for a rather efficient, if primitive, road through the morass.

The wild animals seemed as depressed by the conditions as they were. The team even managed to simply walk past a mud-caked rhino. The creature just gave them a tired huff and continued to munch on a small evergreen growing from a crack on the far side of the pavement.

Another two days and the remains of buildings became more frequent. Soon, their road was cutting a path through a maze of shattered, moldering rubble. On the horizon, the broken, stunted remains of skyscrapers rose like the rotted ribs of a corpse.

Eventually, they were able to make camp in an almost intact-room, missing only one wall. They set watches and dropped into exhausted slumber. Small creatures of the night and ruin, their old friends, the hexrats, and their terrestrial cousins glanced at them disinterestedly, before returning to the matters of life and death.

As the eastern horizon slowly began to lighten, Griffon was celebrating the end of his watch by reheating the last of their coffee. He glanced towards the cavelike opening of their hovel. To see a man standing there, in plain sight, well back from the entrance.

He was tall, only slightly shorter than Griffon, well formed and clean-limbed. His complexion was dark, though not African. His hair was covered by the hood of a short fur-lined jacket. He was dressed in well-worn, fringed buckskin, and gloves of some sort hung from the ends of his sleeves. He held a heavy hunting spear, butt grounded, in his right hand. A small ax or hatchet hung from a beaded belt at his right hip, a combination bowcase and quiver hanging on his left. He was just standing there, silently staring at their camp. Griffon had no idea how long he'd been there, waiting to be noticed.

Slowly, consciously trying to not make any threatening moves, he hissed for the others. Awakening to the warning, the team reacted with the smoothly practiced reactions of veterans. They silently rolled out of their sleeping bags, pulling on their boots and snatching up weapons.

Seeing he had finally been noticed, the man standing outside moved. Lifting his spear, he thrust its point deep into the ground. Carefully he hung his ax and bowcase on its feathered shaft, then faced them and raised both hands to show they were empty.

Griffon whispered quick instructions for the others to keep him covered. Putting down his rifle, along with his pistol, he slowly walked from the cover of their hovel. He carefully held his empty hands out, palms up.

As he stepped out into the growing light, he suddenly remembered the heavy combat knife at his hip. Pausing in consternation, he noticed what appeared to be the hilt of a largish knife peeking from the high buckskin boot of the other.

He came to a halt when he was about four paces from the stranger. They stood looking at each other for a moment, each waiting for the other to speak. Griffon heard a soft crunch of gravel. A bit of weed waived slightly off to the left, standing out in the windless air. *Oh gee, he's not alone. Go figure.*

Just as Griffon was deciding how to begin, the other spoke. His words were English, after a fashion, his accent was thick and blurred. "Dortmund I ham. Speaker for the Oahkee I ham. Who be yea? Reavers be yea or Abataurum?"

Not sure, what either ‘Reavers’ or ‘Abataurum’ were, Griffon decided to take a neutral tact. “I am Griffon,” he said and gestured toward the ruin where the others waited. “We are wanderers.”

The other seemed to be digesting his accent and words. Then a peculiar gleam came to his dark brown eyes. “Want what yea here in the lands of the Oahkee?”

Thinking quick, Griffon answered. “We seek food, shelter, and to speak with the Oahkee. We have goods to trade.”

After another interminable pause, Dortmund seemed to reach a decision and broke out in a broad grin. “Trade we will. Feast yea we will. Tales of your travels you will us tell.”

He turned, raising his right hand to his lips he gave a short, bird-like, warbling, whistle. Three others, similarly dressed and armed, appeared from behind mounds of rubble. They began to cautiously approach the pair.

Griffon turned to see Gillian and White stepping from the ruin where they had made camp, Fineous was nowhere in sight.

Everyone exchanged greetings and introductions. Griffon explained they had to break camp. Fineous finally stepped from the shadows when they returned to the ruin to pack their belongings. Dortmund and his fellows didn’t seem put out at the sudden appearance of another. In fact, they didn’t seem to take any note of it at all.

So, they probably knew how many we were, Griffon thought. *They also didn’t object to us keeping an ace in the hole.* Glancing about, as he packed his rucksack, *I wonder how many cards they’ve kept up their sleeve?*

They made a peculiar-looking formation as they walked through the remnants of a once-mighty city. Dortmund and one other buckskin-clad tribesman walked ahead of the team, with the other two tribesmen bringing up the rear.

They’d been on the trail for only a few minutes when Fineous whispered. “I count at least four others with us, there might be more, but I don’t think so.”

Griffon glanced at the mousy little man before answering. “I’m not so sure. They seem to be working in standard two-man cover teams. They wait for us to pass. Then loop out to either side of our route and race ahead of us. Set up and watch us pass again. That way they can keep us covered while minimizing the risk of exposing themselves. Just pretend that you haven’t noticed them. This is their territory, if they mean to ambush us they will when they’re good and ready. I don’t think they will, but if it does come, we’ll just have to handle it.” Turning, memorizing the trail they were following he said in a low voice to his companions. “Keep your eyes open guys, we’re being followed.”

White, muttered back, “Gee, a revelation. Of course we’re being followed.” Gillian just gave a derisive snort.

As they walked, the team started making small talk amongst themselves and with their escorts. Griffon learned they were heading towards the place where the Oahkee made their home. Dortmund seemed to be especially proud of the tithing the Oahkee had made that fall to the "Abataurum." Griffon also learned these "Abataurum" were the earthly representatives of God himself. Sort of an Angel-Superman-IRS agent all rolled into one.

Dortmund told Griffon that, like all "Speakers," he was not originally from the Oahkee, but had grown up among another people living far away in jungle-clad mountains. Dortmund seemed happy to tell stories of his childhood among the exotic plants and animals of his homeland.

However, he was downright reticent about how he'd come to be here, and why. Griffon was able to glean that, along with the usual "tithes" of food and goods, the Abataurum also took the best and brightest among the youths of the tribe, both boys and girls. The Abataurum provided training. The best became "Speakers" before being sent to act as the headmen of various villages. Others were apparently accepted as servants of the Abataurum. Dortmunder couldn't, or wouldn't speak of what happened to the rest.

After several hours of working their way through the ruins, they entered a region of small, scattered farms. Nineteenth century technology, with ox or horse-drawn plows and wagons seemed to be the best they had. The farm buildings were all clustered within solid-looking stone walls and palisades. The people looked well fed and clothed, if worn and work-stained.

They passed several larger stone towers. Each with a small militia-type garrison.

Soon, they crossed over a long, low ridge and looked down on a small town that had several dozen substantial stone buildings with rain-soaked thatched and wooden, split-shingled roofs. The whole place was surrounded by a high stone wall. Irregular fields and orchards stretched down to a sluggish, muddy river winding its way across the valley.

Dortmunder waived his arm towards the valley. "Home this be of the Oahkee." Speaking with obvious pride, he pointed out the electrical power lines and few rattletrap vehicles in the valley.

Griffon was surprised even these few remnants of technology survived. When he asked how they could keep these remnants of the Old World working, Dortmund replied, the knowledge and parts were the "Gifts of the Abataurum."

They wound their way down into the valley and across the fields. A nervous crowd of townspeople greeted them with fearful stares. The men were heavily armed with an assortment of muzzle-loading, black-powder weapons. None showed overt hostility, just prudent caution.

Dortmunder spoke to the crowd. He told them Griffon and his team, were strangers, to be treated as friends.

He then invited them to explore the wonders of his domain while a guesthouse was prepared for them. He told them there would be a feast of celebration in their honor.

The team huddled together and decided it wouldn't be a bad idea to look around. However, they did decide to stick together.

Griffon bowed as graciously as he could to the Speaker. He told him they would be delighted and they thanked the Oahkee for their gracious hospitality.

Dortmunder beamed, and a sort of whispered thrill went through the crowd. Everyone was smiling as they started their tour of the town.

Four heavily armed men accompanied them. Whether to guard them from the crowd or to protect the town from them wasn't clear.

They saw the communal garages, mill, storage barns, and silos. They were allowed to examine one of the sound, but ancient tractors. These seemed to be the only self-propelled vehicle the Oahkee possessed.

Soon, they asked one of their guards about the house where they would be staying. He led them to a smallish, but comfortable house near the center of town. They apologized to the old couple that had been displaced. The couple smiled, bowed and explained, in heavily accented and awkwardly structured English that it was far from being an imposition. In fact, they had volunteered their home. It was both an honor, and an opportunity to spend an evening with their children's families.

Once safely within the house, Fineous carefully checked all the rooms and pronounced they were alone. He also pointed out their guards had taken up positions at both entrances, and there seemed to be a regular crowd outside.

White carefully looked out the sitting-room window, standing back so he wouldn't be detected by anyone outside. "I guess we've turned this into a sort of holiday for them."

Griffon chuckled. "I guess so. Now, one at a time. What did you see and what do you think about our hosts? Finn?"

The little man settled into a sort of wide chair, or narrow love seat. "Their vehicles aren't of any manufacture I recognized. They seem more like some of the generic vehicles they used to produce in some of the old Communist countries; basic, solid, and dependable. They're made with an eye for maximum interchangeability of parts. I recognized some of the same drive-train components used in the mill's power transfer system." Hesitating, he glanced about, to make sure the windows were shut. "Also, while the guards carried black-powder weapons, both percussion cap and flintlock, I didn't see any sign of a powder mill, nor any facilities for the production of percussion caps. In case it skipped your notice, the guards had night vision goggles hanging from their belts. I can't guarantee they're operational or not, but it wouldn't be wise to discount them." He glanced at Gillian.

The short Scot had settled onto a flimsy-looking chair that groaned alarmingly, but held up gamely under his bulk. "Their electrical generating system is run off the same water-wheel they used for their mill."

Griffon asked again. "So where did they get it? Is this one of those generators the military, or campers used?"

Gillian thought for a moment. "Nooooo, it's much larger than any of them. This is a big, fixed-site version. All manufactured in our day were much smaller, to be mobile. An obvious requirement for any of the people who would want it."

Griffon asked the next question. "So, did anyone manufacture these things?"

Gillian shook his head. "Not that I know of. Why? Fusion-generated power was so cheap, and batteries were so efficient, why bother with manufacturing a fundamentally useless piece of machinery? It's the same reason the blimps were all custom-made advertising gimmicks rather than useful flying machines, they weren't needed."

"So we have someone with engineering know-how, the facilities to produce original designs, and the will to give them to hicks in the out-of-beyond?" Griffon said, thoughtfully.

Fineous shrugged. "Until we can get more details, that's about it."

Griffon looked at White. "What about you Doctor? Did you notice anything out of the ordinary?"

White awkwardly put away his stylus and datacomp. "Well, only a couple of things. First, there were young people, children, adults, even seniors, but did any of you notice there weren't any sick people?" He raised the stump of his right arm. "In a rustic farming village like this, and with the countryside as hostile as it is, you'd figure there'd be at least a few people with missing limbs, the gout, anything." He paused thoughtfully. "But nothing? They must have a really great hospital around here, or..."

Griffon looked at him, "Or what?"

White shrugged, perplexed. "Or nothing, I don't know. I can't make an assessment from one quick tour. Maybe they took off anyone that couldn't run if we turned out to be hostile. Maybe there's a local taboo against showing disfiguring injuries or sickness. Maybe they execute the sick."

Griffon cut in. "And maybe these gift-giving 'Abataurum' take them off to heaven?"

The others just looked at each other questioningly, shrugged, whatever their various natures dictated.

He continued. "Look, something doesn't jibe here. When Dortmunder greeted us out there he asked if we were 'Abataurum' or 'Reavers', as if he couldn't tell the difference. Then, when we get here we're treated like long-lost cousins."

White asked hesitantly. “Yes, but maybe we relieved his doubts as we walked in?” He looked around at the others. “After all, we were friendly and open with him. Any sort of leader of people should have recognized that.”

Fineous smiled grimly. “And any sort of villains worth their loot would be able to fake it. Also, there’s another thing. . .”

Griffon finished his sentence for him. “How did Dortmunder tell the town we were coming and we were friendly?”

Gillian put in. “Well we know we were followed at a distance by Dortmund’s guards. Maybe he sent some sort of hand signal, or something, and one of them ran ahead to warn the village?”

Griffon shrugged, “That’s probably it, I’d have done something of the sort. Still. . .”

It was Fineous’ turn to cut in. “Why are they so friendly? What is it that convinces them we’re not some of these ‘Reavers’ or some such?”

Further discussion was cut off by a knock at the door. One of the Oahkee elders stood there. He bowed and apologized for disturbing their rest. He told them the feast in their honor would start in the second hour of the night. Seeing they were still travel-stained, he again apologized and asked if the house’s bathing facilities were adequate?

Griffon actually blushed in embarrassment. He apologized to the elder and assured him everything was fine. He told him they were simply sorting out their gear and unpacking before washing-up.

The elder smiled and bowed. He reminded them if they wanted anything they only had to ask one of their honor guard.

As he closed the door, Griffon shrugged. “I guess we get ready for a party.” Giving each of them a significant look. “Just remember to keep your eyes open. Right?”

Fineous took the first watch while the others bathed and rinsed out their clothes. A serviceable electric dryer/heater served to dry their clothes in time for the delegation that arrived to escort them to the festivities.

The feast was held in what appeared to be the town hall. The food was plentiful, if uninspired. Home-brew and beer were the drinks of the night.

A musical foursome beat out energetic music on a couple of drums, a guitar and even a beat-up old saxophone, all off-key. Soon everyone was engaged in drinking songs, and rowdy peasant dances.

Once things were running well, the members of the team were pigeonholed by groups of villagers for their story. Griffon, with various input from the others, told of their adventures. The people were seemingly impressed. Being slightly inebriated helped.

As the evening ended, Dortmunder rose, rapping his drinking mug on the table for silence. “Now is the time for the Drink of Friendship.” He motioned toward the kitchen door as a woman appeared, carefully carrying an ancient wine bottle.

The crowd all stood, as Dortmunder pulled the cork from what must be one of their rare relics of the past. He poured a small amount of deep red wine for each guest, as well as for each of the headmen and himself. He raised his mug high. “To friendship!”

Griffon’s wine smelled strangely sweet. *Probably a poor year, but what would they know?*

Following Dortmunder’s lead, they all downed the wine in a long draught.

The townsmen cheered and slapped them on their backs. The music cut in again. Griffon found himself drawn into the dancing throng by a pretty young lady in a tight bodice and full skirt.

The spinning dance, unaccustomed drink, and loud music all seemed to go to his head. Suddenly, he stopped, so quickly his partner bounced off him. He swayed, blearily alarmed. He looked for the others. Fineous was facedown on his table. White was nowhere to be seen. He saw Gillian slide off his bench and under a table, a silly grin on his beet-red face.

What the hell? He glanced towards Dortmunder. The “Speaker” was falling over; townsmen were waiting to catch him. Staggering, Griffon started towards the door. The room began to spin, everything blurred. The floor came into sharp focus. Just before it slammed him in the face. Darkness engulfed him.

Chapter 8

Griffon awoke to profound and total darkness. Animal panic flushed the fatigue poisons from his system. Fearing blindness, he surged upwards, only to feel the strength drain from him, slamming him back as surely as a hand on his chest. He grunted as sharp migraine-spasms stabbed behind his eyes.

Stunned by the pain, he lay back limply. Slowly, reason returned and his training and experience took hold. He relaxed, closed his eyes, and began to take stock.

He concentrated on listening. Filtering out the throbbing of his own pulse and the rasp of his breathing... He heard the familiar buzzsaw snoring of Gillian, and the low muttering of White in his nightmare haunted sleep.

He picked out the drip of water, the sound of wind whispering, dull and muffled as if by thick walls, but not too remote. Low, indistinct voices could be heard from somewhere. A wagon, he guessed, rumbled in the distance. An ungreased axle squealed, irregular, tireless wheels thudding.

He took a deep breath, gasped and choked. Bile surged to the back of his throat.

After an eternal life and death struggle not to choke on his own vomit, he settled down and tried again. Slowly he sampled the air, tasted it with nose, avoiding the rotted-poison taste on his tongue. The stench of mold, rot, vomit, and wet were overwhelming. Slowly he picked out the smell of damp stone, and moldering clay. Then, concentrating on feeling each limb. Slowly, he ran his hands over his body, and the surface he was laying on. Without rising, he gradually ran his hands over a widening circle.

He discovered he was laying on some sort of thick cloth mattress or pad. On one side was a cold stone floor or shelf on which the pad rested. On the other was a rough, damp, stone wall. Both the floor and wall were covered by a thick layer of slimy, rotting mold. He flinched back as his fingers slid over something oozing and oily that slid away from his touch.

He heard a skittering, and squishing crunch near his head, which startled him. Staring wildly, he could now see there was dim light, shining through some sort of grid. A dim form, probably a small hexrat, hissed and scuttled away. He dimly saw it as it squeezed through the grate; something unmentionable gripped in its fanged mouth.

He looked about. He was in a small stone... cell.

He guessed it at about three meters by three meters square, and maybe two-and-a-half meters high. He lay on a ratty bag, rotting straw sticking out through the ravaged cloth. Near his head was a low rope-handled bucket.

Slowly staggering up, steadying himself against the wall, he wove unsteadily to the grating. It was a crosshatch of rusty, but very solid, wrought iron bars. They were held together with cold rivets as thick as his thumb. No space was over fifteen centimeters across. A low door was set in the center of the bars, secured by a heavy padlock. Further exploration revealed nothing else but slug trails and rat droppings.

He managed a weakly croaked. “Hello?” What came out was a rasp, ending in a gagging choke as the miasma of his own breath sent his stomach heaving again. He tried again, stronger this time. “Hello?”

He was mildly surprised when an answer came back.

“That you, Griffon?”

He barely recognized Fineous’ voice. *He must be as bad off as me.* “Yeah, you OK?”

“Yeah, I guess so. Now that’s what I call a Mickey Finn.” Griffon couldn’t help chuckling himself, and immediately regretted it. After a moment, he tried to spit the taste from his mouth. “If this is how they treat their friends, I’m glad we weren’t enemies.” He heard Fineous gag before responding. “Yeah, well you got’ta admire the way they got us to walk right in and hand ourselves over to them. Pretty as you please.” Griffon could only nod, angry with himself for walking into the trap. “Sure, as if we could expect this sort of greeting. I guess White and Gillian are still out of it. You in a cell too?”

“Yeah, I guess we’re in the local ‘Pokey’. I think you’re in the next cell over. I can’t see much, but I guess White and Gillian are in the cells across from us. The light is coming from just past your cell. Can you see where it's coming from?"

Griffon slid to his left and strained against the bars. He could just make out a thin band of light outlining what was obviously a door. "There's a door there. It must be outside, it looks like sunlight." About that time he saw the twin shadows of feet appear at the base of the door, and heard the rattle of keys in a lock.

"Someone's coming. . . Gagh!"

Brilliant sunlight stabbed into his eyes. He staggered back from the bars, an arm across his face to block the glare." Reavers! Fine morning to you!" A very large, burly, and loud man shouted as he strode through the door, swinging a short club on a thong. "Our party did you enjoy? Eh?" Laughing at his own jest, he started rapping against the bars of the cells. "Wakey, wakey, sleepyheads! Missed you your breakfast you have!"

Here's a man that REALLY enjoys his job. Griffon thought as he glared at the oaf, too dry and weak to spit.

Seeing the hatred in Griffon's eyes only sent the jailer into new gales of laughter. Suddenly, the jailer's club lashed out. Stabbing between the bars of the cell to smash into Griffon's face.

Staggering back, blood spurting from his cheek, Griffon caught himself against the wall and slowly slid to the floor. The world spun in bursts of pain. For an eternity, he fought back the waves of darkness and explosions of pain that wracked his head. Eventually the surges of darkness waned, then died. He became aware of the world around him.

Only a few moments had passed. He heard the guffaws of the jailer and the shouts of his companions. The huge Oaf rapped the bars of Griffon's cage with his truncheon. Shouting for silence. He leered at Griffon. "Tough you are not, eh Reavers?"

Griffon could only glare at him, blood from his gashed cheek dripping down his chin.

The Oaf turned to the others. "Word of you we have sent to the masters. A few days you have. Then..." Chuckling. "Here the Abataurum will be."

As he strode out of the jail, he said over his shoulder. "Pray I would if I were you. Mercy your gods may have. The Abataurum will not."

The door slammed shut behind him, darkness returned.

From the cell opposite him, Gillian croaked. "Wha' ta 'ells going on? Are you alright Sahr?"

Griffon wiped the blood from his cheek and gently probed the gash, then tested the set of his teeth before answering. "Yeah, I'm OK." He grinned painfully into the darkness. "Afraid I'll have a 'dueling scar' though."

From the cell to his left, Fineous gave a short laugh. "Yeah, well I'm afraid that may spoil your chance at making the 'Sexiest Man of the Year'." They all got a good laugh at that.

Concerned, White asked him to describe his injury. "It doesn't sound too bad. We need to clean that before infection sets in. Until then, let it bleed free, that may keep dirt from getting into it."

They each took inventory of what they had, and found that they'd been stripped of everything useful. They were wearing their fatigues, their underwear, socks, and combat boots. Everything else, even the laces from their boots and their belts were missing. This turned to a general discussion of their situation. What they might do about it, various escape plans, and a rather offensive commentary on the ancestry of the Oahkies, and the people of this world in general.

Eventually, they heard a creaking of some sort of cart or barrow at the door. When it opened, their jailer stepped in holding a nasty-looking, sawed-off, percussion-cap shotgun. A second man followed him in holding a bucket, wooden bowls, and spoons.

The jailer spoke. "Well, dinner it is you have. Our pigs eat better they will when gone you are."

While the jailer covered him, the second man proceeded to dip up a disgusting slop of leftovers and half-rotten remains into the bowls and handed them to the prisoners. Since the gaps in their bars were too small for the bowls, they had to hold them through the bars while they spooned up the slop. It proved to be as bad as it looked. However, they were all ravenous.

After he served the last of them, the second man left and returned with a large bucket and a cup. He loudly hawked and spat into the bucket before taking their bowls, empty or not, and gave each of them a cup of water.

He produced a key and ordered them to bring their night buckets to the door of the cage and step to the back of the cell. Then, while the jailer covered them with his shotgun he carefully opened the cell door, dumped their bucket into the one in which he'd carried the water. He set the bucket back into the cell and locked the door. After servicing each cell in turn they both left.

With nothing else to do, the prisoners returned to their talk. They ran through every possible plan of escape, examined every inch of their cells, and generally exhausted their topics of conversation. This routine was repeated for three days. They managed to keep their hopes up, though each felt the blackness of despair lurking at the back of their minds.

On the morning of the fourth day, the jailers brought each of them their very own bucket of water and a rag, and told them to clean up. The Abataurum were coming.

Each dutifully, even gratefully, sponged off. They even took the time to clean up their clothing.

They heard the sound like an electric engine approaching, heavy footsteps, then low voices outside the cell. The door opened, and their jailer came in.

He leveled his shotgun at them and tossed sets of ankle and wrist manacles through the bars. He ordered them to put the chains on. The problem of White's missing hand was overcome by fastening the other end of the manacle to the chain between his feet.

Once everyone was secured, he called and the same, silent assistant entered. Under the ominous barrels of the shotgun, the assistant entered each cell in turn and checked their bonds.

The jailer then ordered the prisoners to follow him, and backed out of the jail. The prisoners did as directed, hobbling along and blinking in the weak sunlight.

Their jail proved to be a small, low building near the river docks.

The jailers prodded them into line. Other men were carrying their packs, weapons, and other equipment from a storage lean-to adjacent to the jail. Everything was carefully laid out on a large tarpaulin.

They turned at the sound of heavy footsteps approaching. Three massively armored figures appeared. While of a different design, they were obviously warbots; similar to the one they'd destroyed. Accompanying them were several figures: Dortmunder, the elders of the town, and a woman in a close-fitting white jumpsuit.

Even under the warbots' weapons, the locals directed their obvious fear and deference to the woman. She was tall, with short-cropped, straight black hair, and, while not fat, did appear to be soft and flabby. In fact, the only thing thin about her, were bloodless, sneering lips.

She looked them over with obvious distaste and disdain. Turning to Dortmunder, she said. "These Reavers aren't exactly impressive are they?"

Fineous sneered. "Neither are you sist..."

The jailers truncheon lashed into the little man's groin, dropping him to his knees.

The woman didn't even blink. She stepped before Griffon, grabbed his chin and twisted his head back and forth, examining every feature closely. She repeated this with each member of the party. She seemed to be memorizing every line of their faces.

Then, she stepped back to address them all. "I am Praetor, Olivia Cromwell. I must say, you are truly a surprise. Initial scan indicates that you are original Phoenix personnel. We didn't think that there were any of you left." Now her sneer became really frightening. "Since you all appear to be uncontaminated, you'll have the. . . 'Honor' of donating your organs to our banks. You will be taken to our center. There, you will enjoy the experience of vivisection."

They could only stare. She smiled at their discomfort before continuing. "Don't worry, we've refined our techniques. You'll be alive, and conscious for the whole operation. That will allow you to experience every sensation. You will be able to enjoy the experience as each and every inch of skin, muscle, organ, and bone is removed. Since we cut out your eyes last, you'll even get to watch the whole procedure. Your organs will go into our bank, to be used to improve the life of your Superiors. Your brains will then be mind-wiped, reprogrammed, and...." gesturing to the nearby warbots, "installed as the CPUs for our Battleborgs."

Standing behind her, Dortmunder just smiled. The Elders blanched and seemed to deflate in horror. Obviously, they would have rather died than have anything to do with this particular duty.

When Griffon started to object, he was silenced by a blow from the jailer's truncheon.

She turned to Dortmunder. "I was diverted from my mission by your signal. Since I have no room for them in my vehicle, you'll have to hold them until the Tithing in…" She stared into space for a moment. "Three more days. I want them to be in good shape, we don't want to have to throw away any damaged organs or broken bones." She caught Dortmunder's chin, forcing his face around. "Remember, if it's not perfect, it's not right. If it's not right, it's wrong. If it's wrong, you will be punished."

The Speaker quailed. "Yes, mistress."

She turned to their neatly laid-out gear. She carefully lifted and examined every piece, staring intently at each inch of every item.

Then, she stepped back, closed her eyes, and seemed to go into a trance. She stood that way for several minutes. Nothing else moved, even the town was as silent as a tomb.

Finally, having reached some sort of decision, she gave a sharp nod and turned to the group of villagers.

"Right, in three days, the prisoners will be sent with the tithing. Transportation will be provided." She glared at Dortmunder and shoved a short, thick forefinger into his chest. "Remember, you will be held responsible for their condition. If there is anything amiss, you will ensure those responsible will be sentenced accordingly. Understand?"

His demeanor cracking, sweat stood out on Dortmunder's face. "Y-Yes, Mistress," he said in a wavering and weak voice.

With neither further comment nor glance, she turned and stalked off toward the heart of the town. The Battleborgs automatically assumed an escort position. Obviously shaken, Dortmunder and the Elders followed in a ragged bunch.

Their jailers waited until the assembly was out of sight then herded them back into their cells. The jailers were silent and subdued as they returned the prisoners to their cells and removed their manacles.

Once their jailers had left they all started speaking at once. After a few moments, Griffon called them to order. "Right, White, what the hell was that all about?"

The doctor could be seen to shrug in the dim light. "If you're asking if they can do this..." He paused, thinking, "Why not? They obviously have the technology to do it. If you're asking why..." While the others couldn't see his face they could hear the scorn in his vice. "The Nazis, the KGB, the CIA, all sorts of groups used similar ceremonies to . . . 'dehumanize' their members. Human beings have a tribal, even a 'herd' instinct. Any sane human mind recoils at the thought of torturing, even killing a fellow member of the tribe, or herd. They have to be convinced their victims aren't a part of their tribe. Even soldiers have to rationalize the enemy is out to kill or destroy their side. Criminals rationalize that their victims are less than they are. I'll bet these 'Abataurum' use these procedures as a means of separating themselves from their victims… of 'proving' their superiority over their enemies."

Griffon grimaced. "So we have to take this seriously?"

Fineous said, from his cell. "I'd say that's a big 'yes'. You saw the reactions of the locals. Thank goodness they were wearing brown pants."

Gillian cut to the chase. "So, we take it seriously. What are we going to do about it?"

The silence was deafening.

Fineous finally broke in. "Well I don't know about you guys, but I'm breaking out of this 'Popsicle Stand'."

Griffon could only smile. "And how will we do that?"

"Just leave that to me." A shuffling and grunting came from Fineous' cell. "You guys try to think up something. I can't tell you what I'm planning, you won't react naturally."

"Just what are you trying to do?" a disturbed White asked.

His voice strangely muffled, Fineous replied. "Disappear of course. Now, don't bother me."

The others spent the next several hours speculating. Strange sounds, grunting, and scraping were Fineous only response. Around noon, it started to rain, the low drum muffling the noise. While Fineous continued his efforts, the others continued their speculation. They tried to figure out what the mousy little man had in mind, detailed and discarded a dozen separate escape possibilities, and attempted to make sense out of the mad world where they were trapped.

As the day ended, Fineous' cell grew silent. There was no response to their calls. White, who had the only view into the little man's cell, could make nothing out in the dim light.

Shortly, they heard the sound of their jailers approaching.

Per their normal routine, the senior jailer entered and leveled his shotgun at them. Then his aid came in lugging the bucket of slop and their bowls.

To give the appearance all was normal, each took his bowl in turn, and started eating. When the aid came to Fineous' cell, he gave a sudden start and dropped the bucket.

The head jailer stared suspiciously at his assistant. "What? Hang himself did he?"

"N-no" Stammered the obviously shaken aid. "Gone he is!"

The jailer rushed over to see. Griffon heard him curse as he groped for the keys.

"How ta hell? Tunnel out did he?" The big oaf swung the door open on rusted hinges. The two rushed into the cell.

"Hell! Dead end the hole is!"

"Mean what do ye'?"

"Two feet deep it is! Nowhere it goes!"

"Here he must be!"

They heard the sound of thumping and banging. The mattress was ripped into sodden clots and hurled through the door of the cell.

"Outside he must be! Find him you must!"

"Daft are ye? Tunnel out he did not!"

They heard the sound of a blow.

"Tracks he must have left! Rainin' it is! In the mud tracks will be!"

The lackey ran out into the drizzle.

Their jailer came stalking out of the cell, the shotgun clutched in a white-knuckled grip. He leveled the twin barrels on Griffon.

As Griffon moved slowly to the back of his cell, the Jailer snarled. "Where he is you know? Balls off I will blast!"

As casually as possible Griffon shrugged. "And ruin your precious Abataurum's prize?" He gestured towards the other cell. "He said something about going out for doughnuts."

The jailer just stared, stunned. He started fumbling with his keys and spat out. "Out'ta ya I will kick! Bastid! Reaver you are!"

As the cell door swung open, Griffon braced for action, stymied by the deadly barrels leveled at his midsection.

Then, as the jailer stalked into the cell, Griffon saw shadowy motion behind him. The jailer suddenly lurched to one side, the shotgun tumbling from nerveless fingers. Luckily, it didn't discharge as it fell clattering to the stone floor. A grimy hand, gripping a rock, slammed against the side of his head for a second time.

With the expression of a felled ox, the big oaf slumped to the floor. A dirt-caked Fineous stood smiling in the cell door. The little man put his finger to his lips as he turned and rushed to stand beside the door to the jail, back to the wall. Griffon grabbed the shotgun; and was following when the assistant returned.

He must have been blinded by the darkness because he ran straight into the butt of the shotgun. The blow snapped his head back as Fineous' rock smashed into the back of his head with a satisfying thud. The aid dropped as silently as his boss.

Fineous gestured. “Unlock the others quick!” He raced outside.

Griffon scooped up the keys, where the jailer had dropped them. Then started fumbling with the locks of the other cells.

Grunting and heaving, Fineous pulled a ratty wheelbarrow through the door. Glancing over his shoulder he muttered. “They carried the shit in this, it’s the only thing out there.” Once inside he carefully pulled the door too.

Griffon thought quickly. “Common, let’s truss up these two.”

The jailer and his assistant were gagged and tied spread-eagle to the bars of the cells. Only then did Griffon take time to ask the burning question they all wanted to ask. “How the hell did you do that?”

Fineous, who’d been peeking through the crack of the nearly shut door, gave them a dirt-caked grin. “Like I said, I disappeared.”

In a stage whisper, White said. “OK, I’ll bite. How?”

After another glance around, Fineous turned back, attempting to wipe the caked dirt from his face with the back of his hand. Doing nothing but smearing the mess. “Well, I pried up several of the stones in my cell; then, dug a hole. When they saw it, they thought I’d tunneled out. When they found the hole was only a couple of feet deep, it completely addled them.”

Now it was Gillian’s turn. “So where the ‘ell were you hiding?” He gestured to his recent accommodation. “A titmouse couldna’ hide in there.”

Fineous gave another dirt-smeared grin. “They saw a hole and a pile of dirt.” He started chuckling. “They didn’t notice that the pile of dirt was way bigger than the hole.”

Now it was their turn to chuckle. Griffon asked. “And how did you dig up the stones? They were mortared in.”

Fineous raised his foot, for the first time they noticed that he was barefoot. “Those combat boots have metal shanks.” He grinned ruefully. “That was the toughest part, pulling those damned things apart.”

White again. “Now what? We’re out of the cells, but we’re still in this nest of snakes.”

Griffon had the next step already worked out. “They have our packs and gear in the shed next door. We’ll wait until it’s full dark then slip over there and gear up.” He paused, looking thoughtful. “Then, we slip down to the river, grab a couple of those boats, and drift downstream and out of this place.”

They spent the next half-hour working out the details. Then, as they prepared to slip out into the dripping darkness, their former jailer started to come too.

Fineous stepped up to the big oaf and patted his cheek. “Wakey, wakey shithead.”

The jailer’s eyes snapped open, he glared at them over the gag.

White asked, reluctantly. “Well, what do we do about them? Kill ‘em?” The jailer started to thrash uselessly at his bonds, muffled oaths strained from behind the gag.

Fineous turned to them, grinning. “My, he knows all the bad words!” He faced back to the jailer. “Nooo, we’ll leave these two to explain to the Abataurum how we got out.”

As the import of what he’d said sank in, the jailer went suddenly stiff, staring at them in terror. Then, he went berserk. His bonds cutting into the skin of his arms and legs as he thrashed in panic. He was screaming through the gag. He soon slumped, defeated. They heard him sobbing as they slipped into the night.

Chapter 9

As could be expected, things did not go as planned. They managed to break the lock on the storage shed and recover their gear. Once they’d checked and loaded their weapons, Griffon outlined his plan and they moved out. Fineous took the lead with the grenade launcher, Gillian brought up the rear.

They worked their way down to the river. Few townsmen were out in the cold, rainy night; and they were easily able to avoid the few pools of light streaming from the small dingy windows.

The river formed the western edge of the town with a low stone bulwark along the bank. The stream was in full flood, roiling, muddy, and swift. The party found several small boats pulled up on the low river-wall, well clear of the roiling river. Griffon checked the two at the downstream end of the line, found the oars lain out neatly under each. Then, while White kept watch, he and Gillian flipped them right-side up and drug them to the river’s edge. There was a great deal of heaving and a minimum of bumping and thumping. Fineous went to each of the other boats and used his combat knife to carefully pry out several of the slats making up their flat bottoms.

They froze at White’s sudden hiss. Two men and a boy were walking down to the river. Each was carrying two or three fishing poles and a couple of buckets.

In the gloom they walked right past Fineous, where he crouched between two of the boats. One of the men muttered something, all three laughed.

Gillian and Griffon looked at each other in alarm. Griffon’s mind spun. *Ah frack! If they give the alarm we’ll have to fight our way out. Without the boats we’ll never get out of this place.*

As with most things, hesitation decided the issue. The townsmen froze as they suddenly spotted the two men struggling to hold the boats against the current. They must have thought they were townsmen in the gloom. One of the men shouted something to them over the river's rumble. That was cut off as White loomed out of the darkness, his assault-rifle leveled. Fineous silently slipped up behind them, his grenade launcher slung across his back. The wicked barrels of the jailer's shotgun aimed at the townsmen's backs.

For a moment, the tableau held. Griffon began to think that the townsmen had been cowed by the threat of White's weapon.

At that moment, one of the men spun to run, screaming and flinging whatever he held away from him. He immediately slammed into Fineous, sending both tumbling into a heap. In the crash, both barrels of the shotgun blasted into the sky. At the sound, the other two, who'd been frozen by shock, broke like brace of quail.

Fishing poles and buckets went flying. Screams filled the darkness still ringing with the shotgun's blast. White caught a full load of bait in the face, the boy ran over one of the boats lining the wall, tripped and knocked his head against the next boat, his scream suddenly cut off. The second man ran full-tilt straight off the wall and into the river. They heard him screaming, sputtering, and cursing as the current carried him away.

The three still standing just looked at each other for a moment. Then, started to move. White, wiping worm-laden gunk from his face, turned to see Fineous rising from the ground. The townsman lay unmoving, dead or senseless. The little man tossed the now useless shotgun away and unslung his grenade launcher.

Gillian and Griffon each jumped into a boat, holding them against the breakwater with the oars as the others tossed their packs in and tumbled aboard.

They shoved off. Griffon secured the second boat to the first with the painter. They all lay in the bottom of the skiffs their weapons raised over the gunwale, ready for action.

Lights came on throughout the town, shouts and the ringing of some sort of alarm bell began to sound.

They drifted with the current, hoping to clear the town before the locals figured out what had happened.

But, it was not to be. The Oahkies obviously maintained some sort of guard along their outer wall. The glaring blue-white beam of a carbon-arch searchlight cut through the gloom and began to search across the river. They could make out other lights along the edge of the town begin to sweep the killing ground beyond the wall. Griffon had started to issue quick orders when the river-light suddenly pinned them in its beam. Then, a shout and the roar-flash of a black-powder rifle. A bullet buzzed over their heads.

Three of them cut loose with short bursts of automatic fire. Acentic tracers ripped towards the glaring eye of the light. Fineous' grenade launcher chugged.

The stuttering roar of a gattling gun ripped from the low tower at the river end of the wall. Griffon tried desperately to shift his fire in the wildly pitching rowboat. The rain of heavy lead slugs reaching towards them, a far more immediate threat than the light.

Fineous' first grenade exploded in the town. The glaring fireball of the incendiary round ballooned up behind the light that was his original target. He swung the stubby barrel towards the deadly gattling, it chugged again.

Griffon raised himself to a kneeling position. Aiming carefully, he ripped off a long burst. The spotlight exploded into a shower of glittering sparks. Darkness flooded in. He staggered. Another jackhammer slammed into his chest, driving him to the bottom of the boat. Heavy lead slugs continued to smash into the lead boat. Griffon hovered at the edge of consciousness. Each breath a searing gout of fire. Wood exploded and splintered around him, ricochets splanged off the river and whined into the darkness.

The stuttering roar of the gattling suddenly cut off. White desperately struggled to lift the gasping Griffon in the slowly-sinking craft. Gillian rose in the second boat, firing short bursts at the shadowy forms and gouting flames of gunners sprinkling the shore. Fineous took careful aim with his stubby weapon. The roar and flash of rifles ripped the darkness. Torches sprung out on the tower they were drifting past, the shadowy forms of their boats stood out on surface of the red-glinting river.

Whether it was reloaded, or a jam cleared, the gattling on the slowly passing river-tower began to stutter. Deadly fingers of lead reached for their lives. Fineous' weapon chugged. A balloon of flame exploded from the inner face of the tower. The tearing roar of the gating suddenly stopped, started. . . The top of the tower exploded in a series of rattling explosions and ripping fireballs roaring from the flaming mass of the tower.

Fineous spun, fell backwards in the pitching boat. Gillian dropped and began to snap off single shots at the shadowy forms backlit by the burning tower. Water began to fill both the tiny, overloaded boats.

Rifles continued to bark. Pops and cracks of ammo beginning to cook-off in the flaming tower. The current carried them further down the channel. Bullets whistled and chunked, splintering wood and spatting off the river surface.

The enemy slowly ceased firing, losing them in the darkness of the night. They could still see the flames from the tower as the river swept them around a bend.

Griffon came too, floating along with the others in the freezing cold water. Their erstwhile vessels sank even with the surface of the water. Nothing more than the buoyancy of the wood kept them from settling into the muddy current.

He tried to speak, gasped and choked on the searing bolt of fire ripping across his chest. A form sloshed and wallowed in the water beside him. He made out White's dim features looming just over his face.

The doctor muttered as he worked over him. "Just relax. You've been pretty beat up. But your vest stopped the slugs. I can't tell much more without a light, and we're still too close to those bastards for that to be safe." From out of his line of sight he heard Gillian's gruff whisper. "The Capn' OK? Fineous is still out of it. I think he'll be OK, just had the wind knocked out'ta 'im."

After a bit, Griffon found he could speak, with pain, but so the others could understand. "We'll go ahead and let the river carry us for the rest of the night. I doubt they'll be able to get the hunt up to us before daylight." He paused to catch his breath, and let the spasm's from his chest subside. "Then, we'll have to find someplace to hole up." Fineous, his voice low and rasping with pain. "What about the boats? If those 'Avatars' get some sort of aircraft going they'll spot us in a minute."

Griffon thought for a moment. "At first light we'll sink 'em in the river and find a gully to hole up in."

They took inventory. All of them were cut and riddled with splinters of wood and bits of lead from the heavy slugs of the townsmen. But, only Fineous and Griffon had actually been hit. Their vests had absorbed most of the shock.

Dawn didn't arrive, so much as it snuck up on them, creeping from behind the low, gray, dripping sky. As soon as they could make out the shore, they worked their way to the right bank. They'd debated which side would be safest, but decided it didn't make much difference.

The party pulled up to a small, deep, rain-filled gully cutting through a steep, red-clay bank at the foot of a large, gnarled oak. Tossing their gear onto the shore, they heaved rocks into the boats before shoving them back into the stream to sink.

Nearing total exhaustion, they managed to stagger a few yards up the bank before collapsing. Then, Griffon roused them to change into dry clothing. Luckily their packs had remained relatively waterproof, other than the occasional bullet-hole of course. Since it was raining, and there wasn't any room in the tangled brush for much else, they rolled up in the waterproof mylar emergency blankets from their packs.

It was a few hours later when Griffon started awake, a clammy hand across his mouth. Gillian lay next to him, cocooned in his blanket. In a very low whisper, he said "Shhh, some sorta craft flying over."

Carefully, Griffon rolled over and peeked out from under the bushes. He heard it before he saw it, a low volume, high-pitch, humming. It was slowly cruising about six meters above the surface of the river. He couldn't actually see it, just a sort of distortion in the air. Rain splattered and ran off the surface, providing an outline for a bloated torpedo-shaped craft that was otherwise invisible to the eye.

Memories were triggered, he'd seen this before. Back, before, a craft, a hunter, a. . . Suddenly, involuntarily he tensed, muttering. "Mutter frackin!" He started snaking back under the brush. Frantically he ducked under his emergency blanket. In a gruff, desperate whisper, he said. "Cover up! Now! Dammit!"

The others looked at him incredulously. As he ducked his head under the blanket, "I said cover down!" Finally, they moved. Ducking under the thin mylar and rolling up into tight cocoons.

When they were finally still, he continued, whispering. "It's a goddamn Stalker. They're hunting for us."

Fineous' voice was muffled by the mylar. "A what? Who's hunting for us, the townsmen?" Griffon hissed through clenched teeth. "No, that damned Bitch! The Abataurum, from what we've seen they're the only ones that'd have those damned drones."

"Wha'ta 'ell was it? All I could see was a blur." Gillian, his soft burr made gravely in his effort to keep it low.

Griffon forced himself to relax before answering. "It came out in the last months of the third Chinese war. It's a recon drone used to scout enemy positions and track enemy movements. The reason you couldn't see it was that it's virtually invisible."

"But tha's a practical impossibility! A magnetic field strong enough to bend light waves that tightly would fry any electronics, and anything with enough shielding wouldn't be able to move."

Griffon's smile was humorless, as well as being invisible to the others. "No, it uses magnetic lift plates for flight, and a ducted fan for propulsion, but it's contained in a fiber-optic shell. The skin is like an insect's compound eye. Between each cell is a receiver feeding into an optical fiber. Then it's led through a booster, guided by the fiber around the inside of the shell and projected out of one of the 'cells' on the other side. Basically it hides behind a distorted projection of what's behind it. Unless it's moving or in front of something that'll show up the distortion, you can't see it."

White got to the point. "What kind of sensor array does it have?"

"Anything they want. A microphone would be useless with the background noise of the river." Griffon peeked out from under the edge of his blanket, thanking the good Lord for the steady drizzle that had been making them miserable before. "Also, the patter of this rain would bury any but the loudest noises, as well as making a sniffer useless." He thought hard. "With all the rusting junk, and ruins that must be about, a magnetometer would be jammed by all the false positives. Most likely they're using optical tracking as well as thermal imaging."

After a pause, Fineous put in. “Skipper, this shiny-plastic isn’t the best camouflage.”

Griffon chuckled at that. “True, I’d give my eye-teeth for a real cammo blanket. But these bushes are pretty thick, and the blankets hide our thermal signature. It’s an old trick the grunts figured out after the US’s little desert war in the last century.”

Further conversation was cut off as a low whine penetrated the covering mylar.

The Stalker, or another like it, passed on a reciprocal course. They couldn’t make out the direction, or the distance, covered up as they were. They all knew that it was too damned close.

Long minutes passed, stretching into an hour. They began to relax.

Another sound slowly rose above the rumble and gurgle of the river. It was the familiar deep hum of a heavy, lift-plate transport. Griffon peeked out, but could make out only a dim shadow passing directly above their hiding place. He heard the others rustling, and the click of weapons being readied. The action of his own weapon seemed as loud as thunder.

But, the shadow passed on; never checking it’s slow, steady pace. As the sound died, he told the others to hold tight. The seconds ticked into minutes, the minutes stretched into an eternity.

Finally, Fineous broke the tension. “Uh, Sir? I’ve really got to go.” Puzzled for a moment, Griffon asked, his voice loud in the silence. “What do you mean? ‘Got’ta go?’ Go where?”

Sounding a bit embarrassed. “You know, ‘Go’. I’m sorry, but there’s just some things that won’t wait for the end of the world.”

Feeling the urgency of his own bladder, Griffon finally understood. “I wish you hadn’t said that.”

Each in turn went a short way further up the gully and relieved themselves in field-expedient cat-holes. As he returned, buttoning up his fly, Fineous smiled. “The penalty of being housebroken.”

The tension finally broken, they cleaned themselves up in the rain-swollen creek that trickled along the bottom of the gully and dug some of their last rations out of their packs for a belated breakfast.

When they’d finished, Fineous climbed to the gully’s edge to keep watch. The others settled to figure what to do next.

Fineous, from his perch, said. “Skipper, you’re our military expert. What happened last night? I mean, that last grenade seemed to blow up half the town. What did I hit?”

Griffon thought for a moment. “Well, you hit an ammo magazine.”

Fineous smiled. “Well, Duh! What I mean is. . . How? Aren’t those things supposed to be better protected than that?”

The others waited for Griffon to explain. “I think they haven’t really had much experience with any sort of competent military opponents.” Gillian snorted, Griffon grinned and continued. "What I mean is their precious 'Abataurum' didn't give them much help, and if they'd had any real experience with anyone else with guns or grenades, they'd have never had their gattling-guns on the towers like that."

At the others' questioning looks, he knelt down and as he used a short stick to draw a rough sketch of the town in the wet, hard-packed sand, continued. "I think the only enemies they've had any experience with has been those big animals. What were they, ah..."

White interjected. "The jabberwocks and behemoths?"

Griffon pointed his stick at him. "That's it." Returning to his rough sketch. "Those and the other things, like the big earth animals like elephants, and rhinos, as well as wild herds, and. . ." Thinking. "Some of the more destructive smaller animals, like those tripe-things. Or maybe baboons, monkeys, deer... whatever rips through their crops."

He pointed at the area outside of the sketch. "All of their firepower was placed high up, to cover the fields. From there, they could sweep the whole area and work with the spotlights at night." He drew a quick series of arcs, showing the sweep of the lights and guns from the towers.

He tapped the sketch with his pointer. "Now, while those heavy guns could make even a behemoth think twice, they're liable to need quite a bit of ammo to get the job done properly. And, like most people, I'd guess they'd keep all sorts of ammo close at hand. Since they used black-powder, they probably had it in water-tight boxes."

He paused for a moment, collecting his thoughts. The others looked over the sketch. He continued. "Now most people would put the rest of their ammo close to where it would be needed." He drew in a series of small boxes next to the towers.

Gillian interjected. "So they wouldn't need to waste time in getting it to the guns."

Griffon pointed his stick at him. "Right, now. . ." To the side he quickly sketched out a rough series of boxes at the outer rim of the fields he'd sketched. "If they were worried about an enemy that could shoot back, they would've been more concerned about stopping incoming bullets and trying to catch the enemy in a crossfire by deploying their heavy weapons in outlying... 'Redoubts,' rather than placing them to drive off animals."

From his perch, Fineous put in. "So they didn't have their ammo protected from enemy fire?"

Griffon grinned up at him. "Right, they were only concerned about rain, not about fire. Now, I think they'll correct that little problem."

They all chuckled.

Griffon looked up and asked pointedly. "Now, Fineous, I have some questions about that little escape of yours."

Fineous actually looked uncomfortable. "Sure, what would you like to know?"

Griffon thought on how to phrase his question. "Well, first, why did you dig a hole in the center of your cell? If you could dig, why not tunnel out under the door?"

Fineous shrugged. "Well, I didn't know how hard it would be to dig out. It would have been a lot harder to dig away the flagstones under the door since you had to dig from underneath then drop 'em before your could pull them out." The others nodded, picturing the effort. "Secondly, our jailers never entered together and the first one in would have seen the hole under the door immediately. Even if we could jump him, the one outside would have raised the alarm." The others nodded agreement, the logic of the argument irrefutable. "Also, If I couldn't get enough dug out before they came in, I could always hide the hole under my mattress."

Griffon nodded. "Granted. Now, Why didn't your tell the rest of us what you were up to?"

Fineous' face reddened in embarrassment. "Ah, well you see. . . Ahem. I hate to say this, but... ah. " He glances nervously at the others. "I've been training with you guys for a long time, and, ah... Truth be told, you guys couldn't pull off a decent 'Con' if your life depended on it."

The others chuckled.

Griffon grinned. "Right, well you may not be giving us enough credit, and you took an awful lot on yourself. Gambling on your 'ability' against our lives. Next time, let us know, OK?"

Abashed, Fineous nodded.

"Right." Griffon glanced up at the lightening sky, through the branches of the overhanging brush. "This seems to be clearing. We'll pack up and move out. Any questions?" Gillian raised his hand. "Well Sir'rah, which way will we 'move out'?"

Griffon paused, assembling his thoughts. "Well." He motioned towards the river with his thumb. "Unless you want to swim that, we have to go upstream, downstream, or away from the stream."

Fineous nodded. "Duh."

Griffon grinned. "I'm glad you agree. Anyhow, It's no good going back upstream towards the 'Oahkies', and this river seems to have more traffic than the L.A. Freeway. So, we'll cut uphill, away from the river."

Now it was White's turn. "Ah, sir, shouldn't we wait for nightfall?"

Griffon gestured towards the broken clouds now beginning to scudder across the pale late-winter sky. "No. Our main threats are these 'Abataurum' bastards and these alien critters. The darkness won't protect us from the Abataurum sensors. We'll stand a better chance of spotting trouble in daylight."

The others nodded and set too, packing their gear and burying their trash. Griffon wiped the sketch out with his foot. "Now, let's put some miles behind us."

They were actually sorry to leave the safety of their hideout. The thin brush roof and gully walls had provided them with the safest hole they'd found yet. But, they all realized the safety was illusory and moved out as one.

As usual, Fineous took point. At first, they tried to follow the course of the stream but, the combination of deep rain-sodden mud and choking briars soon forced them back to the rim of the gully. They followed along the edge of the brush, prepared to duck under cover at the first sign of trouble.

The gully meandered through a thick wood of scrub-oak to a low, red-clay ridge to the west of the stream.

Topping the rise, they saw they were back on the familiar plains they'd been traveling before meeting the Oahkies. Gently rolling flatlands cut by periodic gullies and dotted by small stands of scrub. They could see various-sized groups and herds of the wildly varied fauna occupying this wilderness.

For the next two days, they made their way generally south and east, roughly paralleling the river to their far left. Never wandering far from cover, they saw aircraft in the distance on several occasions, but never any form of ground transport. And, while the countryside was covered with ruins, they saw no sign of new occupancy or roads. This whole region seemed to have been given over to the wilderness and the beast.

Early on the third day, they were trudging up another of the interminable low-rolling ridges. Fineous was well out front in the point position, just reaching the crest of the rise, when they saw him suddenly stiffen and drop to a crouch. He hit the quick-release strap, dropping his pack and bringing his grenade-launcher up to the ready.

The others dropped their packs and raced forward, weapons drawn. As they neared, Fineous was looking down the far side of the ridge. Stooping to keep from being skylined, they moved forward to see what lay below.

Before they reached him, they heard the now-familiar hissing scream of a pack of jabberwocks on the hunt. That, and a strangely familiar rhythmic pounding.

Griffon was the first to reach Fineous' side, and what he saw gave him a little start. About two hundred meters down the back side of the ridge, racing madly in their general direction, a horse was galloping flat-out in terror. Even from this distance, he could see the beast was almost done in. Foam streaked sides and, while the stride was still strong, it was beginning to falter. A small figure was stretched out low along the beast's back. It clung for dear life and seemed to be calling encouragement to the valiant steed. Immediately behind it tore a small band of three jabberwocks. Rear legs held rigidly high and swinging as counterbalance to the powerful bounds of the clawed front legs their fang-lined maws gapping and slavering in shrieking anticipation.

The party never saw what made the horse stumble, some irregularity in the ground, or maybe just fatigue. It didn't matter.

The leading Jabberwock gave an incredible leap and managed to rake a massive claw across the horse's hindquarters. Physically twisted by the blow at full speed, the horse screamed and crashed into a skidding mass of broken bones and blood.

With an expert kick, the rider cleared the stirrups, tumbling clear of the horse. Landing hard, the tiny figure rolled into a heap and lay still.

At full speed, the leading Jabberwock tore past the horse. Skidding messily in the soft earth it slipped and smashed to a stop.

The following jabberwocks slammed into the downed animal. They began ripping bloody gobbets of flesh from the screaming, thrashing animal before the leader had even managed to come to a complete stop.

Griffon was already well down the slope, screaming at the top of his lungs and firing wild, unaimed bursts from his assault-rifle to distract the hunters.

He heard curses from behind. Acentic bolts tore past, smashing into the frenzied monsters. The creatures twitched and staggered with each strike.

As if in slow-motion nightmare, Griffon saw each round hit. Divots tore from massively-armored hides. The animals screamed in fury and spun to face their attackers.

Griffon raced directly at the nearest beast.

Crouching over the prone form of the rider, it screamed defiance at the tiny pain-spewing form racing towards it.

The two further beasts sprang forward to the attack. The torso of the one on the left blossomed into a flame-hearted rose of explosion-rent flesh and spattered blue-purple blood.

Then Griffon was upon the monster before him. The creature reared onto hind leg, fore-claws spread wide to receive him, gaping fangs snapping at his face.

Griffon skidded to a stop, assault-rifle up.

SLIP!

Slam! He fell onto his back, sliding under the very jaws of the beast.

The Jabberwock dropped to all threes. Screaming in ecstasy, fangs snapped at the prey and his gun.

The jaws closed on the out-thrust carbine. Griffon triggered the rest of the clip.

Brilliant bolts ripped a massive gap through the top of the creature's skull. Great gouts of putrid flesh and spewing blood flinging a geyser of death.

The dead jaws spasmodically closed on his weapon. Smashing it into flinders as the creature, in a brain-dead, adrenaline dance spun away and collapsed into a quivering heap. Griffon rolled to his stomach, searching for the last creature.

A short distance away, the last Jabberwock stood at bay, reared onto its hind leg.

Fineous, his grenade-launcher nowhere in sight, ducked and wove. Dodging blow, claw, and fang in a desperate dance of death. His pistol cracked time and again, ripping out chunks of flesh, seeking a vital spot.

Griffon glanced back to see White and Gillian still pounding up from behind. Sprint, kneel, fire. Up, sprint again.

They were trying to cover their friend while closing the range. Desperately trying to distract the monster.

Griffon snatched at his own pistol. His hand slapped against the empty holster. The weapon lost in his fall.

Surging to his feet, he ripped his combat knife free. Three quick steps, leaping to the back of the monster. Legs clamped to the heaving, muscular, blood-streaked flanks.

The creature reared, screaming in fury. Desperately trying to reach the tiny figure clinging to it's back.

Gripping his knife with both hands, Griffon plunged it into the right eye of the monster.

Again, and still again! Driving the blade deeper and deeper into the bloody, slime-spewing ruin of the multifaceted organ. The blade bit into bone. Then, a crunch and the creature spasomed into an insane, joint-rending death-dance.

Springing free, Griffon landed hard. Something snapped!

Struggling to rise, an avalanche of russet flesh and putrid blood rolled over him.

Bones cracked, breath driven out in and explosive burst. Darkness closed down,

His mind spun, *Breath!*

PAIN!

Consciousness dissolved into a mass of exploding nerve lights. Tendrils of death! A tidal wave of blackness…

Chapter 10

Dark

Dark

Pain

Dark

DARK

PAIN

GRAY

PAIN

Desperately struggling up a pain-drenched slope to consciousness, Griffon opened his eyes to darkness.

His thoughts spun, stuttered. *Wha' the frack? Ah mutter frackin! Not again!*

The world exploded into blinding, white glare.

"Gaaaa!" Throwing his arm up to protect his blinded eyes.

A husky, and melodious, voice spoke from behind the glare. "Well hello, and how are we feeling?"

"What do you mean 'we'?" Squinting through the glare, Griffon's breath caught in his throat. "Ah, well at first impression, I'd say that I've died and gone to heaven."

Standing in the door was the most beautiful sight he'd seen in a very long time.

She smiled and walked over to the bunk where he lay. "Now that's got to be some sort of record for a recovery."

Griffon ran his eyes down the vision in front of him. Blond hair curled in a tight bob. A soft green jumpsuit that didn't hide a single curve, large bosom, tight waist, and wide hips flowing into long, long, legs.

She was looking at something on the shelf above his head. Then, started punching notations on the datacomp in her hand.

He finally started to get his racing thoughts under control. "Ah, pardon me, Ma'am, but. . . Who the hell are you?"

She gave him another smile. "Well, so much for 'Heaven on Earth'. I'm Chief Medical Officer Tori Stoner." Her grin got even wider. "You are William Griffon, Exploration Team Leader, Challenger Crew." Guessing his next question. "You're in the dispensary of Comanche Base."

Returning her smile, Griffon asked. "OK, I'll bite. How long have I been here? How did I get here? And why am I here?"

She chuckled, continuing to make notes on whatever she was looking at. "You've been here a week. You've been rolled up in an ancient autodoc. We kept you in drug-suspension while we glued you back together."

With clipped efficiency she put her datacomp on the shelf above his head, picked up some sort of nasty-looking medical implement, and bent over him. "I have to check you out. Now, shut up, lay back and relax."

Grinning, complied. “Yes Ma’am.”

After a quick, professional check of his eyes, ears and teeth; she proceeded to flex his arms and legs. Then, she had him sit up and performed the obligatory thumps and prods, turn and cough.

Finally, as she seemed to be finishing up, he decided to risk asking, “And, what about my men?”

She gave him an impish grin. She was big on smiles. “You mean those guys who have been running me, and my staff, ragged for the last week?”

Griffon could only chuckle and nod.

She continued. “They’re outside, I just wanted to make sure you were up to snuff before I allowed that bunch of barbarians in.”

She recovered her datacomp, opened the door, and looking down the hall beyond. “OK, I’ll let you in.” She stepped back as White, Gillian, and Fineous filed in.

She started out, turning back at the door. Pointing the stylus from her datacomp at the three that now crowded the small room. “Don’t get him excited, I’m monitoring him from my desk.” Pointing at Griffon. “Now, shut up, lay back and relax. The moment I see your readings jump I’ll shut you all down.”

Griffon could only grin. “Yes Ma’am.”

After the door slid shut behind her, all four began to talk at once.

Griffon raised his hand. “OK... ok, me first. I’m the one that’s been out of it.” The babble slowly died. “Now, where the hell are we? How did we get here? And of course, what the hell’s going on?”

His friends looked at each other before they all nodded to White to speak.

The doctor clasped his hands in front of his chest and looked up, assembling his thoughts. “I think I’d better start where you left us. When that last Jabberwock fell on you it, well, basically crushed you.”

Grinning, Fineous cut in. “Squashed flat. Next time you go bareback riding, jump the other way.”

Griffon gave him a sour look. “Next time? Bite me.” Then something occurred to him, he pointed at White. “Hey, you’ve got two hands!”

White grinned, flexing the fingers of his right hand. “Well, a full prosthetic.” He rolled up his sleeve revealing what appeared to be a faint line encircling his forearm. He gripped his arm below the ring, pressing a hidden stud, twisted sharply, and pulled the wrist and hand off. Held it out for Griffon to see the contacts. “They’re still tweaking the settings but it works just fine.”

Griffon grimaced. “Uh, no thanks, that thing gives me the willies.” As White grinned and reattached the limb, he asked. “I thought they attached those things permanently?”

White shrugged. "I asked. They said this way I won't have to go into surgery to have it repaired or replaced. I guess it all depends on your circumstances. They've had a lot of experience with prosthetics."

Griffon nodded. "I guess. Go on?"

White nodded, absentmindedly flexing his new fingers. "Well you were so beat up, we didn't even try to revive you. Just sort of pored you into the autodoc and let it put you in full medical suspension."

Griffon grimaced, nodding. "So, then what?"

At White's gesture, Fineous took up the tale. "That rider we rescued turned out to be a courier for the Raiders." He grinned absently. "A right feisty one too. Anyhow, we persuaded her we were friends, and she led us to a pickup point. There we were able to hop an underground tube-train."

Griffon had to interrupt. "They have 'Tubes running?"

Fineous shrugged. "A few. They use 'em to get well clear of their bases before they come up to the surface. It's to keep the others from finding their bases."

Griffon asked. "The Abataurum?"

Nodding, Fineous continued. "That's what they have the villagers they control call them. Actually, that turns out to be a bastardization of 'Avatar'." At Griffon's questioning look. "It's an archaic term for some sort of Angel, or representative of the Gods, or some such." Griffon muttered sardonically. "Well, they didn't seem to be the modest sort."

The others chuckled. Fineous continued. "Yes, well, the Raiders call them the Brotherhood. It's from the name of the original organization formed during the Hiver invasion."

"Who are these 'Raiders'?" Griffon asked.

Fineous pausing for a moment to reset his thoughts. "On that I'd better start from the beginning. If you remember, from when we first awoke, The Hivers started their invasion with a biologic attack. As things went to hell in a hand-basket, several. . . 'Underground' organizations, seem to have, um, 'pooled' their resources in a move to gain control of whatever would be left."

Griffon blinked, perplexed. "Underground organizations?"

Nodding Fineous continued. "Right, well it seems to be the nature of the human beast that society always seems to have secret organizations. Criminal and political, 'Movers and Shakers' get together and form various, 'Star Chambers', or 'Illuminati', 'Syndicates', 'Mafia's', CFR's, Trilats, whatever. They're all the same. Groups organized in secret to aggrandize power and wealth for the members."

The little man paused, thinking. "Anyhow, these groups were normally each other's worst enemies. But, with everything going to hell, several of these organizations, got together, and formed the 'Omega Brotherhood'. They moved heaven and earth to insure their members were placed in the positions they felt would allow them complete control of whatever was left of Human civilization."

He shrugged. "Once the initial Hiver attack was over, they did manage to take control of a sizeable portion of what was left. Their first move was to... eliminate, whatever Human organizations were left that they didn't control."

Griffon nodded. "Like the Raiders."

Gillian stepped in. "Right, while the Brotherhood was able to take over most of the civilian efforts, they had less luck pre-empting the military."

Now White. "Our hosts are... primarily, descended from various elite military personnel that were put in cryogenic suspension to keep from being contaminated by the Hiver biological weapons. To try and guarantee the Bugs wouldn't get them all, they were scattered in small, discreet facilities all over the planet." He shrugged. "The Hivers, and the Brotherhood couldn't find 'em all."

Back to Gillian. "Since they woke up, there's been a three-way war of extermination going on. The Hivers have settled into. . . 'Enclaves', where they're slowly converting the Earth to what we guess is a version of their home world. As their population, and area of 'conversion' grows, they're gradually taking over the planet." Griffon nodded. "What sort of area are we talking about?"

Shrugging, Gillian continued. "According to our hosts, they seem to prefer the tropics. They've, converted about twenty percent or so of the planetary surface, both land and sea." The Scot paused, making a point of glancing at the surrounding walls. "Both the Raiders, and the Brotherhood are paying lip-service to fighting the Hive, but seem to be putting most of their efforts into trying to exterminate each other."

Griffon noted, grimly. "No joy in Mudville huh?"

Now it was Gillian's turn to shrug. "Right, the Brotherhood has the upper hand, the Raiders fight back, and the Hive keeps winning."

Griffon turned to Fineous. "What about that town we came across?"

Fineous shook his head. "What's left of the human population is scattered all over the planet in various groups, clans, whatever. The Raiders and Brotherhood try to contact them and gain control over them. Then, they help with technology and such and try to kill-off the people the other group's gotten to first."

Griffon paused for a moment, collecting his thoughts. "What about the Hivers? Don't they have something to say about these suddenly resurgent areas of technology?"

Gillian answered. "Not really, they seem happy so long as the technology doesn't go beyond a certain level. As soon as anything appears that constitutes a threat they... stomp it out. Hard."

Griffon nodded as another piece slid into place. "That orbital strike we saw."

Gillian nodded. “Right, that was a Raider base the Brotherhood found. The favorite tactic for both sides seems to be to find an enemy base, then to reveal it to the Hivers.”

Griffon could only shake his head. “Cute. . . So, where do we stand with these Raiders?”

Fineous’ sardonic grin was eloquent. “Well, let’s just say that if it was just you and I... we’d be Tripe droppings about now.”

At Griffon’s’ questioning look, he continued. “They seem to feel the threat of... infiltrators outweighed their need for a couple of, ‘Gun-jocks’”.

He waived a hand towards the other two. “However, they seem to have been, ‘Shorted’, on theoretical engineering and life sciences types.” The others nodded.

Confused, Griffon could only ask. “Excuse me?”

White looked embarrassed, the broad Scot just grinned as Fineous continued, “Well, the original Raiders were from elite military combat units. They were quite well educated, had great technicians, and probably some of the finest field engineers in the world. However, they were, ‘shorted’ when it came to doctorate level, theoretical and research types. Add that they’ve had to scratch up their databases from what they could scavenge and steal, and, well. . .” He waived a hand at the other two.

White was positively beet-red in embarrassment. Gillian, grinning even wider, waggled his eyebrows.

Griffon chuckled. “So, we’re dealing with a group of combat veterans who don’t really trust us, but want the services of the academic members of our team, right?”

The others nodded.

He continued, a bit irritated. “If they’re so paranoid you guys must have had a real fun time?”

Now the expressions got positively sour. As usual, Fineous gave voice to their thoughts. “Poked, prodded, scoped, scanned, and. . .” His expression was truly eloquent. “‘Probed’, to death.” He gave Griffon a sly look. “By the way, so have you.”

Griffon snorted. “Great, what did they think, I had a tracking bug up my bum? At least they could have kissed me first.”

They all had a good chuckle. As they got a bit more serious, White responded. “Actually that’s exactly what they were afraid of.” At Griffon’s questioning look. “You see the ‘Brotherhood’ have, made maximum use of their technology. They’re all, well, Cyborgs.”

“Explain.” Griffon was getting very uncomfortable with the path this was taking.

The doctor continued. “They’re all permanently... hardwired into their system. Among other things, they have microscopic cameras and projectors imbedded at the back of their eyes. That, along with transceivers and monitors in the inner ear and the larynx give them full, continuous access to their communications and information nets, as well as allow constant monitoring by the powers that be."

Griffon blinked. "Implants in the eyes?"

Nodding, White went on. "Right, the eye makes an excellent camera, by placing an optical receptor at the back of the orb they get to see everything the. . . 'Brother' sees. Also, since the, camera isn't limited to the visible light spectrum, they also have the ability to see in the UV and thermal spectrums. The camera receives the image, then simply projects an appropriate overlay on the back of the cornea." Griffon had to rub his eyes at the thought. "Nice, that explains the close visual scan that Cromwell bitch gave us."

The others nodded.

Fineous took up the brief. "They use the same system to simulate a computer video monitor. By simply adjusting the picture for the eye's point of focus on the image projected they can do anything a computer mouse can do, scroll, select, deselect, whatever. By using sub-vocal commands they can dictate, access files, process information, do just about anything a normal computer can do."

A question came to Griffon. "How do they handle their communications? Doesn't that sort of thing only work line-of-sight?"

As the conversation entered his realm of expertise, Gillian answered. "They have developed a sub-atomic sympathetic communications system that is digital, apparently has unlimited range, and cannot be intercepted, jammed, or imitated."

Griffon rolled his eyes. "Nice. How does it work?"

Gillian shrugged. "I'm not sure exactly how they worked it out. However, the principle is simple enough. When an atom is split, the various parts have the same rotation. Now, if the rotation of one of the parts is altered, the other parts change their rotation to match it. Since you rotate one direction or the other, it's a perfect means of transmitting digital information."

Griffon was starting to feel a bit confused. "But how does it work?" Gillian shrugged. "I have no idea. Quantum mechanics wer'ra never my strong suite. Einstein was the first to prove the effect mathematically. He just said it was 'weird'. I'm good, but not better than 'im."

Griffon nodded. "Right, well I take it we passed inspection."

Fineous grinned. "We aren't fertilizer yet.'

Griffon looked up, his expression, grim.

Fineous continued. "So, what do we do now?"

Griffon glanced, pointedly at the walls before continuing. "We finish this shit of course. We just have to figure out the how part. Any suggestions? Finn?"

The little man looked thoughtful. "I haven't got anything, but White and Gillian have been working on some ideas." He gestured towards the others; they quickly explained what they had been working on.

Griffon lay back, relaxing. "Great, we have the foundation for a scheme."

The little man nodded. "Right, but if we cobble these together, how do we initiate the action?'

Griffon lay back, relaxing. "That's for you and me to figure out."

They all chuckled at that.

The door opened behind them. The doctor, Tori, brusquely entered, smiling. "Times up. I have to ask you 'Gentlemen' to let my patient get some rest." They said their good-byes, and filed out. Tori checked the readings on the monitor over his head and smiled down at Griffon. He felt the brush of an injection.

The pretty doctor turned, flipping off the lights as she started to leave. Griffon felt the relaxation of the drugs sweeping over him. She turned back, smiling. "You will sleep now. So shut up, lay back, and relax."

Already groggy, he muttered through a yawn. "Yes ma'am."

The next day he had several long hours of being run through the initial rounds of physical rehabilitation.

Afterwards, he returned to his room, sore and aching. He heard a soft knock at the door. Grinning he sat up. "Yes, come in. I'm decent."

However, instead of one of his friends, a stranger entered.

She was hardly one and three-quarters meters tall, man-slim, graceful as a reed, curly, dark-brown hair trimmed in a practical helmet cut. Her otherwise ordinary face was highlighted by a most impressive hooked beak of a nose.

Embarrassed, he could only stammer his apologies. "S-Sorry Miss, I was expecting someone else."

She smiled, lines crinkled at the corner of her eyes, giving life to the brown orbs. "I should be the one to apologize, sir." Still smiling, she looked down, blushing furiously. "I've been told that I owe you my life."

He slowly leaned back, confused. "OK, and who exactly are you, and when did I do this?"

Smiling, she relaxed. "I'm Janine Antoniou. I was the one you saved from the jabberwocks." Grinning, *Ah yes.* "Sorry if I don't remember much. You might say that I left early."

This confused her. "Early?" Nodding as she got it. "Oh, you mean when you were, ahem. . ."

"Squashed?" Griffon interjected.

Embarrassed, she said. "Yes, well, when you were, 'wounded'. Anyhow, your..." She looked confused again, "Friends? Escorted me to the nearest tube-station."

Griffon was amused. "My team, but yes, they're my friends. They told me you were a great help in linking us up with the Raiders. I'd have died, or been crippled for life if you hadn't gotten me to real medical help. I believe that makes us even."

She looked perplexed. "Even?"

Griffon shrugged. *Separated by a common language*. "No debt of honor. The scales are balanced."

He saw she was getting it. She seemed to be quite relieved.

She grinned. "Alright, I understand now. I just wanted to meet my. . . 'Savior?'"

Grinning, he bowed at the waist. "Greetings and well met, Miss Janine!" Her face split in a wide grin, she executed a classic, letter-perfect, curtsey. "And a hearty well met to you good sir."

Seeing his surprise, she said. "I'm a big fan of the tri-vids from your time. I especially love the ones about your knights and ladies."

Griffon had to catch himself. "Those were, fictional. You know, entertainment."

Her smile disappeared as her face turned scarlet. "Oh my, I'm so embarrassed. I... us, I... didn't know. We don't have many, and the library vid-books we've been able to recover have been very, well, confusing."

He relented a little. "I'm sorry, I'm rather new around here myself. I do apologize."

Her smile returned. She started towards the door. "I must be going. I hope we can talk again, I'm really interested in your time. I have so many questions." She stopped in the door. "By the way, your friends have been so, helpful." She got a very peculiar expression he couldn't quite identify. "I'd especially like to ask you about the little one, um. . ."

Griffon had to think a bit. *Little one? Oh yes.* Griffon smiled. "Fineous?"

She nodded vigorously. "Yes, Fineous. He seems to be quite, how do you say, 'interesting'?"

"Yessss, interesting would be one way of describing him." Griffon said, fighting hard not to laugh.

She turned back to the door. "Well, I'll be seeing you. Fair journey."

He was still stifling a laugh. "Ah, fair journey good Lady."

She was smiling ferociously as the door closed behind her.

Fineous is the interesting one? He started laughing. *Yes, that's one way of putting it. . .*

Over the next few days he started on a physical rehabilitation regime. Griffon recognized many of the machines they ran him through, verifying everything was working right, loosening his joints and returning muscle tone.

Tori was the one to run him through his exercises, taking constant notes on her datacomp and monitoring his progress.

After a week of this, she was walking him back to his room and told him he would be released the next morning.

As he climbed back into his bunk, Griffon had to ask. “I have a question. You have lots of technicians around here. How do I rate all this personal attention from the head of medicine?”

The tall blonde grinned at him. “What and miss the chance of examining an original, ‘Pre-invasion’ man? I wouldn’t miss this chance to compare your readings with what we have now.”

She turned, closing the door and turned back to him, smiling. “We have only one more test before I can clear you out of here.” Griffon lay back chuckling. “I was afraid of that. What’s left? A rectal exam?”

She had a rather peculiar, intense, expression. “Nooo, not quite.” She reached back with her left hand, turning the lights down. Her right hand started to undo the top button of her coverall.

Her smile seemed to light up the gloom. Her eyes were smoky pits of pleasure. “We’ve been at war for a very long time. . .”

Another button went. “Lets just say that I’m going to take advantage of having the first healthy, uncontaminated, man to show up here in more than seventy years.”

His thoughts were spinning, going nowhere fast, but definitely spinning. “Oh my.”

Another button went as she stepped towards him. “Now, shut up, lay back, and relax.”

He gave the only response possible. “Yes, Ma’am.”

Chapter 11

Hot, wet fingers of agony etched streamers of ecstasy down his back. Griffon moaned with pleasure as steaming, foaming liquid ran down his leg. His eyes sagged closed.

A heavy pounding began a stuttering roar in his ears.

“Hey, hurry up! There are people waiting!”

Griffon groaned. “Ah shaddup! I haven’t had a real, hot, shower in seventy years!”

From beyond the bathroom door, Fineous’ high-pitched imitation of a little old man. “Yeah sonny, and the rest of us would like to avoid waiting seventy years for our next one! Besides you’re going to be late for your meeting!”

Grumbling, Griffon shut off the water and began the sheer ecstasy toweling-off and shaving can be for someone who hasn’t been able to do either for a very long time.

He checked the clock on the wall as he entered the small room he and Fineous had been assigned. “Ah, I’ve got plenty of time. What kind of world is it where a man can’t enjoy his shower.” Catching Fineous’ eye, he pointed to the nice purpling under the little man's right eye. "What happened to you?"

Grinning sheepishly, Fineous said. "You know that Raider, Janine?"

Nodding. "Yes." The mousy little man did not wear embarrassment well. "Well, I hit on her."

Griffon was now fighting hard to keep a straight face. "And?"

Shrugging, Fineous mumbled. "She hit back."

Failing in his battle, Griffon began to chuckle. "I hope we learned our little lesson. . ."Fineous headed into the bathroom. As the door closed he shouted. "Sure. Next time I'll duck."

Griffon spent a surprised moment, before calling through the door. "So long as you learned a lesson..."Later, dressed in the unmarked olive-green casual coverall of the Raiders, Griffon left for his appointment with the base commander.

The office was spacious, and elegantly paneled in dark wood. Deep beige carpet, large, well padded chairs, and a massive wooden desk dominated the room. The large, beefy, black man sitting behind the desk gestured towards a chair. He spoke with a deep, almost melodious voice, a soft, unplaceable accent. "Have a seat Commander." He gestured to the small oriental man in another chair. "This is my number two, Colonel Tsen." The smaller man rose and offered his hand. Griffon gave his dry, strong grip a shake before they both settled back.

The base commander continued, rhetorically. "What are we to do with you?" His smile didn't reach his eyes.

He held up his hand, cutting off Griffon's reply. "We haven't had any Phoenix personnel. . . 'Sleepers' in a very long time." His smile disappeared completely. "And, we've had some hard lessons with Brotherhood plants."

Griffon had been dreading this. "Sir, we've told you our story. There's not much more we can do. . ."

The Commander cut him off with a raised hand. "Don't worry. If we had any suspicions... you and your team, would be history. What I meant was, we have to decide where to put you and your team." Picking up a small pile of transplex documents, he continued. "Your two scientists have pretty well settled in over at the research division." He put the sheets back down and looked up. "Their supervisors are pretty enthusiastic about their ideas. It's opening up some new avenues. Though I'm not really sure what we'll be able to do with it."

He leaned back in his chair, steepling his hands. "No, I need to find work for you and your driver. We have plenty of. . . 'Shooters'. To tell you the truth, none of our Squad leaders trust you two enough to include you in their teams."

Griffon cut in. "I'm sure we'll be able to integrate, once we've been able to. . ."

The Commander cut him off with a raised hand.

He likes doing that. Griffon thought.

The Commander continued. "No, not yet." He glanced over at his second in command and back at Griffon. "What we have come up with is a little mission for you two." He paused, leaning forwards to paw through the documents again. Picking one out. "We want you to guide one of our teams back to the installation you woke up in."

Glancing up at Griffon he continued. "Your man, White, has requested we obtain samples from the small Hive located there. He feels that since they've been cut off from the others it'll give him a chance to try his ideas and compare them with the current crop." He gave a big grin. "Our data from those days is rather sketchy, to say the least. Also, since the Hivers have proven with their 'Calle-12' virus that they're experts at genetic manipulation, he wants to try and see how they might have changed their own genetic structure over the years. If he can get his own ideas to work, he feels that these might make the perfect . . . 'Vectors' to carry his little, 'package'."

Colonel Tsen put in. "This'll also give us a chance to . . . 'evaluate' the skills of you and your number two."

Griffon nodded grinning. "It'll also allow you to check out our story, and separate us into neat little packages to evaluate our trustworthiness?"

The commander gave a hearty laugh and looked over at his grinning second in command. "I told you he wasn't as stupid as he looked."

Turning back to Griffon. "Yes, and it'll give us a chance to examine the installation. We'll see if we can make use of it, and maybe see if there's anything we can scavenge."

He pressed a button on the desktop com-unit. "Please send in Sergeant Cartier."

The others rose with him. The door to the office opened and a Raider entered. The stripes of a Staff Sergeant glinted from the collar tabs of his coverall.

The commander introduced him. "This is Sergeant Steffan Cartier. His team is just finishing up a training cycle, preparatory to going back on 'Ops'. He'll head up your little expedition."

Turning to the newcomer, he continued. "Sergeant Cartier, you've been briefed about Commander Griffon and his team. Griffon and his number two will be participating in the final rounds of your training. Then, they'll act as guides to lead you to the installation where they were . . . 'stored'." Glancing at the others. "If there aren't any questions? Good, since there aren't." He shook Griffon's hand again. "Good to have you on board."

As they left the office, Griffon checked out his new team-leader. Grey-shot brown hair topped a somewhat short and pudgy frame, dull, lightless, dishwater-blue eyes, crooked yellow teeth. The only glint of expression he could make out as the other gave him the same examination was a mean hostility.

Chapter 12

The eastern sky was just beginning to turn pink as the training officer stepped to the front of the group. Grinning, he waived his pointer and began. "Good morning troops. I am Lieutenant Johnston, I will be officiating the maneuvers today. Before we begin, are there any questions?'

Fineous raised his hand, grinning mischievously. "Yes sir! Why is this a 'good' morning, Sir?"

The Lieutenants' grin got even wider. "Because you get to be taught by me!"

Out-humored for once, Fineous laughed with the rest. "I'll buy that."

The Lieutenant waived for silence. "Now to continue." He turned to the field screen to his right. With a tap of his pointer a cutaway view of the combat suits they were all wearing appeared. "Right, the Mark-Twenty Light Battle-Suit. In fit and weight it's identical to the normal hostile-environment suit. Now, the sealed battle suit can be used as a functional environment suit, just as the environmental variant does provide some protection from hostile weaponry."

As he spoke, each item it was highlighted. "Automatic camouflage: optical sensors adjust overall color tinting to match background and ambient light levels. Thermal shrouding, ballistic cloth protection against shrapnel and small-arms, internal temperature control, and air filtration."

Another wave of his pointer, "The Mark Twenty-A-One Combat helmet, all suit adjustments and helmet functions are controlled by these optically operated toggles located around the inner-periphery of the faceplate, just focus and blink twice." He pointed at each icon in turn. "Suit temperature, air, urine and feces processing, combat rations, and water; here, here, here, and here." Another tap and the next display appeared, he continued. "The faceplate; it's ballistically resistant and protective against low-power targeting lasers. Faceplate functions, open-close, thermal imaging, low-light, and communications."

He proceeded to describe the suit fitting, adjustments, and the full spectrum of modifications available. He almost succeeded in making it entertaining.

Once he'd finished with the suit, he picked up the rifle. "The Mark-Fifty combat rifle. This is a semi-automatic, nine-millimeter, electromagnetic railgun, firing from a twenty round clip." He picked up the magazine and went over loading, aiming, firing, strip-down, maintenance, the full weapons manual.

Fighting back a yawn, Griffon could only think. *The Army proves that some things never change. Even when they out'ta.*

The instructor went on with the pistol, grenades, emergency pack, medkit, autodoc, etc.

Finally the Lieutenant finished up the standard equipment brief and got down to the meat of the exercise. "Your suits are the training version of the standard Light Battle-Suit. It is identical to the standard suit in all ways, with the addition of damage sensors that, in case of a hit, or other indicated injury from the training weaponry, will simulate wounds via electrically induced pain simulation. Yes Private?"

Fineous had raised his hand. "Uh yes . . . sir . . . Pain simulation?"

The big Lieutenant grinned. "You get hit, it gives you a mild electrical shock."

Fineous asked thoughtfully. "Just how strong is 'mild' . . . sir?"

The instructor's grin got bigger. "Strong enough to simulate the wound indicated. For example, if you loose an arm, the suit will incapacitate the limb and simulate the pain you could expect. Short of lethal levels of course."

Griffon raised his hand. "Sir, what about a, 'lethal' hit?"

Now the Lieutenant was actually chuckling. "The suit will render you unconscious."

Nodding, Griffon traded looks with Fineous before commenting. "Right, rough sport."

Lieutenant Johnston nodded, still grinning. "Combat's a rough game soldier. If it'll ease your mind we have very few fatalities."

"Right, I hope we don't ruin your statistics, Sir." Was Fineous' quick response.

Johnston shook his head in mock seriousness. "You have no idea how much paperwork is involved." He picked up a training rifle. "Now, speaking of hits. Let's go over the weaponry. This is the training rifle, it's identical to the normal combat rifle, with the proviso that it shoots bolts of ultra-violet laser energy instead of bullets." Putting down the rifle, he indicted the other items on the table with his pointer. "The same for the pistol and frag-grenades. The smoke grenades are normal full-spectrum obscuring, with the exception of UV." He grinned at them. "That way, the smoke won't block the shots from the weaponry."

He tapped a stud on the screen, replacing the equipment diagram with a rough map of the training area. "Alright, enough for the standard training brief. Now we get down to the range brief. Sergeant Cartier. . ."

The Sergeant snapped to attention. "Sir!"

"Have you decided on your teams?"

Sergeant Cartier saluted. "Yes, Sir! I will command the first fireteam with..." Giving Griffon a hostile glare. "Griffon. Corporal Sanchez will have the second team and...." He gave Fineous a distasteful glance. "Fineous."

Nodding, Johnston waived a hand indicating the surrounding woods. "Right, well you all know the game. But, for our newcomers. . ." He gestured towards Griffon and Fineous. The rest of the squad grinned. "This is our version of the old game 'Capture the Flag'. There are two teams, each has a flag to protect and the requirement to capture the enemies flag to win."

He continued. "At the end of the game, we'll debrief the. . ." grinning at the squad, "survivors. The others will get to learn the lessons. Any questions? Good, head for your deployment areas. The game will begin in..." Glancing at his wristpiece, "One hour twenty. Sergeant! Move 'em out!".

Sergeant Cartier flipped up his visor and knelt. Clearing a flat space in the dirt. Quickly he scratched a map of the training area. "Alright, we're here." Looking up. "Excuse Me! Would you like to join us Mister Griffon?"

When the others had gathered together, Griffon had automatically moved off to the side and taken up a sentry position under the nearest tree. Reluctantly, he rejoined the group.

Griffon managed to keep a straight face as he thought What *an Ass!*

Glaring at Griffon, Cartier continued. "Now that we're all here..." More scratching, "They're over here. Stream, hill, hill, hill, rocks here and here, forest." He leaned back, pointing a nearby clump of trees, separate from the main body of the forest.

"That's where we'll set up our base, and prepare our position." He checked his suit-clock. "After we dig in, I want Phillips to take Jacobson and Sittai..." Three of the team glancing at each other, nodded. "Check the area from here to the stream and set up an O-P..." Pointing at his map, "here. The rest of us will dig in a defensive perimeter around our base." Giving Griffon a sarcastic sneer. "You do know how to dig a hole don't you?"

Griffon didn't rise to the bait. "Yes Sergeant, I assume you want us to camouflage our positions too?"

Immune to irony, Cartier just gave a gap-toothed grin. "Yes, we always do. My people know what they're doing, but I'll be sure to check your work." The rest of the team laughed as they started pulling out their entrenching multitools.

Asshole, Griffon thought. But he managed to smile as he said. "I'd appreciate it."

It took well over an hour for the team to dig in. Sergeant Cartier kept changing his mind about how to get the most efficient interlocking fields of fire. Then, he went to great lengths to ensure their camouflage was up to par.

The sun was approaching noon by the time he was satisfied with the deployment and released his recon team. The others settled into their holes and began to scan their perimeters.

The crack of heavy rifle fire jerked them all to their feet.

"Ambush! We're taking fire!" Screamed from their comlinks.

The team status read-out on their helmet's heads-up display showed Sittai dead and Phillips wounded.

Another fusillade of shots rang out from the woods.

Jacobson's voice screamed from their suite speakers. "We've been ambushed! I coun..."

Sergeant Cartier over-rode the transmission. "Remember your communications procedures! Identify yourself and use proper reporting format!"

Jacobson's tactical icon now flashed red. . . Dead.

Griffon could hear the agony in Phillips voice. "Base, this is Phillips. We've been ambushed. I count at least fou... Gaaaaah!" His icon now flashed red.

Sergeant Cartier's voice now came over the radio. "Assume defensive positions. Prepare for an attack. . ."

Griffon thought, *Oh, for the love of Pete*. . . He started to move.

Griffon had heard enough. He scrambled from his foxhole and sprinted across the clearing and into the woods, keeping at least twenty meters to the right of the point where the others had entered.

Carter started screaming over the radio. "Griffon! Get the frack back here! You mother frackin' son of a bug! I said. . ." Griffon switched off his radio.

Once he was well under the cover of the woods, he stopped and moved left several meters, before settling down under a large oak tree.

He sat on the ground, leaning back against the bole of the tree. He was careful to keep the tree between his position and the clearing.

Once settled down, he carefully lay his rifle on the ground and covered it with some of last winters' leaves. They still lay thick under the tree. The weapon had a dull, camouflage-pattern matte finish, but it wasn't light variable like the suit. He leaned back, relaxed, and got very still.

The camouflage of his suit quickly assumed the color pattern of his surroundings. Only his eyes moved behind his non-reflective visor. He concentrated on scanning the area between his current location and the point where the trail the recon team had followed entered the clearing. He turned up the sound receptors in his suit and waited.

It was several minutes before he spotted the approaching enemy. The camouflage of the suits was almost perfect. From any distance at all, he could only spot them through their movement. Once he had their location, he upped the telescopic power of his visor to make them out.

He saw two, moving in quick bounds from cover to cover. They alternated sprints so they could provide covering fire for each other, if needed.

Griffon didn't move.

As they approached the edge of the clearing, Griffon saw one of the figures gesture towards the other. Then, the first dropped into a classic "High-Crawl", and, ever so carefully, squirmed his way to the edge of the clearing.

Griffon sat and watched. He alternated between scanning the woods and checking out the two enemies he could still see. Just as an experiment he switched his visor to Thermal, they were even more difficult to pick out. He switched back to normal light.

After a few minutes of checking the clearing, the apparent enemy leader carefully backed into the woods. Once he was well inside the cover of the trees, he rose and moved off towards the trail, waiving the other to follow.

Griffon waited until they were almost out of sight before he pulled his rifle from under the leaves and rose to follow.

Moving quickly and quietly he followed them. Instead of trailing immediately behind, he moved diagonally off, deeper into the woods, keeping them just in sight. He noticed that they continually turned to check the treeline of the clearing, but never their "Six".

Griffon watched as the enemy leader reached the trail and squatted. Several enemy soldiers appeared from the woods and clustered around.

Griffon counted the figures. *Five from six leaves one to guard the flag.* He thought.

Moving slowly and carefully, he grounded his rifle, butt down, leaning it against his hip. Slowly, pulling out two frag grenades, flipped up their safety caps and tapped the primer button on the first...

Slowly he counted seconds - One... Two... Three... Throw, tap the primer on the second and throw. Grabbing his rifle, he dove to the left, rolling into a prone firing position as the first grenade exploded just above the cluster of "Enemy" troops.

They dropped; a couple were still thrashing in electrically induced agony. The second grenade bounced among them and exploded. They all lay still.

Griffon rose and went forwards to check them out. He switched his radio back on.

"...pid greener! Son of a bug! Piece of shit! Got himself killed. Get ready! They're. . ."

Griffon couldn't help grinning behind his visor as he keyed his mike. "Base, this is Griffon. I have five, I say again, five enemy K-I-A's. How copy, over?"

The silence on the line was deafening.

"Base, this is Griffon. I say again, I have five enemy K-I-A's. How copy, over."

Sergeant Cartier's voice came shakily from the speaker. "Um, Griffon . . .uh . . . this is base. Did you say you had five enemies K-I-A'd? . . . Over."

Griffon was starting to have serious problems with not laughing out loud. "Base, this is Griffon, let me see... one, two, three, four... yep, I've got five of em here."

Cartier was still a bit shaken. "R-Return to base... um, over."

Griffon flipped up his visor and nonchalantly strode back to their perimeter. Sergeant Cartier and Private Morales were waiting for him.

Sergeant Cartier was fit to be tied. "What the frack happened out there?"

Griffon grinned. "I'd say that while we were digging in the bad guys went ahead and laid an ambush. Then, after they took out half our team, they moved up, and checked out our perimeter."

He couldn't help getting in a dig. "Then, Corporal Sanchez called them all together to brief them on his plan of attack." Grinning. "He forgot to leave a sentry while he was briefing his team."

Morales was nodding, the irony went right over Cartier's head. He was still too angry. "So what th' frack did you think you were doing, taking off like that?"

"I was really hoping they didn't already have snipers set up." He nodded towards their entrenchments. "A fixed perimeter like that's just dandy, but without some sort of flanker or patrol, it's just a fixed target for the enemy. Also, once they took down our recon patrol they had us at two to one."

"So you took it on yourself to break our perimeter, on your own hook?" Cartier sneered. "What kind of soldier do you think you are?"

Griffon felt his face burning. *This is getting old.*

While he kept his voice even he couldn't help getting in a dig. "A live one." Seeing Cartier start to swell up like a blowfish, he continued. "That's old news. They're dead. We're not. What do we do next?"

The Sergeant had apparently not thought much beyond being mad. The question caught him off guard. Sputtering a bit. "Well, we, um, ah, ahem. . ."

Griffon was fighting his own battle to keep a straight face.

Cartier managed to finally collect his thoughts. "Well, ah, yes, you said you dropped five of them?"

Nodding, Griffon smiled meanly. "Yes, Sergeant. The only one unaccounted for is Fineous."

Cartier got a really sour look on his face. "Oh yes, your little 'Greener' buddy. Sanchez probably left him as rear guard while he attacked with the rest of his team. Good idea." Glaring at Griffon. "If you can trust that little shit to do what he's told."

Griffon just looked back blandly, shrugged.

You could almost hear the ungreased wheels turning as Cartier attempted to think.

"Well, since the object of the game is to capture the enemies flag, and since there's only one of them left. . ." He gave a gap-toothed grin. "We'll just go take his flag away from him." He gestured towards the woods. "We'll spread out and sweep the woods. Morales on the left, Griffon on the right." Griffon turned, closing his visor and moved out. He thought. *Just take the flag away from him. Just take the flag away from Fineous?* He glanced over towards the Sergeant. *Oh Yeah. Just got'ta remember to stay out of the blast radius.*

The sun was well down the western sky by the time they located the enemy flag. It was at the base of a large overhanging rock spur. Which was in turn, at the head of a steep-sided draw.

Since there were only the three of them left, Sergeant Cartier decided to bypass the obligatory planning briefing. Instead, they carefully moved up to a spot just within the edge of the forest.

"You can just make out his fighting position there. . ." Sergeant Cartier said, using the muzzle of his rifle as a pointer. He gave Griffon a gap-toothed grin. "You're little buddy isn't very good at camouflage, is he?"

Griffon dialed up the magnification on his visor. Just below the enemies' flag, and a bit off to one side, he could make out the freshly-turned earth of a foxhole's berm. It was peeking out through the poorly -laid covering of grass and brush. In a harsh whisper, "I don't know Sergeant, he's usually the best there is at hiding and camouflage. I can't help feeling that it's a trap."

"Why would he bother?" Cartier was capable of a remarkable sneer. "He's got an almost perfect defensive position." He gestured with his rifle towards the draw. "Steep rocks to each side, anyone coming over the rim would be skylighted, and the backside is even worse."

Motioning for them to follow, he slid backwards into the forest, maneuvering so that there was a large pine between them and the draw. "That's why the Corporal felt so secure in leaving his base security to only one man." Griffon started, "Um, Sergeant, I thin..." He was cut off by an angry slash of the Sergeants' hand.

Cartier glared at him. "Yes, I know you old-timers are good at ambushes and back-shooting, but, trust me, we can handle a simple bounding overwatch. Now, Morales, you take the left. I'll go down the right. Griffon, do you think you can give us covering fire from back here? Will that be a safe enough for you?"

Griffon smiled. *Yep, well clear of the blast radius.* He just shrugged.

Cartier snorted. "Right." He rolled towards Morales' side of the tree so he could point out his intended route. "Now, I'll make the first bound, to that bit of brush over there." He pointed with his right hand. "You cover me from behind that oak over there..." Shifting his position, "Once I set up I want you to bound up to that big rock. See it, on the left there about twenty meter's up?"

Carefully checking out his route, Morales gave a short, sharp nod.

"Good, once you're set up I'll bound over to that last, fallen log." He twisted around to face Griffon. "You're to cover us from back here. I want you to lay down continuous fire on his fighting position. Do you think you can keep his head down?" At Griffon's nod. "Great, once I get in position, I'll start tossing grenades and we'll rush in and finish him. Any questions? Good. Now, get in position."

It only took them a few moments to move to their assigned places.

Cartier raised his arm. "Ready. . . Set. . . Go!"

Griffon began laying a steady series of shots. Firing quickly, but irregularly, trying to blanket Fineous' fighting position.

Cartier jumped up. Racing forwards in a tight combat crouch, head up, legs pumping.

Just short of his destination he dove forwards, hitting on his side and rifle-butt, rolling into a prone firing position. He started to fire his own rifle towards the head of the draw.

As soon as he brought his rifle to bear, Morales began his sprint. In a mirror-reflection of the Sergeant, he hit in a well-practiced roll, coming up firing.

Cartier had just jumped up and started his second sprint when there was a flash and explosion.

Morales was tossed flopping, from behind the rock he'd been using for cover. His tactical icon tripped red.

Griffon flinched. *Mother frackin...* He thought as he keyed his radio. "Sergeant, he's boobytr..."

The Sergeant cut him off. "Just cover me you piece of shit."

Griffon saw the Sergeant resume sprinting towards the log he'd indicated before. *That stupid ignorant* . . . he thought as he started firing again. Carefully placing his shots as the Sergeant closed with his angle of fire.

Cartier dove behind the log, rolled... and disappeared from sight.

"Gaaaaaa...Urk!" Griffon flinched at the burst of noise from his headphones. He was only just able to see Cartiers' heels disappearing as his yell was suddenly cut off. Another Icon flashed red.

Griffon started racing forwards, pulling a grenade and tapping the primer. As he could just make out a head and rifle rising from the camouflaged spiderhole, on the near side of the log.

Instead of lobbing the grenade, Griffon threw it like a fastball. The long-lost pitchers of old would have been proud as he drilled it towards his target, and dove to the side, rolling.

The grenade flew past Fineous, slammed into the log, and bounced back, rolling into the hole with him.

Griffon continued to roll as several shots flashed past him.

There was a muted 'Pop' and smoke began to billow from the hole, blanketing the area around it in a heavy, dirty-yellow fog.

Griffon leapt up and sprinted forwards, holding left to clear the log as he raced blindly by through the smoke.

He slid to a stop, flat onto his back, rolling over into a prone ready position. Facing towards the back of the fallen log as the smoke began to clear.

Silently he waited. The smoke gradually lifted. He began to make out the line of the log, the shadows of the trees beyond. Finally, despite the camouflage, he could just make out the statue-still figure now crouching on his side of the log. He put a single round in the middle of Fineous' back. The little man spasomed and dropped. His rifle falling from nerve-dead hands.

Griffon carefully rose up, keeping the little man covered. Slowly, he approached the prone form, rolling it over with the toe of his boot. Fineous' blank faceplate stared at the sky.

Satisfied the little man was down for the count, he walked up to, and looked over the log, into the tiny, but deep, and heavily camouflaged, 'Spiderhole'. Through the still clearing wisps of smoke, he could just make out Sergeant Cartier's crumpled form.

Ass! He thought as he shouldered his rifle. He walked over to triumphally lift the enemy flag...FLASH!

Chapter 13

Griffon carefully flexed his arm; grimaced. "It's been three days, and I still ache."

That earned a hearty laugh from those around the table.

Tori smiled, leaning forward, massaging his arm. "You're too old for these silly games."

That earned another round of laughter.

Janine stood and started clearing the table. When Tori objected she responded with a smile. "You cooked dinner, I'll serve dessert." She gave Fineous' chair a kick. "Ahem!"

Fineous gave a long-suffering sigh, rolling his eyes. "Honey, would you like some help?" He dutifully headed towards the kitchen, accompanied by another round of laughter.

Tori stood. "Anyone need their drinks freshened? Griffon? Another glass of wine?"

Griffon, shook his head. "No thanks, another glass and I'll never make it through the tri-vid."

She glanced at the doctor. "White?"

The doctor nodded. "Please. I'm afraid I'll have to pass on the vid. I have to write up my notes on today's work."

Nodding, she turned to the last member of the party. "Gillian? Another mug of beer?"

The broad-shouldered Scot grinned and shook his head. "I'm afraid I'll have to also pass. I have a date with the gym."

With a shrug and a smile, she poured the wine for herself and the doctor.

Griffon glanced at White. "By the way, how's your project coming?"

White, looking a little embarrassed. "I've about shot my bolt. I've plotted the required sequencing. But once I cross-check with any changes in the Hiver genetic structure with samples from the old hive, I'll be at a dead end."

Puzzled, Griffon asked. "What do you mean? I thought you had the run of the laboratory?"

White, sipped his wine, shrugged. "I do. But. . ." He glanced at Tori. "While the Raiders have everything I need to do the theoretical work and planning, they don't have the facilities to do the actual sequencing and genetic development for the required mutation."

Griffon turned to Tori as she sat back down. "Oh?"

She nodded, sipping at her own glass. "Certainly, you have to remember. Our original facilities were little more than glorified emergency rooms. Since then, we've been able to expand our research capabilities." She shrugged. "However, complex Xeno-geneticics haven't been at the top of our priorities."

Griffon scowled, thinking hard. "If the Raiders can't do it... can the Brotherhood?"

"Almost certainly." White shrugged. "But how do we get them to buy off on it?'

Fineous and Janine returned, carrying trays with slices of chocolate cake and real coffee.

Gradually a familiar expression, come over Griffon's face. He turned towards the Scott. "How's your little project coming?"

Gillian nodded. "I've developed the virus, and even worked out the activation sequence. But. . ." He raised his mug to White. "We've got the same problem. How do we get it delivered?"

Tori looked puzzled. "A computer virus? We've tried that; you can't get past their screens. Even if you do, they have firewalls and backups to minimize any infection."

The broad Scott grinned impishly. "Aye, your viral screens are formidable." He nodded towards Fineous. "But Finn gave me an inspiration. His little idea slips through normal screens like grease through a goose. Since I've designed it to mimic a general systems upgrade, it should bypass their firewalls. All we have to do is hold on activation until the normal backup procedures have infected the whole network." The two women glanced at each other, puzzled. Janine asked. "How?"

Gillian bowed to Fineous. The mousy little man looked a bit sheepish. "Weeellll, you see. When I was assigned to station Io, I had this security chief who was giving me a bit of a hard time." He shrugged. "I had an idea on how to screw up his computer system by sending a set of time delay reset commands. Since it didn't target the software, hardware, or files it went right past all the viral protections."

He stared into space, grinning. "As a matter of fact, it was a bit more successful than I expected. It shut down the entire system. Since the computer controlled all base functions, you might say we had a bit of a problem."

Glancing sheepishly at the others, he continued. "As a matter of fact, it almost destroyed the base." He shrugged. "We were far too dependent on our automated systems."

He went on to describe exactly what he had done, much to the entertainment of the others.

Sipping his coffee. "Anyhow, the World Space Agency decided it would probably be a good idea for me to, uh, be 'banished', to the, 'Outer Darkness'. That's how I got assigned to the Challenger crew."

Laughing, Janine gave him a hug and a kiss. "...And aren't we all happy they did!'

Gillian returned to the hub of the problem. "Yes, but that still doesn't solve the problem. How do we infect their system?"

Griffon grinned, turning to White. "This genetic code you've worked out for the mutation, how is it actually recorded in the computer?"

White shrugged. "Basic machine language, it takes up about a million lines of code. . ."

Griffon glanced at the Scott. They both grinned.

The team leader shrugged. "I'll have to figure out how we're going to, ah, 'give it,' to the Brotherhood. You two work out how to integrate the program into the genetic file."

The doctor nodded, looking at his wristpiece. "Well, I have to go."

Gillian also stood, bowing to the ladies. "I must also be leaving. I thank you for the excellent meal, and fine evening." He nodded to Griffon and Fineous. "I'll be seeing you off in the morning."

Once the two had left, the others sat around the table, in no particular hurry to break things up.

Janine was a bit hesitant. "Um, If it doesn't seem too ignorant." She nodded towards Fineous. "You mentioned you were all members of the 'Challenger's' crew. I remember studying all about how it was the Earth's first starship and all that. But, one thing I was never able to figure out was. . . How it was supposed to work?"

As Griffon and Fineous chuckled, Tori stepped in. "After the attack, and all the destruction in the fall, we lost almost all the old records. Also, a lot more was lost before our ancestors got around to assembling a database."

Griffon shrugged. "We were one of the planetary exploration teams. What do I know about Warp mechanics?"

Fineous nodded. "I can't do the mathematics, but I did spend a lot of time with magnetodynamics and all."

He continued. "Ok, what do you know about the workings of magneodynamic lift plates?"

"Not much." Tori shrugged. "I know they use superconductor material only the Brotherhood can produce."

Janine nodded. "We've been able to scavenge some for systems, weapons, and vehicles. The Brotherhood can produce new vehicles. The best we can do is keep a few of the old Maglifts going."

Fineous nodded, "Right, well the magnetodynamic lift plates are the key to the whole thing. They're simply a superconductive wire that's been spun out into a flat, disk-shaped coil. The whole purpose of the design is to produce the strongest magnetic field in the most efficient package."

After another sip of coffee, he continued. "Now, according to my flight briefing, it was known for ages that a magnetic field had a distinctive, ah, 'pull' in the direction of it's positive pole." He shrugged. "It's supposed to have something to do with that law of physical motion, 'every action has an equal and opposite reaction.' The magnetic field pushes out electrons at one end and pulls them in at the other. Make the magnetic field strong enough and the magnet will 'pull' itself along."

He took a bite of cake. "Anyhow, they found it really didn't take that much. As a matter of fact, my manuals said even nineteenth-century Victorian technology would have been technically capable of developing limited magnetic lift capability."

He shrugged. "The first experiments with magnetic lift plates took place in the... nineteen-sixties. The University of California-Berkeley, was working on developing new types of magnetic coils. They discovered that running about a thousand volts of D.C. current through a disk-shaped copper coil would produce a powerful enough magnetic field to lift itself off the ground."

He glanced at the others, grinning. "It seems they'd stumbled onto one of their governments 'Black Secrets', they were shut down real quick."

"Later, with the development of high-temperature superconductors, some scientists remembered the experiments and managed to create liftplate technology using a fraction of the power required for the old copper coils."

"That's where our magnetic, interplanetary vehicles came from. They were much, much safer and far more efficient than the old chemical-reaction rockets that were used in the early days of space travel. Since the magnetodynamic system worked by simply running an electrical current through the coil, we actually had to find ways to use the excess electricity."

He stared off into space, remembering. "Plenty of power for atmosphere processing, water and waste reprocessing, everything. Most important of all, these vehicles avoided the debilitating effects of long-term weightlessness, and cut down the time of interplanetary travel by providing for continuous acceleration that simulated gravity and greatly speeded the trip."

Another sip of coffee, "Anyhow, that's how we explored the Solar-system. But it was another 'accident' from history which gave them the clues on how to reach the stars. The problem was Einstein's theory of relativity. Under normal circumstances you can't accelerate past the speed of light. And with that limitation, even the nearest stars would have taken years, decades, even centuries to reach. However, there was a shortcut. . ."

Holding up a synthi-silk handkerchief. "Imagine this is normal space." He lay it out flat on the table, smoothing out the wrinkles.

Placing a finger in the center of the handkerchief he traced an imaginary line to the edge. "To get anywhere you have to travel along the surface. But, space is curved. . ." He lifted the handkerchief, continuing to run his finger to the center on the back side.

"To get anywhere from anywhere is a horribly long distance. That, and the fact you can never accelerate to anything near the speed of light. Even with the Einsteinian relativity time-shift, it would take too long to get anywhere to be practical."

"Now, towards the end of the twentieth century they came up with the theory of the 'Warp', where you can take a short-cut from one point to another."

He picked up his fork and pushed one of the prongs through the center of the cloth, connecting the two points. "By 'Warping', or spreading the universal lines of force you could move from one place to another, by 'cutting across' the curvature of space and still avoid violating the limitations of Einsteinian space." He leaned back, thoughtfully playing with the handkerchief and staring into space. "Now, at the end of the Second World War, in the middle of the Twentieth Century, the old United States Salt-Water Navy was experimenting with creating an 'Invisible Ship'."

Janine looked confused, "You mean like in 'Stealth' technology?"

Griffon commented, while Fineous took a bite. "No, they actually wanted to make a major warship invisible."

Nodding vigorously as he swallowed, Fineous said. "They new a strong enough magnetic field could, ah, 'bend' light waves, radar, whatever. Their problem was to create a strong enough magnetic field. Instead, they decided to use two magnetic fields running along either side of the hull. They knew the interface area where the fields overlapped would accentuate the effect of the field."

He shrugged. "Anyhow, when the US Navy fired up their magnetic fields they effectively sheared the lines of force. They created the first known Warp."

Fineous gave a lop-sided grin as he continued. "However, they weren't prepared for it. They hadn't even bothered to shield the crew or ships systems from these hyper-powerful magnetic fields. That, and the fact they weren't able to keep the fields in 'synch' caused the bubble to collapse uncontrollably."

Shaking his head. "It was another item the government hid in its 'Black files'. But, you can't hide the truth. Also, they were forced to reveal the facts when the development of industrial superconductors threatened to create the same problems by accident."

Looking perplexed, Tori asked. "No, that doesn't hold up. What about the magnetic repulsion trains? They use opposed magnetic fields without any problems."

Fineous shook his head. "You're talking about a power difference of several levels of magnitude. The fields used for the magtrains were nothing compared to what's required to warp time and space itself. Also, the fields used in vehicles and rail-guns aren't even close to being synchronized."

He sat back, shrugged. "Sorry to go on like this, I guess you hit a soft spot." He stared off into space, his expression taking on an intense sadness. "You know, I may be the last person living that's had any real time in space. How can I describe Earth-rise on Luna? Or tell of the thousands of rainbows caused by sunlight filtered through the rings of Saturn?" He shook his head, his eyes glistening.

Janine leaned over and kissed him. He flinched, snapping back to the present.

She stood, gathering the dishes, kicking his chair. "Come on, give me a hand cleaning up."

Grinning with relief, Fineous rolled his eyes melodramatically. "K.P. again!"

They all laughed as the two disappeared into the kitchen.

Tori and Griffon stood and walked into the living area. He glanced at his wristpiece. "I think we've missed the start of tonight's tri-vid." He gave her a hug and eased down onto the sofa. "Any ideas on what we can do instead?"

She kissed him deeply. Then pulled back, grinning. "Sir! We have company!"

There was a loud crash from the kitchen. Janine shrieked. "Oh! You! Ooh!"

Griffon nodded towards the kitchen door. "I don't think that's going to be a problem."

The sounds of giggling could be heard from behind the door.

Tori chuckled. "Maybe we should give them a hand?"

Griffon shook his head. "Nooo, I think she pretty well has things well in han..."

Fineous' "Gaaarrrk!" reverberated through the kitchen door.

Griffon smiled. "Yep, she definitely has things well in hand."

They collapsed into each others arms, laughing.

Soon the kitchen door opened. Fineous and Janine bounced into the main area of the quarters, linked arm in arm, laughing.

Fineous made a great deal of a massive and obviously faked yawn. "I guess we'll have to pass on the tri-vid movie." Janine dissolved into laughter. The little man had to grit his teeth to get out. "I think we'll go ahead and turn in."

Griffon nodded, trying vainly to keep a straight face. "Good idea. Um, just remember, we have to be standing-too at oh-six-hundred."

Fineous and Janine were working their awkward way towards the door, still arm in arm. "Right-O Sir! I'll be up." Janine glanced back, over her shoulder, grinning. "Wan'na bet?"

Chapter 14

Wham!

"Ow! Will you please hold it down to a hundred K's!"

Griffon could hear Sergeant Cartier's yell without having to be plugged into the vehicles intercom.

Which was quite surprising, considering how loudly his ears were ringing from having his helmeted head slammed against the armored side of the vehicle for the umpteenth time.

The nose of the Multi-purpose-Armored Combat Vehicle (MACV, naturally nicknamed the "Mac-Vee") suddenly gave a sickening diagonal, diving twist as the lunatic driver dropped over the edge of yet another gully. He'd obviously taken it at a well-practiced angle, since it hit the bottom with a jarring roll to the left that didn't quite send them tumbling 'ass over teakettle'.

Griffon braced against the wall as, sure enough, the front end surged upwards. The driver roared up the far side and shot out of the gully. All without ever touching the brakes.

Griffon managed to think, h*e must be loosing his touch. . .* Ooof! *We didn't even come close to 'Orbital Trajectory' that time*, between jarring impacts.

Sergeant Cartier's voice took on a tinge of panic as he yelled, "All right! Pull it over! Pull it over now! Right now! Dammit! I said stop!"

Griffon quickly shifted his feet, just in time for the nauseating lurch and slide as the driver slowed the vehicle into a 90-degree sideways skid to kill the excess velocity. He did note the driver still hadn't bothered with more than a tap on the brakes.

However, Sergeant Cartier hadn't been expecting the corkscrewing and was thrown from his seat in the turret basket. Well, that is he would have been thrown, if it weren't for his safety belt. Unfortunately, while his belt had been buckled, Sergeant Cartier hadn't really tightened it, and ended up hanging ass end up from his seat.

Corporal Sanchez tripped the lever dropping the rear ramp and the team scrambled out of the vehicle as a wall of reddish dust rolled up to fog the world around them.

It was only then that two of the team noticed Sergeant Cartier seemed to be stuck in his awkward position and returned to release him.

In the front-end of the vehicle, the drivers hatch popped open and Fineous sprang out like the proverbial 'jack-in-the-box'.

Once everyone had sorted themselves out; and managed to keep Sergeant Cartier from killing the grinning little fiend, they went about breaking out their noon meal. Soldiers everywhere quickly learn the 'Holy Trinity' of field operations- Food, Sleep, and Dry Socks.

Griffon handed a steaming 'Meal, Self-heating, Lunch or Dinner, Menu Number 21D' to Fineous. He dropped next to the driver, sitting on the shady-side of the armored vehicle. "Went kinda overboard on the 'Mad-Max' driving demo, didn't ya?"

The mousy little man was still a bit scarlet around the edges, but managed a calm-toned response, "Hey. I told that . . . idiot I haven't had any sleep for the last two nights. I was too tired to drive after he had us pulling duty all last night." He paused to shovel down some of the steaming glop from the foil pouch. "Just what's got a cob up his ass anyhow?"

Griffon shrugged, trying to chew a spoonful of his menu number 16C, "I asked Tori about that. She told me some of the Raiders hold a personal grudge against us for loosing the war with the Hivers." He grinned, "Besides, you can't blame him for the night before last can you?"

Fineous grinned, "OK, well I'll give you that. However, on the other hand . . . you're kidding right? We slept throughout the whole thing! How the hell can they blame us for this mess?"

Griffon shrugged, "She said it didn't matter. As far as they're concerned our time was some sort of 'Golden Age'... and we degenerated into some sort of hedonistic orgy of waste, sin, and corruption. They believe the Hiver invasion was some sort of 'Wrath of God', and they've been left holding the bag."

Fineous snorted, shaking his head, "Great, we're stuck in a post-Apocalyptic world with an asshole that blames us personally for everything from the ozone layer to foot fungus."

Griffon chuckled, "Hey, anyone that'd include Ronald MacDonald and Zippy the Wonder Slug in his pantheon of old gods can't be considered to be all there."

Fineous gave him a sly grin, "Yeah, maybe that's reasonable for an Officer but, dammit, this is a Sergeant!"

"Rankist!" Chuckling Griffon choked down the last of his ration. He then carefully crumpled the pouch into a tiny ball and tossed it into the trashbag that had been hung off the side of the MAC-V.

He stood, rubbing the small of his back, "I think that little driving demo you gave busted a kidney."

Fineous waived his spoon, grinning, "Ah what the hell, you've got a spare."

Still wincing, Griffon gave a mock-solemn shake of his head, "Uh-huh, I'll let you explain to Tori why I'm pissing pink and can't get it up."

Fineous was trying to drink from his canteen; any reply was choked off when the water went down the wrong pipe.

Having finally gotten the last word, Griffon proceeded to walk around the vehicle, checking it out.

He couldn't help admiring the design. Thinking, *Not bad, seven meters long, three meters wide, two meters to the top of the hull. Eight-by-eight independent drive, self-regulating tires, amphibious. Filtered overpressure for biologic and chemical protection. Ceramic-composite armor, reactive camouflage, screened for thermal and electromagnetic emissions. Turret-mounted armament of one three-barreled gattling HELBORe* (Hi-Energy Laser Beam ORdinance)*; coaxial automatic 40-millimeter electromagnetic rail-gun; and a parascoping multi-spectrum sensor mast.*

He stuck his head through the rear ramp to check out the rear-crew-compartment. *Humph, ten of us, with all out gear are a bit cramped. Still, all in all, it's a hell of a lot easier than traveling by 'Leather Personnel Carrier'.*

He turned as Corporal Sanchez came up, grinning. "Well, I think Sarge's cooled off enough he won't be trying to shoot your little buddy any time soon."

Griffon, grinning back, "Well, he's the one that won't lighten up." He shook his head. Automatically he glanced around, checking the perimeter security, and that everyone was keeping the trash policed up. He shook his head, thinking, *Hunh; some habits never die, even if it's not my responsibility.*

He glanced at the Corporal, "I know we're not on Sergeant Cartier's hit parade, but what do the troops think?"

Sanchez shrugged, tipping a watercan out of its rack to refill his canteen, "Oh, they're letting it run." He set the can back and gave Griffon a searching look; "You guys are a bit of a puzzle. We really haven't had much experience at trusting strangers." He chuckled as he twisted to hook his canteen on his belt.

Turning back, he added, "But, you guys did great in training. So I guess we'll give you a chance to prove yourselves." He gave Griffon a grin, walking back towards the others, "If you don't mind, we'll wait and see how you and Cartier sort things out. He's a capital-A Ass, but he's still our boss. Hope 'ya understand."

Griffon could only grump, “Yeah, well thanks.” He went back to sit with Fineous before they had to load up again. He noticed this time Sergeant Cartier had Private Phillips drive.

For the next two days they continued to make good time. Spring was well underway; everything was green, and the roving herds had large numbers of calves and young.

The predators were also out in force. However, they either avoided or ignored the massive armored vehicle.

Griffon had been told they had emerged from the Raider tunnel system in the area of the old United States Military base at Fort Hood, Texas. Everyone assumed, from their descriptions of their wandering, that the old base they were looking for was somewhere in the huge area of the old artillery base at what used to be Fort Sill, in Oklahoma. Not bad, but he realized they still had several hundred square miles to search.

On the second night, they spotted a formation of aircraft flying at extremely high altitude. When he asked, he was told they were relatively safe, so long as they didn’t go near any of the Hiver bases. The bugs apparently didn’t consider single vehicles to be much of a threat. Though Griffon noted they did go to the trouble of camouflaging every time they stopped for more than a few minutes.

He also found out the Raiders were tracking two Hiver ‘Battlecruisers’ in polar orbit. They told him that, while the Hivers didn’t have any permanent bases, or satellite nets, they always had at least one and usually several of their massive warships in orbit. There were often a variable number of other ships, cargo, transport, and others whose purpose the Raiders hadn’t been able to identify. These came and went on an irregular basis.

The campfire discussions on the matter generally split between belief that the Hivers didn’t want to clutter up the near-Earth orbits with unneeded satellites; and this was a Hiver backwater that didn’t rate more permanent basing.

Late on the fifth day of their cross-country trek, they came to the Red River. With the collapse of the old flood-control and irrigation system, as well as the apparent changes in the weather patterns, the river had reverted to its ancient status of being a significant waterway that an old Texan or Okie wouldn’t have recognized. In addition, it was still swollen and fast flowing with the spring runoff.

After pulling up on the inside-arc of a bend in the river, the team went into their well-practiced drill.

While the rest of the team began to lay out heavy tow-cables, Private Jacobson began to don his heavy battlesuit.

Once encased in the heavy ceramic armor, he looked a lot like the Hiver Combots and the Battleborgs of the Brotherhood. Positive feedback-controlled, power enhanced joints giving an equivalent strength many times that of a normal man.

The suit was equipped with a full compliment of sensor, communications, and internal environmental controls. It also mounted a plasma torch in the left forearm (leaving the right hand free for 'delicate' manipulation) which combined the utility of a cutter and welder, along with providing a highly efficient weapon. For a primary weapon, the suit was also provided with an oversized, and very heavy, 40-milimeter electromagnetic automatic rifle that used the same rounds as the vehicles' turret gun (these were loaded into ten-round 'clips').

Once suited up, Jacobson simply tied the forward tow-cable around the suits' waist and walked across on the bottom of the river.

He proceeded to drag the cable to the upstream side of the bend and secured it to a large stake that he simply pounded into the ground with the suits' power-augmented fist.

After securing a second and third cable, (for safety and backup), the crew loaded up the vehicle and drove it into the current. The cables kept the vehicle facing upstream, while the force of the current gently pushed them to the far bank.

Within a remarkably short time, and with minimal effort, they'd managed to cross a major river obstacle the vehicle's limited swimming capability couldn't have safely managed.

Another three days travel brought them to the target area of their search.

Griffon started to sudden awareness. A heavy hand across his mouth.

The sentry, Corporal Sanchez, was kneeling over him. He was staring off to one side, his rifle ready in his other hand.

Without a word, Griffon rolled over, snatching up his own rifle as the Corporal moved silently to the next sleeping figure.

It was a clear, warm, and humid spring night. The moon was down, but the galaxy of stars provided good light.

The others were up now, weapons ready. Corporal Sanchez was the only one in his battle-suit.

Griffon snapped around as a familiar hissing shriek ripped the night.

Somebody switched on a spotlight. Seven meters away, the massive; hulking form of a Jabberwock flinched back from the brilliant spear of light.

Roaring and hissing, it reared onto its rear leg, tearing at the air with its glitteringly sharp foreclaws.

Three more lights snapped on. The team formed a firing line as the creature began to duck and bob, tearing at the brush on the edge of their clearing.

Griffon glanced to the other members of the team. A feeling of unease came over him, *What the frack? Something . . . something's wrong.*

Keeping an eye on the beast, he sidled over to Sergeant Cartier's side.

The beast continued to smash and tear at the brush. It seemed to be whipping itself up into a berserk frenzy.

Griffon leaned towards the Sergeant, asking in a low voice, "Ah, is this normal? I thought these things were always ready for a meal?"

Cartier quickly checked his team before answering, "No, it's not. Maybe it's covering for a youngster or something. Maybe it's some sort of mating thing." He shrugged. Then louder "Stand ready! It's liable to charge."

It didn't. Seconds stretched into a minute, then two. The creature continued to rip and roar. It even seemed to be drawing back a few yards.

Griffon started and spun as somebody grabbed his arm. It was Fineous.

"Jesus Finn!" His voice a too harsh, too loud whisper.

Surprisingly the little man was looking the other way. His head was jerking back and forth, as he tried to look everywhere at once. "G-Griff, don't you remember..." He stuttered in his nervousness. Griffon couldn't help wondering that the little man now really looked like a frightened mouse.

Griffon's attention snapped back as the creature smashed into the clearing in an aborted charge.

Fineous seemed to be on the verge of real panic. He continued to stare into the darkness, never looking at the creature to their front. His grenade-launcher clutched to his chest with both hands. His voice was showing real panic. He was almost shouting, "G-Griff! These are pack hun . . ."

The second Jabberwock bounded off the top of the MAC-V, bringing down the camouflage, and smashing one of the team to the ground. Pinning the struggling, figure facedown, its third leg ripped the man's spine out. His dying scream tore through the tumult.

A third and fourth Jabberwock charged from the darkness, into the flanks of the startled group.

Acentic bolts ripped blazing streaks across the darkness. A grenade launcher chugged. A hundred razor-sharp flechetts blowing one of the creatures into a fountain of torn flesh and spewing blood.

A soldier that had been knocked sprawling rolled and staggered to his feet, clutching his side where the claws had sliced. He pulled his pistol with blood-dripping fingers . . .

Griffon dropped into a crouch and emptied his clip, slamming the first Jabberwock in mid-leap.

He spun, searching for another target in the reeling, chaos of melee.

Rifles blasted, pistols barked. Sun-bright bolts shredded the darkness. Burning slashes of purple-blue into his night-blinded eyes.

Blinking furiously to clear his eyesight, he spotted Fineous wielding his launcher one-handed, like an over-sized pistol. A hundred flechetts blasted a monster into oozing hamburger.

The Corporal, standing out in his battlesuit, and Sergeant Cartier blasted the last Jabberwock into oblivion.

For a minute silence reigned as the remnants of the team searched for targets. They made sure the area was clear before they lowered their weapons, chests heaving, and started to tend the wounded. Private Phillips leapt to the turret of the vehicle, firing up the sensors and searching the darkness for threats.

Two were dead, one was critically wounded. Corporal Sanchez and one other were hurt to a lesser degree.

They gently slipped the wounded Private Sittai into the team's autodoc and heaved the remnants of the creatures into a heap with brush and wood. A blast of the vehicle's HELBORe fired a funeral pyre for the dead.

Chapter 15

Once the wounded were tended, Sergeant Cartier decided they would continue their mission. It took six days of searching to find the gully holding the hidden entrance to the installation.

Cartier decided he would take Griffon, Fineous, and Private Morales to explore the shattered bunker. The others were left to secure the camp and care for Private Sittai.

Slowly, they made their way, level by level, into the darkness. Since they inspected each level completely, it took two days for them to reach the huge vault that was their first destination. Several times, they had to fight off packs of Tripes and once even a horde of hexrats.

Finally, they stood at the entrance to the chamber. One of the causeways stretched arrow-straight before them.

Cartier and Morales were stunned by what they saw. They had never been to one of the Hiver enclaves. Thus, they had no idea what the aliens had in store for their world.

Carefully, they worked their way towards the center. The causeway was crumbling and worn, rockmoss and alien plants eating away at the shattered remnants of mans labor.

When they reached the edge of the central lake, Cartier directed that he and Griffon would provide cover. Fineous and Morales went forward, intending to collect samples of the Hivers scuttling around the area.

Rifle in hand, Griffon scanned the jungle and lake. The expected mass of Hiver nets were spread thickly around the area. Periodically, his eyes caught the thrashing of smaller animals trapped and struggling against their fate.

While still a few meters from the central mass, Fineous knelt and carefully lay his launcher down. He had the stasis-sample box ready as he reached to collect a couple of the bugs scuttling along the causeway.

Griffon caught sudden motion from the corner of his eye. He heard a grunt as he turned to glimpse the sole of the boot that smashed into his faceplate.

Stunned, he went spinning off the causeway. Smashing through the Hiver nets, his breath was crushed from him as he crashed and tumbled to the ground three meters below.

Gasping he glimpsed the flash as rifle-fire crashed and roared. His suit's tactical display flashed red as Morales died.

A momentary silence stretched through the massive chamber. Then, the jungle roared, hissed, and shrieked in startled reaction to the noise. He heard twin muffled thumps of grenades. Fineous' icon flashed red, dead. Struggling to free himself from the nets, he saw Cartier's feet through his faceplate.

The Sergeant knelt and rolled him over, yanking at the nets to ensure he was safely bound.

Helpless, Griffon could only look up at Sergeant Cartier's sneering face. The traitor reached down and ripped Griffon's faceplate from his helmet.

The Traitor leered down at him, "What? No snide comments or cheap cracks? I am disappointed."

Still a bit stunned by events, Griffon shook his head, "Wh-Why?"

Cartier snorted, still sneering, "Why? Because Milady Cromwell directed that I give you a 'properly poetic' death."

He looked around at the Hivers beginning to swarm. "I think letting the damned bugs eat you by boring through your face fulfills that nicely." He shrugged, "Too bad that little shit died so quickly." He shook his head, "But, I think that feeding him to the daggerfish will work."

Tightly wrapped in the nets, Griffon could only stutter and sputter in rage, "B-But why? I thought . . . I mean . . . She's Brotherhood! Dammit!"

Cartier gave him a big snaggle-toothed grin, "Yes, and they are going to win! You see, the Brotherhoods' the only hope humanity has of defeating the Hivers." He spat out the next words, "The 'Raiders' can only impede and cripple their efforts. Besides, those bandits only hope to return to the days of corruption and waste." His boot smashed into Griffon's helpless face, breaking his nose and starting blood to spurt. "Your world!" His face reddened his voice a shrill shout, "The same frack that allowed the damned bugs to win in the first place."

Griffon shook his head, trying to clear it as nerve-lights and darkness spun behind his eyes. "I-I thought everyone was routinely scanned for Brotherhood implants. H-How . . ."

Cartier chuckled, "Oh come on! Do you take us for idiots? A simple switch of frequencies and I can use any of our radios to call in." He snorted, "Our own communications-security technology ensures that the traffic can't be tracked."

He stood, "I just head back to the surface. Tell everyone you're all dead. Then, we head home." He chuckled, "I'll call in and let Ms Cromwell know I got you, and your little friend too."

Griffon started to thrash when he spotted movement behind Cartier and froze.

A figure in a tattered battlesuit was sprinting up behind the Sergeant.

Cartier saw him staring and had just begun to turn when Fineous flashed by. The little man slapped the Sergeant's helmet and ran on by.

As the little man dodged through the brush and ducked behind one of the pillars supporting the causeway, Griffon heard him shout, "Tag! You're it!"

With a snarl, Cartier snatched his rifle to his shoulder to fire. However, the lithe little figure was out of sight. He cursed and crouched, watching for the refugee to show himself.

Griffon saw the huge form heave into view behind the Sergeant. While starting to die down, the screaming noise of the jungle still covered the sound of the horror as it awkwardly heaved it's mass towards the two.

Griffon froze in shock.

Massive slime-covered, metallic scales glinting in a splintered rainbow; great welts oozing blue-black blood. The creatures battered multifaceted eyes gave a greenish gleam as the massive head swayed with the strange waddle of the creature.

In outline it was like a great sealion, two forward fins supported the huge head and shoulders. The rest sloped downwards to a third fin at the end of the wide, flat, truncated tail.

Only Griffon's eyes moved as he glanced at the traitor crouching over him.

Cartier was still looking for Fineous. Concentrating on any sign of sudden attack or ambush from the little man. He failed to 'Check-Six'.

With a final heave the monster thudded down immediately behind the Sergeant and glared down at the pathetic human. Cartier stiffened and slowly turned to face a demon from hell.

Cartier's surprise and shock were total. His eyes went up and up, his nerveless hands lowered his rifle.

The creature opened its maw.

Twin lower jaws swung downwards and back, forming a near-perfect tripod with the upper beak. Great curved daggerlike fangs glinted in the artificial sunlight. The creature's roar blasted the frozen figure backwards.

Cartier stumbled and tripped over Griffon's body. His rifle went spinning into the brush as the traitor threw up his arms and screamed.

With lighting speed a massive tentacle-like tongue snapped out and gripped Cartier around the waist.

The man was yanked into the spiked maw.

His screams ripped the sudden silence of the jungle.

However, he was too large to be swallowed in one gulp. He caught at the jaws and struggled against the pull of the tentacle attempting to draw him into the throat.

For an eternity the tug-of-war stretched.

Cartier screams rang repeatedly.

The tongue yanked and jerked, the humans' breath was driven out as his ribcage cracked and splintered under the strain. Then, the jaws slammed shut, snapping Cartier's spine backwards. The creature gulped and swallowed. Each spasm, each snap of the jaws drew the battered, shredded form into the beasts' gullet.

Griffon froze. His only defense was to remain perfectly still, and hope the creature overlooked him.

The monster slowly finished gulping down Sergeant Cartier's tattered corpse.

It swung its head from side to side, scanning the jungle for enemies, for prey.

Griffon felt the first of the Hiver warriors begin to crawl across his face. It took all his willpower not to shake his head, not to blink.

The creature must have decided the coast was clear. It began to heave it's bulk around. Slowly it returned to the lake.

The first Hiver crawled across Griffon's left eye. He blinked, trying to dislodge the bug. The monster could still see if he made any significant move.

Slowly, oh so slowly, the monster continued to turn. **PAIN!** Griffon jerked and twisted. Acid needles stabbing into his eye.

He twisted and rolled in his agony. Tangling himself deeper and tighter into the nets.

He opened his mouth to scream.

Bugs, dozens of bugs, swarming warriors flooded across his face in a wave. They surged into his mouth, across his eyes began to bore into his nostrils.

Venom-dripping jaws snapped and twisted in the flesh of his face, driving acidic poison into his flesh, into the soft linings of his mouth, his nose, his eyes....

Griffon jerked awake. Darkness, silence, and dizziness overwhelmed his senses. He felt like he was . . .drifting.

Gradually he explored his body. Feeling the roughness of clothing against his skin. Tingling in his hands and feet.

One by one, he tried to flex his limbs, and felt the immediate pressure of bonds. He heard the soft beeping of a medkit, muffled. He tried to open his mouth; his jaw was bound shut. He was gagged. Breathing deep, the air smelled mediciny, filtered.

He forced himself to be calm. Collecting his thoughts, *well, only one thing to do.*

He yelled, muffled and deadened by the gag, and started to thrash against his bonds.

Strong hands gripped him, holding him. Feeling them working at his bonds, pulling them free. He relaxed.

Finally, the gag and blindfold were pulled away from his right eye. His bonds were loosed.

Fineous, dressed in his coveralls, was squatted over him, grinning. "Well, welcome back to the world of the living."

The little man reached down and pulled the Medkit from where it was clutching Griffon's' thigh.

Griffon glanced up. He was no longer in his battlesuit, but he was still in his olive coveralls. "Um, gee thanks."

The little man handed him a steaming cup of coffee.

Griffon gingerly felt the heavy bandage covering his left eye as he glanced about.

He was lying near a small fire. The rusting heaps of the topmost, garage level surrounded them.

He saw other forms laying around, rolled up in their sleeping bags, snoring. Corporal Sanchez was sitting by the fire, turning a large chunk of something on the spit.

Griffon shook his head, sipping the rich, smoky taste of Scotch laced coffee.

After draining a good part of the brew, he shook his head and asked, "Ok, so what happened?"

Fineous settled back, staring at the fire, "I was going to ask you the same thing. All I know is that I was collecting samples when all hell broke loose." Picking up a stick, he poked absently at the fire.

Fineous shrugged, "Sergeant Cartier shot Morales first. I guess it was because he was the one holding the gun. I didn't wait to ask, I dove off the causeway into the lake."

The little man reached over, lifting the tattered sleeve of his battlesuit where it lay next to him. "Those little fishie things decided I was the main course. I came up just under the causeway and saw that there were all sorts of vines hanging under it. I started to pull myself up out of the lake. There was footer-ledge just above the water." He shrugged, "I pulled myself up on it. About then grenades started to explode in the water."

Griffon cut in, "Yea, I saw you die on the tactical display. What was that all about?"

Fineous gave his familiar grin. He lifted something out of a pouch on the battlesuits' harness. He popped open a small access panel on the inside of the suits' left upper arm. He showed Griffon the tiny bit of plastic and metal he held before snapping it back in place. “Fuses. The suite transmits a signal based on what its internal sensor-nets tell it. Cut the sensor circuit and it transmits that it’s not reading any life signs.”

Griffon nodded, “OK, yeah I remember something about that in the suit maintenance briefing.” He gave the little man a serious stare; “Not that it mentioned anything about using that little thing to spoof the tactical display though.”

Fineous chuckled, “Well, I guess everybody picks up what’s useful to them. Don’t they?”

Nodding in surrender, “OK. So you faked being dead, then what?”

Fineous turned back to the fire, picking up a cup, and using a rag to pour from the steaming pot. Then, leaning back, he continued, “Well, I sat back and sorted through things a bit. I could pretty-well bet it wasn’t you that’d tried to frag me, and Sergeant Cartier was the only other guy back there with a gun.” He shrugged, “Though that didn’t mean somebody else hadn’t been around. Anyhow, I was trying to work out a plan. I’d forgotten to grab my grenade launcher before I went swimming, and I did remember that my pistol was pretty well useless against a light battlesuit. But, since whoever was out there had a rifle, I was toast.”

He shrugged, staring off into space, “Anyhow, there I was, perched on the ledge, trying to sort things out, carnivorous perch floating up dead from the grenades and all. When I saw the biggest hummin’ mother of a fish I ever saw coming around the bend. It was making tracks and looked really very pissed.”

He gave Griffon one of his famously sardonic grins, “I decided that I’d better find a perch a bit further from the water and followed the footer ledge around the edge of the pillar, using the vines for handholds.

The little man shrugged, “When I got around the edge I saw Cartier standing over you. I could see you were pretty well tied up in Hiver nets, and I saw him give you a kick.”

Fineous’ smile went sly; “That pretty-well made up my mind about who was the bad guy here.”

Shrugging, he took a sip, “Anyhow, old ‘Fishzilla’ started up out of the water behind me, and I saw Cartier still had his rifle.”

He glanced over at the Corporal, who was listening in, not saying anything. “I decided that if I was caught between a rock and a hard place I’d introduce the two and see which cracked.”

Griffon nodded, “Yeah right.” He gave the little man a mock-glare, mimicking, “‘Tag you’re it’?”

Fineous chuckled, “Well, it seemed the thing to do. After I ducked back under the causeway, I snuck around the pillar and peeked back. I saw Cartier get chomped and the critter head for the water.”

He pointed at the medkit. "When I got to you, you were unconscious, and Hivers were swarming all over your face. I picked them off, popped one of the emergence seals on your suite and slapped a medkit on you. Then, I cut you out of the net."

Griffon took another sip, "What about Morales?"

"After I got you cleared I went to check him. Cartier had hit him in the back of the head." The little man shrugged, "Those battlesuits aren't designed to take a heavy rifle round at point blank."

Remembering the sight of Hivers swarming over the splattered mass of brains, the little man gave a shudder, and glanced at Griffon. "Anyhow, I saw you'd been pretty-well chewed up so I drug you out of the Hiver area, and sealed you up with my helmet. Then, I buried you under the heaviest rocks I could find and made tracks up here to get help in hauling you up." He shrugged, "That's about it." Glancing at Griffon, "What's your side of it."

Griffon glanced at the Corporal, wondering how he should phrase it.

Ah hell. He told what had happened, and what Cartier had said.

Corporal Sanchez spat in the fire; "I never liked that piece of shit." He grinned at the two adventurers; "I checked out the site and recorded it on the tri-vid. Everything checks out. So I guess that's about it." He turned back to the meat, snorting, "Traitor! I never figured him for having even that much class."

Griffon slowly stood, a bit unsteadily. Fingering the bandage over his left eye. "So what's the story on this?" Sanchez nodded, still turning the meat, "Your medkit took care of the poison from the stings, the shock, and prevented infection. But, your eye was cut up pretty badly. We'll keep it bandaged until we can get you to Hospital."

Fineous, with a nasty grin, "I hope you don't mind being under Doctor Stoner again?"

Griffon sat back down, groaning, "That's not the problem. I just hate the idea of another two weeks of hospital food."

As the three laughed, Fineous managed, "Yeah, probably the only thing that'll make you miss field rats."

The little man gestured towards Griffon's discarded bindings, "Sorry about, hog-tying you. We didn't want you to hurt yourself by thrashing about."

Griffon shook his head, giving a theatrical groan. Once the laughter had died he asked, "So, Corporal, what's the pla..."

Sanchez was holding up his hand, grinning, "That's Sergeant Sanchez." He chuckled, "Blood-stripes count."

Griffon nodded, "Riiiight. OK, 'Sergeant', what's the plan?"

The new Sergeant paused to turn the spit, before answering, "Well, when we went back down to fetch you, we gathered a bunch of Hiver samples." He gestured at the darkness around them, "And I can pretty-well verify this place is too wasted to bother recovering. Since this base uses Geo-Thermal power, we can't even scavenge a reactor. So, I guess we call it quits and head back to the barn, to get our wounded taken care of."

It took Griffon a moment to realize what was wrong with what Sanchez had said, "Wait a moment? What do you mean 'Geo-Thermal Power'? In Oklahoma?"

Checking to see if the joint of meat he'd been roasting was done, Sanchez didn't even turn. "Sure. Hey, any place on earth can use Geo-Thermal energy, all you need is a deep enough hole, and Thermal-Bore technology makes that easy. After all what can be more dependable than the heat deep in the Earth's crust? It'll be there until the Earth itself cools."

Griffon nodded, thinking fast, "I guess, it just took me a bit off-center is all." At the Sergeants' signal that the meat was about ready, he decided to get ready for dinner. Starting with a quick trip to the slit latrine.

As he took care of business, his thoughts clicked into place. *So they have Thermal-Bore technology? That's what I needed to know. Well back home and "ShowTime".*

Chapter 16

Griffon stood at the head of the table. He looked at his friends, smiling. The half-healed, pinkish scar across the corner of his left eye pulled and twitched as his eyes crinkled. Not painful so much as irritating. "I assume you're all wondering why I've called you together?"

A chorus of, "No, not really. Not a bit. Hey! I'm just here for the beer!" Greeted him.

Chuckling, he nodded, "Ok, Ok, I deserved that. First, how do we stand on 'Vector'? White?"

The doctor leaned back, picking up his datacomp to double-check his notes before responding. "It's up to speed. After checking the Hivers you guys brought back I found there were some modifications of the intestinal fungus they use for digestion. Apparently, they initially modified it to allow them to digest terran food. This was similar to the changes they did to the other species they brought to Earth. Supposedly, the exact biochemical makeup of proteins in terran flesh and plants was slightly off from what they were used to. In addition, there were some of the common chemical compounds they ingested that were actually toxic to their metabolism. These changes corrected for that."

Using the stylus, he scrolled down the page, "Now, they appear to be in the process of regression. Returning to the original makeup as the area they've converted to what is norm for them has reached the point of being self-sustaining."

He glanced about the table, "The good news is that this actually gave me a broader template to work with, and simplified my efforts."

Griffon nodded, "So, it's ready to run?"

The doctor nodded, "Correct."

Turning to the broad Scot, Griffon asked, "Good. Gillian, have you been able to integrate the virus?"

Gillian nodded, "Right. All's ready on that score."

Griffon smiled and nodded, "OK. What's the trigger?"

Now Gillian picked up his own datacomp and brought up the appropriate page. "I couldn't use any form of codeword or fixed date."

He nervously looked around the table, "I couldn't guarantee that we would be able to access their system to activate the virus, and several of their viral scans were keyed to search for such time-activation codes. Instead I decided to go with activation upon our performing a relatively easy, but unlikely, series of actions they would automatically note."

He grinned about at the others, "To prevent accidental, or inopportune triggering of the virus, the actions needed to be quite specific, easy to set off, and... Well, stupid. To say the least."

With great reluctance, Gillian explained.

Griffon was a bit stunned, "Well, I guess that meets the parameters you've laid out. It does seem a bit risky for the person in question though. Don't you think?"

Gillian grinned, "I said it would be stupid and unlikely didn't I?" He glanced nervously around the table again, "No offense Doctor, but, I couldn't count on the effects of your genetic experiment. I-I mean, that I couldn't pre-select a set of variables without knowing what exactly will happen."

White nodded back, chuckling, "No offense taken. I can't be sure it'll work, nor how well. I'm only hoping to knock them back a bit to give us a chance of taking them out."

Griffon, steering the conversation back, "Right. Well, I've broken down the operational plan of action we need to ensure widespread downloading into the Brotherhood network. It's in seven distinct phases. First, we need intelligence. I think I can handle that. We have to locate a major Brotherhood base and determine it's exact layout. This is to give us the greatest possible chance of successfully kidnapping at least one, and preferably two or more full . . . 'Brothers'."

He nodded towards Fineous, "Since we've returned with verification of our story, the Raiders have really loosened up with what they'll let us access. Second, administrative preparation, obtaining the resources we need, and getting everything in position. Again, I'll have to ramrod that. I have to sell the Raiders on the plan and get them to buy off on it."

He checked his datacomp before continuing, "Third, to gain access to the Brotherhood base, with minimum risk and at minimum cost. We'll have to work out some means of getting around the Brotherhood security."

He nodded towards the mousy little man across the table, "Finn, you've shown, how do we say . . . a facility for screwing with security. Can you take that?"

Fineous nodded, "I'll have to know what I'll have to work with, and where the target base is located."

Nodding, Griffon made a note on his datacomp, "Right, for now the most likely scenario is targeting a major underground facility. Like the Raider bases, it'll have access only through a long tunnel complex, and with a full spectrum of sensory systems."

Fineous nodded, "Ah yes, I suppose it will have the normal thermal and optical motion sensors, along with ground sensors. There will also be at least one perimeter of outlying Observation Posts, as well as defensive bunker-complexes at the tunnel entrances. Also, further security posts and self-destructs along the corridors." He gave Griffon a big grin, "Correct?"

Griffon could feel that his face turning red, "Ah, yes. You've been checking these things out?"

Fineous shrugged, "Well, let's just say I have a habit of checking out what I'd need to get out of any place I've gotten myself into. Since these Raiders use the same basic technology and have installations with the same origin as the Brotherhood, it isn't hard to figure out what I'll have to deal with. But, I still need to know where the target is most likely to be . . .?"

Griffon used his stylus to bring the appropriate page on his datacomp, "The most likely target is the area of the old North American base at Fort Riley, Kansas."

Nodding, Fineous started tapping on his own datacomp, "Kansas huh? Well in that case we'll need to develop several . . . 'special' packages. I'll be able to piece those together. Two Raider teams, several miles of Fu-line, a Thermal Bore, and an MDC truck."

Griffon could only nod. *Just a truck-driver huh?* He added the items to the list, "Right. Well, I'll have to see if I can get the Commander to cut those free for us."

Hesitantly, almost like a kid in class, White raised his hand, "Excuse me. But, what exactly are Fu-lines and Thermal Bores?"

Griffon nodded, "Well, as with all of our technology, their development history dates back to the last century . . ."

He caught himself, chuckling, "OK . . . The century before last. Fu-gas was an early form of pyro-explosive material developed from simple jellied gasoline. Fu-line is the latest form of this material in long, very small diameter hose. It's used for starting long lines of fire."

Remembering, he continued, “It wasn’t originally designed with military applications in mind. It was actually intended for fighting forest fires. It would be used in starting controlled, long-lines of backfire to destroy fuel in the path of the wildfire.”

White nodded, thinking. He glanced at Fineous, “So you’re planning to distract the Brotherhood by starting a forest-fire in Kansas? I’m pretty sure that would take them by surprise.”

Laughing, Fineous tried several times to speak. He failed miserably. Finally, he managed to collect himself. “N-no, actually I’m looking at starting several prairie fires.” He raised his hand, preempting the questions of the others. “Yes, I know, their fortifications will be pretty-much immune to a grass fire. But trust me, this’ll work.”

Griffon nodded, “Ookay.” Shaking his head, “Anyhow, the ‘Thermal Bore’ was specifically designed to bore the tunnels for the tube-train system. It’s a heavy, mining machine using atomic technology. It consists of a large, cylindrical body carried on caterpillar treads. It has a high-temperature ceramic cone at the front. This melts its way through the earth by emitting a high-powered laser or stream of fusion plasma from the tip of the cone. The tracks move the machine forwards, widening the hole by pressing the molten material back along the cone, and melting the surrounding matrix.”

“As the molten material finally flows past the edge of the cone, it’s flash-cooled by liquid nitrogen. This forms a continuous wall of compressed ceramic material that acts to shore up and seal the tunnel.”

White nodded, “Yes but what about all the dirt and rock, where does it go? If you were at any depth at all, the material would be compressed already. How did they handle the excess?”

Griffon grinned, “In almost all cases, natural rock matrix consists of a compression of formerly molten material that cooled under extreme pressure. Much of its volume is made up of crushed crystalline structures and microscopic gas bubbles fixed in place as the mass cooled. Under the incredible temperatures of the Thermal Bore much of this material is, well, vaporized and drawn off. It’s also run through a magnetic separation filter to isolate selected elements.”

Gillian stepped in, “If I remember right, since many of the more valuable minerals; gold, silver, platinum, and such actually have rather low melting temperatures. This meant that even the miniscule amounts found in granite, marble, and other common matrix, allowed the tunneling to actually pay for itself.”

White was nodding, “Right, and if these machines were used for drilling the long tunnels for the tube-trains, the Raiders should have a few around.” He looked up at the ceiling, “Otherwise, how did they dig out this place?” Glancing at the others, “Right?”

Griffon grinned, "Elementary my dear Doctor." Looking around, "Any more questions? Good."

Consulting the notes on his datacomp, "Next we have the 'Assault Phase'." He gave Fineous a sardonic grin. "I assume that if we're going to bore into the complex, we'll be able to select the level of the main complex we'll be able to break into and avoid the fight down the tunnels and upper levels?"

The mousy little man nodded, "If things work out right, we should be able to mask their ground sensors and get in before they really know what we're up to."

Griffon nodded, his stylus tapping away on his datacomp, "Good, that'll allow us to cut our manpower for the assault to a minimum." He looked at his notes, "As a matter of fact," looking at the others, "we can make it with just four or five. Hope you're up to it."

Groans sounded from around the table. Griffon continued, "OK, minimum personnel gives maximum security, and maximum chance of successful evasion."

Still tapping notes on his datacomp, "That takes care of steps four and five." Looking up at the others, "For step six, 'Implementation'. We need a secure place to take our. . . 'subjects'. White," the doctor glanced up from his notes, "Keeping them healthy, but incommunicado will be your job. Gillian, you'll have the responsibility for setting up a system to tap into the Brotherhood implants. I don't want to have to depend on having them read over a few million lines of code. OK?" The Scot nodded, not looking up from his own datacomp, his accent brought out by his distraction, "Nah problem, Sahr. They'll have'a designed 'a effective, 'contact port' for the direct input and downloading of information." He glanced up at the others, "It'll be a backup, in case of interruption of their normal communications."

Griffon nodded, "Fine. Now, for the last part, 'Follow-through'. To get this to work we'll have to convince our 'guests' we're running a 'Rogue Operation' in violation of the Raider High Command. That means we'll have to . . ." His explanation of the plans took several more minutes. When he finished, the others just sat there for a few moments.

Fineous was the first to speak, "You said Gillian's activation plan for the virus was risky? This is a bit of a long shot, don't you think?"

Griffon shook his head, "No, not at all. The Brotherhood should buy off on it completely."

Fineous shook his head, frowning, "No, not that. I mean that it's liable to be a long shot for us to get back."

Griffon nodded, "Well, you can't gamble without putting your money down."

Fineous grinned, "When I put my money down, it's never a gamble."

Griffon chuckled, "OK, I promise, we'll make sure to rig the game as much as possible. Any other comments? Questions? No? Good. Now, lets go get some dinner, I'm starving and the ladies await."

As the group broke up, White and Gillian went their own way. Fineous joined Griffon in the elevator.

The mousy little man was the first to speak, "So, the girls are planning a dual ceremony now?"

Griffon shrugged, "Hey, whatever. It's not like any man has ever really worried about his wedding day."

Fineous chuckled, nodding, "So, how do you feel about getting 'hitched'?"

Griffon shrugged again, "Oh, I guess it's the right thing to do. I hate to say this, but it's not like we're going to have much chance at shopping around. I think we've both been really lucky. Besides. . ." He stroked the pinkish scar across the corner of his eye, "With my track record I really like the idea of living with the best saw-bones around. How about you? How do you feel about it?"

Fineous gave a long-suffering sigh, "I'd really have preferred them to ask us first." Chuckling, "But really. . ."

He paused long enough for Griffon to glance over, concerned. His friend had a strange, empty look in his eyes, "You know, I've been all over and done most everything. But, really, I can't ever remember having a . . . well, a home." The elevator came to a stop. The door sighed open. "Maybe having someone there for you is what makes it a home."

Chapter 17

Griffon lay at the lip of the dry wash. Carefully raising his head above the sun-scorched grass of late summer. He scanned his surroundings to the softly undulating horizon. A few scattered bands of plain animals and one sizeable herd of long-horned cattle grazed in the distance. A gusty wind sent wavelike ripples across the sea of grass. He turned to look at the swollen sun as it slowly slid into the west. Another figure in the shifting camouflage of a battlesuit crawled up and lay beside him.

Griffon turned, snapping up his visor, nodding towards Fineous.

The little man lay next to him and raised his own visor. "Both Raider teams have checked in, everything's in place."

Griffon nodded, "Right, how long for the burn?"

Fineous scanned the area as he answered, "If the weather people are right, and these winds hold, we should be reaching maximum concentration about twelve hours after ignition."

"Good, then we'll tell 'em to fire it up about midnight. That way we'll be able to hit 'em about noon, when at least their thermal sensor's are the most useless." Griffon looked at his mousy little friend, "You know if this doesn't work we're toast?"

Fineous gave a derisive snort, "Sure it'll work. These gomers are soooo dependent on their mighty widgets." Now it was his turn to ask, "Are you sure that monstrosity will be able to get into their complex?"

Griffon nodded, patting the ground, "Pretty sure. Gillian told me the 'Bore'll do between five and ten clicks an hour through this stuff."

Fineous snapped his visor down to scan something in the distance. His voice was muffled by the suit speaker, "How'd you ever persuade the Commander to cut this free? I thought they were short on this sort of stuff?"

Griffon glanced back down the wash towards the heavily camouflaged camp, "Don't tell the others, but the Raiders are loosing. Counting Comanche base, they've got three whole major installations left." He shook his head, "According to the Commander, the way the Brotherhood's been going, there's about one chance in ten they'll still be a viable force in two years." He shrugged, "He doesn't give us much of a chance of pulling off this little escapade or making any real dent with our scheme. But, well it's about the best deal they've got going right now. Besides, I gave him a good trade for his generosity."

Fineous raised his visor again before glancing at Griffon, "Oh?"

Griffon couldn't help smiling, "Sure, their problem was that the Brotherhood and the Hiver aircraft have been virtually undetectable to the Raider radar."

Fineous' brow crinkled, "Stealth? I thought that'd been a major bust?"

Griffon nodded, "It was. However, the answer, like so many other things, was lost in the fall. The Raiders have been on the short end of the stick in recovering lost records and technology. I told him how to beat the Stealth technology."

Fineous nodded, "I guess there's some advantage to having a History minor after all. How's it work?"

Griffon turned back, scanning their surroundings. With his own eyes this time. "It was one of the things that caused the fall of the old 'United States of America'. They'd spent decades and over a trillion dollars on developing stealth technology. In fact, they based the aerial branch of their combined-arms concept of warfare on super-expensive stealth aircraft. The problem was that the powers that be had known that the answer to combating stealth had been around almost as long as the airplanes had been."

He lowered himself, turning to the little man beside him, his face grim; "It was civilian weather radar."

Fineous frowned, "Weather radar? You mean Doppler Radar?"

Griffon unhooked his canteen and took a sip before continuing, "Yep, you see in the weather mode, the computer interpreting the Doppler signal was programmed to ignore anything moving faster than about one to two hundred kilometers per hour. Make it sixty to a hundred milers per hour. That's why they could spot a tornado by the 'hook' on the radar. It was the cloud matter and debris accelerating into the cyclone. Well, some technician figured if the Doppler could pick up raindrops, snowflakes, and clouds, it could pick up an airplane with the radar cross-section of a bumblebee. All they had to do was reprogram the computer to look for a bee doing six hundred knots at thirty-five thousand feet."

Fineous snorted, "Wasn't it easy to jam or spoof?"

Griffon nodded, "Sure, until they redesigned it to meet military specs, frequency agility, and phased array and all that."

Fineous gave him a sardonic grin, "You mean the old US government knew about it and still put all their eggs in that basket?"

Now it was Griffon's turn to grin. "Yep, it seems the old American Constitution said 'Provide for the common defense' was the top of the governments' responsibility. It never had any prohibition on how many tax-dollars it would cost to buy it off. The real break in their nasty little secret came when somebody did a check of the American targeting priorities in their famous 'Gulf War' in the last decade of the twentieth-century."

Griffon returned his canteen to it's holder as he thought back. Recalling his professor's comments. "It was noticed that with all the Iraqi Headquarters, SCUD missile parks, air-defenses, airbases, radars, and all they had to take care of, one of the first targets was the weather shack at the Baghdad International Airport. Like the Iraqis couldn't look out the widow to see if it was raining."

Fineous shook his head, "Shit, no wonder they shot themselves in the foot. But why?"

Grimly, Griffon continued, "A trillion dollars was a big reward for mendacity. And, enough of it was funneled back to the politicians to make sure nobody messed with the gravy-train."

Fineous forehead scrunched in thought, "But, wait, I thought you persuaded the Raiders to use ground-penetrating radar to locate and map this place. That requires high-altitude over-flights. If the Brotherhood knows how to beat stealth, how did they do it without getting shot down?"

Griffon smiled, "Any knife can twist in your hand. If they've programmed their radar to look for aircraft, they've also programmed it to ignore anything moving below a certain speed. That's to keep from becoming cluttered by the clouds and such that it was originally designed to track. I simply had the Raiders mount the radars in old-fashioned helium balloons. Since the balloons were moving at the speed of the wind, the radar decided that it was a cloud and ignored it. Being filled with helium they were even invisible to thermal sensors, and there was no magnetic footprint to trip a magnetometer."

"Great, you beat the twenty-second century version of twentieth-century technology with nineteenth-century technology." Bemused, Fineous could only shake his head, "And, people call me a 'Sneaky Bastard'."

Griffon chuckled, "Yep'er. Well, you'd better get that signal off to the Raider teams." As the little man started to back down into the wash, "Oh, Finn, tell 'em thanks for the assist, and to get the hell out 'ta here once it's going good, OK?"

Fineous waved an imitation salute, "Sure thing Skipper."

The team prepared throughout the day, trading off the watch and resting.

At midnight, the signal was sent to the support elements located far beyond the horizon. Detonators were fired. Tiny lines of flame exploded across the prairie to be quickly whipped into broad walls of roaring firestorm. Fed by the tall, sun-scorched grass, the fire raced before the wind.

At first, only the nearest animals noted the fire and began to trot clear. Faster they ran, faster... and faster!

Soon, like the bow-wave of a great ship, the mass of panic-blinded animals raced before the crackling flames.

In timed sequence, new lines of fire exploded into being. Angled to funnel the panicked creatures into a tighter and tighter mass.

The team awoke in the pre-dawn darkness. The first waves consisted of the birds, fleeing before the streams of choking smoke. They could feel the ground begin to vibrate, to shake, to quake!

Quickly, they leapt to their feet and began to clear the camp. Looking up into the pinking dawn, they saw a wall of flame-tinged, black-cut, brown-grey stretching across the horizon.

Far ahead of the fire, the stampeding wall of life surged towards their position.

Clumps and knots of the fleetest creatures raced by. Larger beasts, greater knots, whole herds, intermixed in a panicky mass roared by. Screaming, biting, surging, and dying, the creatures came.

As the last of the team climbed into the massive vehicle, Fineous fired the next in a series of explosions.

Lines of flame sprang into life around the enemy installation, trapping the surging mass of panicky life.

Horror and hell exploded across the plain.

Around the base, gapping doors opened in the earth. War machines roared out to face an enemy assault.

Brotherhood cyberplanes screamed into the air, searching for the attackers. Massive Battleborgs stomped into the open. The first were smashed into splinters by the tight-packed avalanche of screaming, tearing flesh.

More machines rose from beneath the earth. Ripping lines of sun-bright nuclear flame tore into the fear-ravaged animals. Acentic bolts tore and smashed, and still the avalanche of terrified flesh rolled across the plains.

In the driver's seat of the Thermal Bore, Gillian fired up the Fusion torch at the tip of the forward cone. He engaged the tracks. The massive metal beast slowly nosed forwards.

To camouflage the glare of the torch, Fineous tripped another set of triggers. Around the installation, Fusion Flares sparked and burst into life. Unnoticed in the roiling cauldron of hell they incinerated, knots of terror-blinded beasts adding to the man-made inferno.

The massive Bore tore into the Earth. Gillian drove blind, watching his instruments, guided by a holographic schematic that formed in his 'Heads up' display.

In the cramped crew-quarters behind his seat, the others readied for the assault.

One hour passed another. The Bore rocked; dull thuds and rumbling roars penetrated the thick sides of the vehicle.

The team automatically looked at the ceiling, startled. Grim-faced Griffon nodded, "They're blasting the stampede. Sounds like heavy artillery." He shrugged at the others; "I'd be using airbursts to flatten it if I were them."

Fineous, for once doubt crossing his brow, asked, "Will we make it before they quiet things down?"

Griffon shook his head. Reaching forwards, he punched Gillian in the shoulder.

The broad Scot was hunched over his controls, sweat dripped from his brow. Without looking back he snarled, "What?"

To be heard over the noise, Griffon had to yell, "How much longer?"

Gillian shrugged, shouting back, "Not long, we're making better time than I expected, we're just reaching the . . ."

With a screeching roar, the Bore slammed to a stop. Gillian cursed and snarled at his controls, yanking levers and pounding switches. The Fusion torch at the nose flared and roared. The treads seemed to stutter, shriek, and then bite. The vehicle lurched forwards, again and still again.

Through gritted teeth the Scot snarled to the others, his accent coming to the fore, "We're cutting through the outer walls. Te'a musta incorporated armored-plate in the outer shell." Again the vehicle lurched and stalled. Gillian slammed the controls to their stops. The others could see the meter-bars creep into the pink, then red. A flashing yellow strobe appeared. A siren began to whoop. Gillian snapped a switch, cutting off the alarm. "We're at one-hundred-twenty percent on the reactor."

Griffon rose to squat behind his seat. He gripped the Scots' backrest and roared over the noise that reverberated through the cramped chamber, "Go!

Go! Go! We'll never make it back now." He turned to glare at the ceiling. The others saw the familiar red-faced snarl of his 'Game Face'.

Smoke began to seep from the ventilators, sparks splattered from behind panels, whole boards began to blink and flash in warning.

With a surge that threw them to the back wall, the Bore gave a last heave and smashed into the clear.

Gillian whooped, "We' arra ta'rrrru!"

The vehicle lurched to a stuttering, rocking stop.

Gillian started shutting down the systems. Grinning ferociously, he roared, overloud in the cramped quarters, "Last stop! Eva' body oot!"

They popped the side hatch. It swung up smoothly. A wall of white heat and choking fumes rolled into the compartment.

Griffon snapped his faceplate down. Leading the way in edging around the rim of the Bore's drill-cone, and froze in place.

The Plasma and compressed gasses of the Bore had exploded into the area beyond the outer wall with the force of a sizeable chemical bomb.

The fusion torch had burned through the flimsy structures beyond.

Griffon was brought up short. Reinforced concrete and steel had been melted and blown back like butter before a blowtorch. Distantly sparking power lines and flickering emergency lights highlighted a circle of blackness that stretched from complete incineration through blast damage into simple carnage. He could see the flickering flames down the wreckage-strewn corridors, barely touched by the smashed lines of the overhead sprinkler system.

Shaking himself, he moved forwards to allow the others to pass.

The team quickly recovered from their shock.

Griffon thought, *Showtime!* "Right! Lets roll. Gillian, you've got our six. Get the magtruck ready and hold the exit. White with me. Finn, you're sure you can make these Gomers think you're an entire army?"

He could just make out the sardonic grin behind Fineous' faceplate. Nodding, "Oh right. Forget I said anything. Let's move out . . ."

"I want visuals, and I want them nowwwww!" Praetor Cromwell stood on her dais, screaming at the frantic control-room technicians.

"Praetor! The sensors in the breach area are gone." The sweating male in the orange coverall of Internal Systems quailed at the glare.

The chunky figure in white snarled down at him, "Well get them back on line you pathetic lit. . ."

In his panic, the tech presumed to interrupt, "My apologies, Praetor. B-but the sensors aren't down. They're completely gone. The enemy attack has destroyed the sensor system."

A derisive snort, and a dismissive waive of a plump, manicured hand, "Whatever."

She turned towards the next technician. "What's the status of the surface engagement?"

Now it was the turn of the female in the charcoal and black colors of security. "Mistress, um, s-surface combat units report . . . great disruption on the surface, and s-some casualties. However, they are also reporting no, um, enemy units in evidence."

The Praetor's voice was very, cold now, "How could there be casualties if there's no enemy?"

Sweating the security tech hesitated before answering, "Um, well, Mistress, even a Battleborg can be crushed by a frantic Behemoth."

"So, you're telling me we deployed our main combat units, and risked Hiver retaliation for a bunch of stampeding cattle?" The Praetor rubbed her forehead as she sat down. Turning towards the orbital control station, "What's the status on the Hiver Battlecruiser?"

The technician in dark blue was too intent on his screen to show fear, "Praetor, it's shifted orbit. It will be reaching optimum firing position in..." Frantically double-checking the numbers scrolling across the screen, "Thirty-five minutes, sixteen seconds."

Her face flushed in fury, but voice very quiet, the Praetor nodded, "Of course."

Cromwell snarled back to the internal sensor station, "What is the status of the station?"

Nervously, the tech began to read his status board, "Breach on level four, sector thirty-six, Gamma ring. Enemy small arms and explosives reported on levels three, four, and five. We've lost elevators one, two, three, and five. Emergency stairways Alpha and Beta are blocked. All levels are reporting that the activation of the sprinkler systems is dropping the water pressure throughout the complex. Dialing up the pumps to compensate."

The Praetor leaned back in her chair, thinking, *At least he had some good news.*

The female in black reported, "Praetor, security reports they've trapped at least one enemy assault team in sector fifteen, Delta ring, level four. They've activated the emergency bulkheads to trap the enemy units."

Cromwell began to spit out orders rapid-fire, "Ready all batteries. Instruct surface combat units to clear and secure all exits, then form escort. Order two Battleborgs down to reinforce the security team in assaulting the trapped enemy units. I want live prisoners. Other internal security teams will continue cordon and search operations."

She paused, considering what else needed to be done, "Have them work their way towards the breach. It won't do any good to initiate a major engagement with the Raiders until we've cleared all these damned infiltration teams!"

Frantic typing and low-voiced commands started going out.

She turned to the tech at the communications terminal, "Contact all members of the Brotherhood to initiate immediate evacuation. All sections will continue operations. Once the mobile command element comes on-line, begin evacuation of all vital equipment and technical personnel. Non-combatants . . ."

Behind her, the guards at the entrance stiffened, one sprang to the central dais, screaming, "Mistress! Enem..."

A massive explosion ripped the bulkhead hatch apart. Flaming shards of jagged debris tore across the control room.

The guard rushing towards the dais was torn apart by shrapnel. His tattered torso slammed into the Praetor knocking her to the deck, stunned.

Technicians that were still up leapt towards the weapons arranged neatly in their racks.

The racks were next to the door.

Acentic bolts ripped the smoking haze that filled the room. Shadowy forms sprang through the shattered bulkhead.

It was a massacre....

Rifle at the ready, Griffon snapped his visor up; wrinkling his nose at the death-stench of seared flesh and loosened bowels.

Quickly, he glanced about the room for any remaining threat.

Seeing none, he strode to the nearest consoles and began to scan the controls and screens. "Right, this looks like it. You check these Gomers, see if any of them are full Brothers. I'm going to check . . . Great, here's the security station."

White knelt over the huddled mass before the central throne-like seat, his eye caught by a glimpse of blood-streaked white.

Rolling the shredded remains of a body in the remnants of a security coverall he shouted, "Skipper! Found one!" He quickly grabbed the throat, feeling for a pulse.

Griffon turned from the console he was bent over, "Is it still alive?"

White nodded, quickly pulling a medkit from a belt-pouch and slapping it on the arm of the unconscious figure. The machine began to run a diagnostic check while the doctor gave a quick and rough cursory examination.

Within seconds he turned to Griffon, "Still alive, hardly has a scratch."

Griffon nodded. Turning back to the console, muttering, "Finally found one."

He scanned the screen, "Looks like we're running out of time. Get it ready to travel, I'll . . . Ah, frack!"

White glanced up from where he was adjusting the controls on the medkit, "What's happened?"

Griffon just shook his head. Triggering his transmitter, "Fineous this is Griffon... Fineous, this is Griffon, come in... Finn come in... Dammit! To much concrete and conduit, I can't reach him."

Hefting his rifle, he turned towards White, "They've got Finn trapped. I'll go get him."

He pointed to the blood-splattered figure at the doctor's feet; "You get that back to the Bore. Help Gillian get everything ready. When we get there we're liable to be in a bit of a hurry."

White nodded, bending to heave the white-clad figure up into a classic 'Fireman's Carry'. Griffon headed out the shattered door, pausing to check the corridor beyond was clear. He nodded and waived the doctor forward.

As he turned down the corridor, following the memory of the layout he'd scanned from the security station, he turned back; "Doctor, you and Gillian have everything to complete the mission. If things get too hot, you two will leave us behind. Understand?"

White nodded; he freed his right hand, holding it out to the tall figure standing before him.

Griffon gripped the others hand. White's voice was gruff, "Yes Sir. Just make sure you guys make it. OK? I don't want to have to tell your women we had to leave you."

Griffon grinned, "Right, I'd hate to cause you any embarrassment."

He turned away, snapping his visor into place.

White stared at the figure disappearing around the next corner, mumbled, "Good luck." Then turned in the other direction.

Chapter 18

Griffon moved quickly, threading his way through the corridors of the complex. He attempted to route himself around the security points that had been identified on the screen he'd studied.

He arrived at the long corridor leading towards the area where the enemy had trapped Fineous.

At the mouth of the hallway he knelt and, slowly, peered around the corner at knee height, his rifle at the ready.

He saw at least a dozen figures in the monotones of Brotherhood Battlesuits positioned along the corridor, weapons ready, concentrating on the blank wall of the emergency bulkhead at the far end. That was bad enough. However, the massive forms of two Battleborgs at the head of the hallway were what caught his attention.

There was another, in the yellow coverall of a Technical Command Officer giving directions. They seemed ready to open the bulkhead.

Mother frackin! Griffon pulled back around the corner and keyed his transmitter, "Fineous, this is Griffon, come in."

A seconds' pause then he heard a familiar voice in his ear, "Griffon, this is Finn, welcome to the party! Where are you?"

Finally, Griffon 'checked six' before responding, "I'm at the end of the corridor beyond that bulkhead. I count at least thirteen enemy troops and two Battleborgs about to break in on you."

He heard his friend give a derisive snort, "Are they about to open the door?"

After checking on the progress of the enemies activities, Griffon keyed his mike, "Affirmative, any time now."

The response came quickly, "Well, just stand back and watch the fun."

Griffon thought before asking, "Finn, what've you done?"

He could visualize Fineous' sardonic grin as the little man answered, "Just watch. Finn out."

Griffon slid into a prone position and slowly eased his rifle around the corner.

The enemy commander had finished his dispositions. Griffon saw him step to the panel beside the emergency bulkhead and start punching in the security code to open.

Powerful motors engaged, the bulkhead slid quickly upwards...

Revealing a wall of water.

Like the enemy, Griffon froze.

The flood slammed down the narrow corridor.

The two Battleborgs, and the Commander, who'd been standing directly before the bulkhead were smashed back, and dropped under the flood.

The debris-choked wave surged down the corridor. The closest troopers had no chance. They were swept aside and went under. Those further back began to scramble for safety. Several began to sprint towards Griffon.

Griffon desperately looked around. The wave was still head-high as it reached the cross-corridor. Griffon saw his chance. He scrambled to the top of a tall locker against the wall, and jumped up; grabbing at the maze of pipes and conduits running just under the high ceiling.

He managed to pull his legs up as the wave crashed into the wall opposite the corridor and began to wash down both directions of the cross-corridor.

He saw figures trapped in the flood, some still struggling, others twisting limply in the stream, unconscious or dead.

After a few moments, the flood started to recede. Griffon's sound receivers picked up . . . an off-key rendition of 'How high's the water Mama'?

He twisted to see Fineous floating down the stream, laying on several floating cushions that had been tied together in a rough raft.

Fineous spotted him as he floated by in the rapidly dropping flood, and gave him a derisive wave.

The stream still had enough force to tip the little man's raft as it hit the far wall, dumping him into the now knee-high water.

Griffon dropped beside him as he came up sputtering and gasping. Fineous gave him a huge grin, "Got'ta remember to close my faceplate next time."

Griffon could only shake his head, reaching down to help his friend up, "You idiot!" He glanced back up the corridor, a couple of figures were staggering to their feet, a few others were either squirming or laying in place, very still. One of the Battleborgs was attempting to stand, one leg twisted and broken, the other wasn't moving at all.

As Finn rose, Griffon gave him a friendly shove in the direction of the Bore.

They began to splash down the corridor, Griffon couldn't help commenting, "There you go again! Ruining my heroics! Spoiling my rescues."

They had to get past one security checkpoint, behind a wave of grenades and gunfire before they could reach the blast-scarred area surrounding the Bore.

Gillian and White were waiting for them. The Magtruck was unloaded and floating in the tunnel behind the Bore. Their prisoner securely strapped in the rear storage compartment.

Griffon glanced around, "Right, lets move out people. It's about to get really busy aroun... Finn! Where are you going? Finn?"

The little man ducked back into the Bore's hatch. Griffon followed, finding his friend bending over the display of a box jury-rigged to the fusion-bottle of the massive vehicle.

Griffon knelt beside him as he asked, "What're you doing?"

Fineous gave him a quick smile before turning back to the keypad, "What do you think? I borrowed this TacNuc from the Raiders. This'll keep 'em from following us any time soon."

Griffon nodded, "Right, how much time?'

The little man snapped the panel cover back into place, "Ten minutes. I hope that truck's up to snuff." He grabbed another box and followed Griffon out of the hatch. As Griffon started towards the back of the Bore, he glanced back to see Fineous close the hatch and affix the box he was carrying above the door.

Griffon came back, "Now what?"

Fineous, finishing what he was doing, carefully affixed a placard to the short chain that hung from the box on the outside of the door.

The little man turned to go, "They might get here in time to diffuse the bomb. This oughta give them a bit of pause."

As the little man edged past him, Griffon couldn't help but look at the placard . . .'Pull This STUPID'

Griffon could only stare for a moment, before turning to follow his friend. "You've got to be kidding!"

Fineous climbed into the driver's seat of the truck, Griffon twisted himself into the small weapons-ring behind Fineous' seat and strapped himself into place. White and Gillian were already in their places on the bench-seat just in front of the box-like space where they'd secured their 'guest' and packs.

Fineous fired up the drive and sent the Magtruck skimming back down the fused tunnel, towards freedom.

The fume-laden air rushed past them as they roared down the tunnel. Fineous skillfully handled the controls as they ripped down the mildly- rolling tunnel.

Griffon saw the bright dot of the exit swiftly swelling ahead. When a white-hot glare sprang into being behind them.

Twisting in his seat, he saw a wall of flame roaring down the corridor.

With a neck-snapping wrench, the shock wave flung them twisting and spinning out of the opening.

Luckily, the Bore had entered at a slightly downward angle. They were tossed upwards and outwards, avoiding being smashed into the far wall of the wash by almost a meter, maybe.

Frantically, Fineous and the stabilizing gyro of the Magtuck tried to regain control. The damned truck twisted and spun through the air.

Finally, the little man got the machine under control and leveled off, two meters above the plain.

Griffon freed his seat and spun to look back at a large 'Bubble' of earth rising over the site of the installation. With a last heave, the mound cracked and split. Smoke and dust spurting out as the whole began to settle back into itself.

Griffon turned back, and slapped Fineous on the back. Over the vehicle intercom, "I thought we had ten minutes?"

Without turning, Fineous shrugged, "I guess one of 'em was stupid."

Befuddled, Griffon could only stammer, "Y-You mean? I mean . . .That idiotic booby-trap?"

Fineous twisted in his seat and grinned back at him, waggling his eyebrows.

Griffon could only sputter, "You idio..."

Gillian's yell cut in, "Cyberplanes! Coming down! Now!"

Griffon spun automatically freeing the tri-barrelled HELBORe and swinging it around.

High to their left rear he spotted splintered sunlight glinting off the flat, angular shapes of Cyborg piloted, Brotherhood strike-fighters as they spiraled into a turning dive. Lining up to pounce on the speeding Magtruck.

As soon as the sights came on line, Griffon tripped off a short burst.

Instantly, long fingers of flash-blasted atmosphere reached towards the diving craft.

Griffon swept the fingers of energy through the trio of enemy craft.

In a fantastic spiraling ballet they spun apart, dodging the HELBORe's blast.

Without taking his eyes from the weapon's sights, Griffon yelled into his suit microphone, "Break left! Now!"

Fineous slammed the magtruck hard over, swinging the belly-coils up, using the power of the lift magnet against the force of inertia. Everyone felt the snapping force as the truck pivoted through a right-angled turn.

On the enemy craft, twin energy cannon pivoted from their lock positions and fired. The ground to the right of the vehicle exploded and flashed into vapor.

Griffon swung the laser around to fire up the enemies' ass as it blurred past.

The second and third Cyberplanes dropped hard and pulled up in line abreast, neatly bracketing the hard-dodging target.

Griffon ripped the HELBORe across the pair, one staggered and swerved, breaking lock before recovering and whipping up into an impossibly fast turn. The other dodged away from it's damaged companion.

Almost in synchronization, the two snapped up and around, roared out and away.

Griffon heaved the weapon around. Spotting the first Cyberplane as it started it's next run.

Desperately he tried to bring the heavy laser to bear. His eyes locked on the twin circles of black death as they lined up on the wildly dodging magtruck.

The world strobe-lit into black and purple. His faceplate immediately blanked. His back and neck whip-snapped, as the magtruck slammed into the earth, hard. It bounded back into the air then back to a hard skid.

His faceplate cleared to a growing mass of bubbling white-hot fire.

He managed to think, *What th' FRA . . .!*

An instant's vision of shock wave racing across the ground. It slammed into the vehicle. Tossing it, spinning, into the ground.

Chapter 19

The world grayed and swam. Dust billowed in Griffon's vision. A spasm of pain ripped up his spine, "Ow! Muther frackin!"

It took a force of will, but he managed to open his eyes. The world swayed, upside down.

Carefully, he turned his head. He was hanging from his safety strap. The HELBORe had been crushed back to the top of the mini-turret.

He keyed his microphone, "Finn? White? Gillian? Are you guys all right?"

White was the first to respond, "I'm fine sir. Just a bit shaken up."

Gillian's broad Scottish accent colored a series of curses, before he answered, "Aye, Sahr. Just a bit battered around the edges."

Griffon waited a moment. Fineous failed to respond. "Finn? You OK?"

"Urgh!" The voice was a bit blurred, "Yessir, feeling like a pair of dice in the cup, but, OK. I guess... Sorta."

Griffon was carefully freeing his legs from the wreckage, paused, "What? Are you OK or not?"

Fineous chuckled, "There goes my insurance points. They'll never let me drive again."

Amid a general round of chuckles, Griffon managed to respond, "Right. Well don't sweat it. You're seventy years behind on your premiums anyhow. OK, people, let's get the hell out'ta here."

Carefully he reached up and hit the quick-release buckle.

Bad idea! He groaned as the top of the turret slammed into his head, under the heap of his body.

Carefully, painfully he unfolded himself and crawled out from under the wreck of the magtruck.

Strong hands reached in to drag him free.

Griffon stood swaying and took a quick headcount. Fineous, Gillian and White were all there. He looked at the huddled form in the bloodied white jumpsuit. "How's our guest?"

White gave a sardonic grin and a shrug, "Slept through it like a baby. I've set the Medkit to keep her out until we're ready for her to wake up." He shrugged again, "I can't jam her commo link. However, I figure if we can't jam it or intercept it they can't home in on it. Besides, if she's out she can't see where we're at or where we're going."

Nodding, Griffon looked into the faces of his friends, "How are you guys?"

Nods and shrugs all around. Gillian rubbed at the massive bruise on the right side of his face, "A bit beat about Sahr, but, we'll live." His broad face split in a toothy grin, "For now."

Griffon turned back to survey the wreckage of their magtruck. "Any chance of getting that thing running?"

The squat Scott shook his head, "No way Sahr, the fusion bottle held up. Otherwise we'd a' been crispy critters. But the whole drive trains shot and the lift coils all broken up."

Grimly, Griffon nodded, flexing his back, "Looks like we're back to L-P-C's." Grimly, "Let's saddle up people." Pointing at their unconscious prisoner, "Doctor, can you go ahead and download our little package into that?"

White nodded, “Yes Sir, I can. Gillian’s rigged a port-contact interface that’ll allow us to load anything we want into her system.” He gave Griffon a lop-sided grin; “I do have a surprise for you. You know our guest.”

Griffon’s thoughts were still a bit befuddled, “You mean?”

The Doctor grinned, “Yes sir. Who else would you expect to find in the main control center for a Brotherhood base but the district Praetor Herself.”

Chuckling, Griffon gave an exaggerated bow, “Then go ahead good sir. While you’re at it we’ll salvage what we can.”

As the others turned to comply, Griffon caught White’s arm, “And, Doctor. Once you’ve delivered our little ‘package’, could you please wake her up? We’ll let that Bitch carry her own weight.”

Soon, they were able to prod their whining, complaining charge into motion, heading south.

Several miles later they made camp in another dry wash. Carefully hiding their small fire under the overhanging bank.

Over the tasteless goo of his dinner, Griffon was finally able to start asking the questions that had been eating at him. “All right Fineous, how did you manage to flood the corridor like that?”

The little man grinned, “Well, I was trying to evade when I made a wrong turn and they were able to trap me in that corridor. I didn’t realize it was a dead end until after they’d dropped that emergency bulkhead. I plugged all the drains I could find and shot out the water lines for their sprinkler system.” He shrugged, “I was hoping to trigger an automatic release on the door. It didn’t work out that way. I thought they would figure something was up and shut off the water. Instead, I swear it started coming in even stronger.” He chuckled, taking another bite. “I was glad they opened it up when they did, I was about to drown in my own cleverness.”

That brought a laugh to all but their sullen captive, who just gave a sarcastic snort and continued to eat the ration they had given her.

Griffon nodded, still chuckling, “OK, and what about that nuke you set? I thought we had ten minutes? Or did they trip that inane booby-trap you set?”

Fineous shrugged, “I also had it set to trigger the nuke if they tried to open the hatch or fooled with the box.” Again with the toothy smile, “For myself, I prefer to think that they were just Doofus enough to yank it’s chain.”

“Uh-huh.” Griffon, looked about the group, “Anybody have any idea what that last blast was? I mean did their reactor blow, or what?”

Again Ms. Cromwell gave a derisive snort.

Gillian answered that, “No, that was a surface detonation. I believe that little shindy alerted the Hivers and they dropped one a their little rocks on’na the target.”

Griffon nodded, “Makes sense. What about our little airborne escort? They catch it in the blast?”

Nobody had seen what had happened to the Cyberplanes. Consensus was that they were there before the blast, and gone afterwards.

Once they were finished with the meal, Griffon turned to their prisoner. "Ms. Cromwell, or should I call you Olivia?"

Another disdainful snort and the waive of an imperious hand, "Whatever."

Griffon grinned, "OK, Olivia, I guess you're wondering what you're doing here?"

Her chubby, thin-lipped face seemed made for sneering, "I never try to understand the actions of idiots or other animals."

Such a charming creature. Griffon just grinned wider, "Well, before we went in with the Raiders, we decided we wanted to capture one of you. We have a gift for you." He shrugged, "The Raider High-Command didn't think we should give it to you, but . . . they can't use it, and we thought you could."

No response, just a suspicious glare.

Griffon held a datachip up and gestured towards White, "Our Doctor has developed a little, um, 'surprise' for our Hiver visitors. It's biologic in nature."

He could see a greedy gleam of interest start in her eye. He gestured to White, "Doctor."

White nodded and picked up a stick to poke at the fire while he spoke, "The Hiver digestive system uses a particular type of fungus in its digestive track. It aids in the final digestion of food, much like the equivalent intestinal bacteria that's found in humans and other terrestrial creatures. I've done a slight genetic modification on it."

She positively sneered at that, "And they're supposed to poison themselves with your little trick?"

White nodded, "Yes, actually that's exactly what they will do. You see, for a biological weapon to work you have to catch the enemy by surprise, or with a weapon they're not prepared to combat, or..." He gave her a big grin. "Offer them a biological weapon they'll want to infect themselves with."

He continued, "Now, as far as I was able to figure, they might be highly evolved and intelligent insects, but the key is, they're still insects. They have no consciousness of self, individual life, or anything but hive. As far as the Hive is concerned, all things are divided into four categories- Dangerous to the Hive, kill it. Good for the Hive, use it. Useful to the Hive, abuse it. If of no interest to the Hive, ignore it."

"I believe, if we can convince them a mutated form of their intestinal fungus has developed, say, in a small group of Hivers that have been cut off from the main community for several insect generations. A mutation which significantly increases the amount of food digestible to the Hivers. They will actually, actively, try to spread it throughout the Hive community."

She seemed to be actually thinking about what he was saying, "What do you mean, 'Increase the amount of food' digestible by the Hive?"

"Well, as can be expected, Hiver creatures fill much the same ecological niches as their Terrestrial counterparts. One area where they seem to have a bit of a gap, at least in the creatures we've found so far, no Hiver can eat and digest cellulose, um, wood fiber."

He prodded the fire again, sending up a shower of sparks, "They have several plants, funguses, bacteria, and such that break down wood fiber, but no apparent counterparts to Terrestrial termites."

She nodded, "Go on."

"Well, I altered the genetic structure of the Hiver intestinal fungus to match that of the particular intestinal bacteria termites carry. The bacteria that allow them to digest wood fiber." White laid his stick aside, glancing at the Praetor, "Now, considering the Hiver plants we've sampled have a very large number of 'woody' plants, along with their Terrestrial counterparts. This modification would significantly increase the amount of food the Hivers can digest from a given eco-system."

She sneered, "So that's your plan? Give them more food? What, so you think they'll overpopulate themselves into extinction?"

White grinned, "Well, no. I've also provided a slight modification of the reproductive system of the Hiver fungus. The new version causes a slight, and innocuous, change in the Hiver blood chemistry. So long as there are uninfected Hivers around, and the fungus can tell when the Hivers . . . physically 'join' for their exchange of information, it continues normal reproduction. Once a period of approximately six months have gone by without the fungus detecting an uninfected Hiver it... goes into a brief period of uncontrolled sporation."

He stared directly into the Abataurum's eyes, "Their intestinal track literally explodes from the inside." He gave a surprisingly nasty snarl, "A rather painful means of death I must say."

White reached back into his pack and pulled out a small stasis container. "Here I have several Hiver Workers and Warriors recovered from such an isolated community. . ." He pointed at the datachip Griffon still held in his hand, "and that holds the genetic coding for the new fungus." He gave an embarrassed glance around, though the ruddy light prevented anyone from seeing if he blushed. "I've also taken the opportunity to directly download the information into your data system."

He grinned at her surprised start, "Check you files."

She stared into space. In the dim light Griffon could see her eyes glitter and shift as she read the 'Heads-up' display projected onto the inside of her corneas.

She positively snarled, "You Bastards! How dare you . . ."

Griffon cut her off, "All's fare in love and war', Sister."

Her reaction was expected. She jumped up, screaming, "You pathetic little shits! You and your kind are sooo self-centered. You couldn't care less about the human race or anyone but yourselves. With your sick, greedy, whining about your individuality, and rights, you can never care enough to do a job right!"

Griffon was surprised at the amount of venom a human voice could hold. "Sorry if we're too self-centered to declare you and yours our lords and masters. But, I really don't like the thought of being . . . Salvaged to provide spare parts for my betters."

She was a positive expert at sneering, "Now, look you . . ."

Griffon cut in, "No! You look Bitch! We don't have to be friends; we don't have to be allies. I'll be happy as sin to see the last of you and yours die slow, agonizing deaths. But, we have an enemy that's killing us both off." He gestured with the chip he held, "This offers a chance of really setting the bastards back. The Raiders do not have the facilities or expertise in xeno-biological research to pull this off. You do. That's why we're disobeying instructions in giving this to you. We've done our part, you do yours!"

If her mouth had actually dripped all the venom that oozed with her voice they'd all be dead, "That's it, you people do a half-assed job, then dump it on us. I'm sooo impressed with your humility! You don't even do the job right and expect US to save you all."

That puzzled Griffon, "What do you mean by that? We did all we could with what we had."

She sneered back, "And that's why you will fail. You believe a job done well enough is a job done right. We hold axiom that 'If it's not perfect it's not right, and if it's not right you have failed.' That's why we will win. We get the most from whatever we do."

Griffon just shrugged. Answering, with a derisive flip of his hand, "Whatever."

Conversation pretty well petered out after that.

For the next week, they continued their trek south. Griffon had discussed their next step with the others. Minus Ms Cromwell's input, of course. Deciding that they would drop her off with her serfs at the Oahkee town. It was roughly on the line of march to the nearest entrance to the Raider tube-system.

After a week of Ms. Cromwell's whining, sneering, and venom, everyone in the group would have been happy to slit her throat and call it a day. However, duty and discipline did manage to override disgust.

She was hardly pleased when they told them what they planned. She didn't have anything better to offer. She just accepted another topic to whine about.

They had finally gotten Ms. Cromwell to agree to use her communications link to set up a meeting with the Oahkies. She agreed that they would hand her over to her servants in a safe meeting, along with the Hiver samples and datachip. They agreed they would hand her over unharmed.

Naturally, it was a trap.

Though the team knew it was a set-up, even they didn't figure on being ambushed by the full levy of the Oahkies, over sixty heavily armed men.

After Griffon ordered his team to lay down their arms, Ms Cromwell had been quite viscous in taking out her petty revenge. Even Dortmunder and the Oahkee warriors had seemed embarrassed as she giggled and pranced as they pummeled the members of the team.

It was only the intercession of Dortmunder. He pointed out that if they were killed now she wouldn't have the full satisfaction of taking part in their vivisection. This thought was so attractive to her that she didn't have them tortured to death then and there.

As it was, they were bound in manacles and hauled back to the Oahkee village.

On the trip to town, Griffon noted several changes, with some satisfaction. The Oahkie warriors were now armed with new single-shot, breech loading, center-fire rifles. (still black-powder), rather than the odd assortment of muzzle-loaders they had carried before.

Also, the town had new defenses, the wall and towers were still there, but now there were several low-lying bunkers surrounding the village.

Then again, there were the decorations. Griffon had guessed the identity of the two rotting skeletons impaled on either side of the gate. Olivia was happy to point out to them that this time their guards would be far more attentive.

One of the bigger surprises, were the new security procedures for holding prisoners.

They were hauled into a low, heavily walled stone building. It had obviously been a stable until recently. The interior partitions had been removed, creating a single large room. However, the heavy iron rings that had been used to secure livestock were still situated around the walls.

Each team-member was secured to the wall by his wrist manacles. They were spaced around the room, far too far apart to be able to reach each other. Also, an armed guard was detailed to remain in the cell with them. The guards had a lantern and were relieved every four hours.

Olivia took great relish in informing them their transport would be there the next morning. Then, she went into nauseating detail about what was in store for them when they got to where they were going.

The crowd left them, without food or water, to their thoughts, and the petty torments of their guard.

The prisoners had been searched and stripped of their boots, belts, and anything other than their coveralls. The cell was sun-heated, the air thick with humidity and stench. Perfect accompaniment to their thirst and hunger.

Griffon was at a loss. He'd tried to think of everything, and nothing. Any plot or plan he could come up with had one basic flaw, they wouldn't work.

Then he caught White giving Fineous a surreptitious wink.

Griffon kept a straight face as he thought, *What now?*

Fineous sat up straight, his arms suspended above his head by the short chain of the manacle that passed through the large iron ring, deep-set in the stone wall. The little man glared at their guard where he sat in his chair by the door. The lantern on the small table was the only light in the room.

Fineous managed to crack at the guard, "Yo, Goat-breath, did it make you mad when they ran Yo' mamma out of here to make room?"

The heavily muscled oaf just gave the little man a slack-jawed glare, "Huh? What say you, Reaver?"

Fineous gave him his best sneer, and croaked, "I said, that your Mama was a broken down old she goat, and your Poppa was any one of several stray animals. Because your Mamma wasn't particular."

Griffon was becoming a bit alarmed as the very large guard slowly stood, gripping his heavy rifle with white-knuckled hands.

Because of the angle of the light, Griffon couldn't make out the guards expression, but he did figure it wasn't what you would call pleasant. He tried a stage whisper, "Um, Finn, Don't . . ."

The mousy little man cut him off with a grin. Then turned back to the guard as he slowly stalked up to him, "Ooohhh, lookey! You can teach any animal to walk on two leg . . . Ooof!"

After doubling the little man up with a deliberate kick to the stomach, the guard carefully leaned his rifle against the wall. Making sure it was well out of reach of any of the prisoners.

Then, turned back to lift the scarcely conscious man's head by the hair. The Oaf doubled up his other fist and slammed the little man in the face . . . again . . . and again.

His knuckles were glistening with Fineous' blood. Griffon saw at least one tooth knocked free.

The guard ignored the shouts of the other prisoners as he let the little man's head drop back and turned to return to his chair.

He turned just in time to catch the butt of his rifle in the face. Surprised, he staggered backwards, blearily seeing the rifle swung-batlike to smash into his skull. He dropped where he stood.

As the guard had started towards Fineous, Griffon spotted White quickly reach up with his left hand and roll back the sleeve of his coverall on his right arm. Quickly the doctor gripped the silver ring at the base of his prosthetic, press the hidden catch, and twist, deftly disconnecting the artificial arm.

The Doctor then passed the manacle, prosthetic and all through the large iron ring and re-secured the limb in place. Then, as the guard was pummeling Fineous, he stepped up behind him, grabbed his rifle and proceeded to smash his skull in.

Quickly, he dropped the weapon, grabbing the keys from the guard's belt; he proceeded to free the others.

It took some time for them to revive Fineous. His blurry-eyed response when asked if he was all right was, "All this and a retirement plan too."

With that, they knew their little friend would be OK.

As soon as Fineous was feeling better, they dowsed the lantern and opened the door of their latest jail.

Griffon quickly scanned the area. Since it was early evening, there were still several people about, and golden light streamed from many buildings.

He stepped back into the stable and motioned for the others to gather around. "Finn, are you up to a little skullduggery?"

The little man gave him a truly ghastly gap-toothed grin; "I'm always up to a little skullduggery."

Griffon could only chuckle, "Great, now here's what we're going to do. . ." He proceeded to assign duties to each team member, "Fineous do you think you can find their armory?" At the others' nod he continued, "Great, I don't think they'll be nice enough to put our gear where we'll be able to get at it, and besides, we haven't the time to look for it. So Finn, see if you can appropriate some weapons for us. Gillian," the broad Scot gave a curt nod, "I want you to head down to the river. Tie a couple of boats together, and shove them off into the current. Since that's how we got out last time, it'll make a perfect decoy this time. White. . ." The doctor gave a nod in turn. "You'll come with me. We're going to see about lifting some food, blankets, rope, that sort of thing."

Griffon turned back and peeked out the door, "We'll meet at the foot of the tower at the upstream end of the ring-wall. From there, we'll see about climbing out of here and heading upstream while they chase our decoy downstream. Any questions? Good, Lets go."

The companions slipped off into the night, each on their own mission.

After a bit of exploring, dodging from shadow to shadow, they found they had no problem gathering up all the supplies they could carry. Several of the houses had unlocked root cellars, with all sorts of foodstuffs being stored for the winter.

Heavily loaded with the fruits of their efforts, the pair worked their way to the foot of the last tower at the upstream-end of the wall. They noted there was a single guard in the tower. Apparently he chewed tobacco with all the spitting he did.

They waited tensely in the deep shadow under the tower, when an immanently recognizable, short and broad, shadow slipped up beside them. Gillian had a long coil of rope over one shoulder and a heavy bag that clinked alarmingly when he set it down.

Keeping it low so as not to alert the guard above, Griffon asked him how it went.

"It went fine, Sahr." The Scot nudged the bag with his foot, "There were'ah couple of Oahkies a walkin by the river. They wer'ra carrying several useful items."

Griffon nodded, "What did you do with them?"

Even in the darkness he noted the complete deadpan of the Scot's face as he responded, "Well ah Sahr, I was a thinking the boats would make a better decoy if they had'da bit 'o ballast as it were."

"Ugh, well anyone seen any sign of Fineous . . . What the . . ." Griffon almost choked as the little man came huffing up, just walking in the middle of the street without any attempt at being secretive.

Fineous was struggling with four heavy rifles and several large pouches draped over his slight frame.

As they relieved the little man of his load, Griffon couldn't help hissing in his ear, "Do you think you could be a little more blatant?"

Fineous gave him a gap-toothed grin, "Ever think they can't see who's who in this gloom and you would only look suspicious if you act suspicious?"

"Ummnnn!" Griffon really wanted to scream now. However, they still had too . . .

A crashing explosion ripped the night. Blasting into the sky, a red-orange fireball soared to the stars, lighting the entire town in a hellish glare. Large chunks of masonry and wreckage began to pelt the village. Flaming bits went crashing into the roofs of surrounding buildings.

Rather belated, and totally inadequately, alarm-bells began to ring. Shadowy figures streamed into the darkness.

Several fires had started with the flaming debris dropping onto sun-dried wooden and thatched roofs.

Panic, running, shouting, screaming, and such seemed to be the order of the moment.

From his side, Griffon heard Fineous mutter, "So that's where I left my torch."

Griffon's most coherent thought, at the moment, was *Unnnnnhhhhhhh*!

Quickly he gathered his team into a huddle, "So much for sneaking out. We still need to take out the guard before they get their act together and . . . Finn! Come back!"

The little man had started pounding up the wooden steps to the tower. The guard was dutifully, and uselessly, ringing his bell and shouting at whomever he saw in the street.

The guard didn't even turn as Fineous climbed through the trap door to the tower, "Well, its about time... What ta' 'ell's goin' on?"

Griffon didn't hear the response, but he did hear the thump of the guard falling to the floor of the tower.

He glanced up to see Fineous' grinning face and his motion for them to climb up.

By the time they reached the top of the tower and were lowering themselves outside the wall. The Oahkee flares and gattling were ripping the dimly seen forms of their decoys.

As Griffon began to take his turn at the rope, Fineous caught his arm.

The little man pointed at the panic and ruin laid before them. Griffon could see him grin in the hellish light; "Don't you just love it?"

Griffon paused to stare at the spreading fires and panic.

Suddenly, he felt as if he was looking over the edge of a vast abyss. Sadness welled up at the work of years going up in flames. He glanced at his little friend and caught his eye. "No, I don't." He waived his arm at the spreading chaos, "Every time this happens, the Hivers win a bit more. Their victory becomes a bit more complete."

Fineous gave him a peculiar look, "Hey sir! Snap out of it. We're caught between the lions and the jackals. Whichever wins, humanity looses." He waived his own arm towards the flames, "Don't fret over the death of a jackal."

Griffon nodded. They dropped over the wall and slid down the rope.

Chapter 20

Once on the ground they went into a quick huddle.

Griffon gestured towards the burning town; "We'll never make it to the tube now."

He pointed at Fineous, "I remember hearing Janine telling us the Raider couriers have 'Bolt-Holes' they can hold up in when things get hot. Think you could find one?"

The little man gave a curt nod, "Yessir! As, a matter of fact I got her to give me a complete map of sites in this area." He glanced up, embarrassed, "Not that I expected any problems. But. . ."

Griffon gave a sardonic grin and nod, "Right. Can you find the nearest?" At Fineous' nod he gestured towards the night, "Then lead on Good Sir."

They made good time through the ripe, sun-dried fields surrounding the town. The spreading flames and occasional flare of an explosion lighting the way.

At Fineous' direction they made their way towards one of the outlying towers they'd passed on the way in.

They had no trouble surprising and capturing the eight-man squad manning the outpost. The entire garrison was on the wall facing the town, staring slack-jawed, at the glow of flames in the distance.

While White and Gillian bound and gagged the guards, Griffon selected and saddled four horses.

When he asked Fineous what he was up to. He just got the cryptic comment, "Flaming pigs."

Along with being a defensive outwork for the town, the tower also acted as a stable, corral, and storage for livestock and farm implements. This allowed all the stock and machinery to be secured each night without the need of driving them all the way back to town each night.

Once the other three were mounted and ready to ride they got a chance to see what the little man had been up to. . .

He'd quickly made up bundles of brush, straw, blankets, whatever he could gather. After dousing them with lantern oil he'd found in the tower, he quickly cut lengths of rope to tie each bundle to one of the animals in the corral.

Then, having opened the gates he ran about touching a lit torch to the bundles and cracking a bit of knotted rope like a whip.

In no time, the whole panicked herd was stampeding through the surrounding cropland.

Each animal left a trail of flaming debris that quickly caught in the sun-dried grain.

As Fineous mounted, the others could only stare as more than three dozen animals streaking like flaming comets into the night. Each dragging it's flaming bundle behind it.

Gillian shook his head at Fineous, "Yer a cruel, cruel, little man."

Fineous, leading them into the night, just grinned and shrugged, "I didn't make the rules. I'm just making sure they'll have a dickens of a time finding us."

Griffon nodded grimly, the panicked screams and bellows echoing in the distance. *Dickens is right.*

They managed to make it to the bolthole and safety before dawn.

The heavily camouflaged bunker was cut into the base of a hill. It was marked by the ruins of some sort of transmitter tower. Which jutted like a rusted horn, from the peak of the hill.

The "hole" proved to be quite comfortable and well stocked. With what they'd brought, they could hole up for several weeks.

Which was fortunate, considering all the activity the hole's hidden cameras showed on the surface.

Well camouflaged and even better screened, they could sit back and watch Brotherhood vehicles and Oahkee patrols combing the area.

After breakfast, they were lounging around the table in the single large room that made up the crew/work upper-level of the hole. (Stable, garage, and storage made up the lower level.)

Griffon glanced at Fineous as the little man was savoring a hot cup of coffee. "OK Finn, what was all that about 'Flaming Pigs'?"

The little man leaned back in his chair and grinned over the rim of his cup. "You're not the only one that's studied history."

He sipped before continuing, "Way back when the Romans were fighting the Greeks, or Carthaginians, or somebody, they were at the disadvantage. Their enemies had elephants and the Romans didn't. So, somebody had the bright idea of dousing pigs with oil, setting them on fire and running them through the elephants to stampede them."

Griffon nodded, "Mean. Did it work?"

Fineous shrugged, "I don't remember. I just thought of it when I was trying to come up with a way to cover our escape."

Nodding, Griffon turned towards the doctor, "Speaking about escape." He gestured with his cup at White's arm, "How did that Cromwell bitch miss your prosthesis? She knew you were missing an arm from last time. Even if she forgot, aren't they all 'wired' into the system? Wouldn't the computer have remembered?"

White emptied his cup before answering. "I'm not sure. I guess it's like one of those people with a photographic memory. They can memorize a book just by glancing at the pages. But, they can't understand it unless they actually read, or process the information."

He got up and refilled his cup at the pot, "I guess she either didn't ask the computer for details, or assumed that my replacement…" he wiggled the fingers of his right hand at them, "was permanent, like theirs." He shrugged, "Either way, they missed it."

Fineous gave a derisive snort, "Great, Cyborgs can have a brain cramp too. Skipper, how long are we gonna stay in this hole?"

Griffon waived his cup at a monitor showing a Brotherhood magtruck with a pair of Battleborgs go by. "I'd give it a good month, to let the heat die down."

He grinned at the little man, "In a hurry?"

Fineous grinned back, pulling a small box from a pocket of his coveralls, "Noooo. I just found a pack of cards and thought you-all might like to play a little…"

Groaning, the others all started bombarding him with scraps of food, bits of trash, etc.